BY COLUM MCCANN

FICTION

Twist
Apeirogon
Thirteen Ways of Looking
TransAtlantic
Let the Great World Spin
Zoli
Dancer
Everything in This Country Must
This Side of Brightness
Songdogs
Fishing the Sloe-Black River

NONFICTION

American Mother (with Diane Foley)
Letters to a Young Writer

PLAYS

Yes! (with Aedin Moloney)

TWIST

COLUM McCANN

TWIST

A NOVEL

RANDOM HOUSE | NEW YORK

Published in the United States by Random House, an imprint and
division of Penguin Random House LLC, New York.

RANDOM HOUSE and the HOUSE colophon are registered trademarks
of Penguin Random House LLC.

Published simultaneously in the United Kingdom
by Bloomsbury Publishing.

LIBRARY OF CONGRESS CATALOGING-IN-PUBLICATION DATA
Names: McCann, Colum.
Title: Twist: a novel / Colum McCann.
Description: First edition. | New York, NY: Random House, 2025.
Identifiers: LCCN 2024040667 (print) | LCCN 2024040668 (ebook) |
ISBN 9780593241738 (hardcover; acid-free paper) |
ISBN 9780593241745 (ebook)
Subjects: LCGFT: Novels.
Classification: LCC PR6063.C335 T95 2025 (print) |
LCC PR6063.C335 (ebook) | DDC 823/.914—dc23/eng/20240830
LC record available at lccn.loc.gov/2024040667
LC ebook record available at lccn.loc.gov/2024040668

International ISBN 9780593978528

Printed in the United States of America on acid-free paper

randomhousebooks.com

2 4 6 8 9 7 5 3 1

FIRST U.S. EDITION

Title and part-title page image:
Andriy Nekrasov/stock.adobe.com

Book design by Simon M. Sullivan

For Christian

Meanwhile, let us abolish the ticking of time's clock with one blow. Come closer.

VIRGINIA WOOLF, *The Waves*

Those of us who reject divinity, who understand that there is no order, there is no arc, that we are night travelers on a great tundra, that stars can't guide us, will understand that the only work that will matter, will be the work done by us.

TA-NEHISI COATES

The sea, though changed in a sinister way, will continue to exist; the threat is rather to life itself.

RACHEL CARSON, *The Sea Around Us*

PART ONE

1

We are all shards in the smash-up.

Our lives, even the unruptured ones, bounce around on the sea-floor. For a while we might brush tenderly against one another, but eventually, and inevitably, we collide and splinter.

I am not here to make an elegy for John A. Conway, or to create a praise song for how he spent his days—we have all had our difficulties with the shape of the truth, and I am not going to claim myself as any exception. But others have tried to tell Conway's story and, so far as I know, they got it largely wrong. For the most part, he moved quietly and without much fuss, but his was a lantern heart full of petrol, and when a match was put to it, it flared.

I am quite sure that I will hear the name of Conway again and again in the years to come: what happened to him, what strange forces worked upon him, how he was wrecked in the pursuit of love, how he fooled himself into believing that he was something he was not, how we fooled ourselves in return, and how he kept spiraling inward and downward. Then again, maybe Conway was just being honest to the times, interpreting the present in light of the past, and perhaps he got it correct in some way.

I am not sure that anybody, anywhere, is truly aware of what lay at the core of Conway and the era he, and we, lived through—it was a time of enormous greed and foolish longing and, in the end, unfathomable isolation.

When all is said and done, the websites and platforms and rumor mills will create paywalls out of the piles of shredded facts, and we will piece together whatever sort of Conway we can to suit ourselves. Still, I'd at least like to try to tell a small part of his story, alongside my own, and alongside Zanele's too, and if I take liberties with the gaps, then so be it. Like so many people nowadays, I'd prefer to sweep the memory of those days under the carpet. That I have made my mistakes is hardly unique. Maybe I tell this story to get rid of it, or to open up the silence, or to salve my own conscience, or perhaps I tell it because I am scared of what I too have become, steeped in regret and saudade. I often lie awake wondering what might have been if I had done things just a little differently. The past is retrievable, yes, but it most certainly cannot be changed.

———

In January 2019 I boarded the Georges Lecointe, a cable repair vessel. For a struggling novelist and occasional playwright, it was a relief to step away from the burden of invention onto a ship that would take me out to the west coast of Africa, a place I'd never been before. The center of the world was slipping, my career felt stagnant, and frankly, at my age, I was unsure what fiction or drama could do anymore.

I thought I would spend a few weeks on the ship, then return to Dublin and write a long-form journalistic piece, shake out the cobwebs. My first two novels had been minor successes, and I had written a couple of plays, but in recent years I had fallen into a clean, plain silence. The days had piled into weeks and the weeks had piled into months. Not much sang to me: no characters, no plotlines. The world did not beckon, nor did it greatly reward. As a cure, I had thought that I would try to write a simple love story for the stage, but it turned out to be a soliloquy of solitude, not a love story at all. I shut the laptop one morning. All my characters slipped into a chasm. I cast around for new ideas, but mostly it was fall and echo, echo and fall.

Everything felt out of season. I was drinking heavily, breaking covenants, refusing my obligations to the page. I bought myself an antique typewriter in an attempt to get back to basics, but the keys stuck and the carriage return broke.

So many of my days had been a haze. In my most recent novel I had been treading memory: the farmhouse, a small red light from the Sacred Heart, my father rising early to tend the farm, my mother trapped by shadows on the landing, my rural upbringing, my escape to London, the sunsets over the Thames, the journey home, the descent into suburban Dublin where the streetlamps flickered.

Some of the novel had been autobiographical, but the fictional elements were truer. *All the truth,* my father told me, *but none of the honesty.* I recall him stepping rather apologetically from the Galway theater where the book was launched. Rain on the cobblestones. Exit ghost.

I had a feeling that I had exhausted myself and that if I was ever going to write again, I would have to get out into the world. What I needed was a story about connection, about grace, about repair.

———

I had no interest in cables. Not in the beginning, in any case. In the one article I eventually wrote, I said that a cable was a cable until it was broken, and then, like the rest of us, it became something else.

Sachini, my editor at an online magazine where I did occasional work, called me one cold autumn afternoon. She spoke in long, looping sentences. She had happened upon a news report of a cable break in Vietnam and had been surprised to learn that nearly all the world's intercontinental information was carried in fragile tubes on the seafloor. Most of us thought that the cloud was in the air, she said, but satellites accounted for only a trickle of internet traffic. The muddy wires at the bottom of the sea were faster, cheaper, and infinitely more effective than anything up there in the sky. On occasion the tubes broke, and there was a small fleet of ships in various ports around the world charged with repair, often spending months at sea. Was I interested, she asked, in exploring the story?

It was fascinating to think that an email or a photograph or a film could travel at near the speed of light in the watery darkness, and that the tubes sometimes had to be fixed, but my sense of the technology was limited, and it was all still a perplexing series of ones and zeros for me. I demurred.

Flattery has a double edge. I was not sure if I should be offended when Sachini called me the following week and insisted that I was one of the few writers capable of getting to *the murky underdepths.* She told me that, in some of her ongoing excavations, she had found a ship, the Georges Lecointe, that was purported to be among the busiest cable repair vessels in the world. It held the record for the number of deep-sea jobs in the Atlantic Ocean. She reminded me that I had specifically said that I was interested in the idea of repair. *Tikkun olam,* she called it, a concept I was not familiar with at the time. But repair was certainly what I craved. She also corralled me with the simple fact that the boat had been called in to help recover the black box of Air India Flight 182, destroyed by a bomb off the southwest coast of Ireland in 1985. More than three hundred people were killed and most of the bodies were never recovered. I had been fourteen years old at the time of the bombing, and I recall a photograph of an Irish policeman carrying a child's doll through the airport. It intrigued me to think that a small black box stuffed with statistics and information could be hauled from the bottom of the ocean, but the bodies could not.

I walked along the Dublin coast. So much of my recent life had been lived between the lines. All the caution tape. All the average griefs. All the rusty desires. I had been an athlete once, a middle-distance runner. I had taken risks. Gone distances. Now I watched those in swimming togs who actually braved the cold water, and I envied them their courage. The sea tightened my eyes. For how long had I been walking around in the same set of clothes? I called Sachini. She hardly buoyed me when she said that a stint at sea might freshen me up, but she salved my mood with a decent word count and a generous budget.

I began my descent into the very tubes I wanted to portray. The owner of the Georges Lecointe was a telecommunications company in Brussels. The press department told me they were open to a visit from a journalist working in the international sphere. This, in retrospect, was quite naïve on their part, but they had languished publicity-wise in recent years, and they were engaged in several cable-laying bids with Facebook and Google—both of which were due to lay huge cables in the seas around Africa—and possibly thought that an article might raise their profile. It turned out that they owned a number of the world's working cables: their insignia was a purple globe wrapped in spinning coils of wire.

I sublet my flat in Glasnevin, put my furniture in storage, and caught a plane to Cape Town, where the Georges Lecointe was docked. I arrived in the first week of the new year. I had decided to take a few days to acclimate. My only fear was that there would be a cable break and I might miss my chance if the boat was called out to sea, but the publicity team had assured me that they would alert me in the event of any news. I found myself a hotel where I thought I might unwind for a couple of days. Some sardonic copywriter had quoted Oscar Wilde in the hotel's brochure: *Those whom the gods love grow young.* Such sweet irony. It was the weekend of my forty-eighth birthday.

———

After apartheid, I had thought Cape Town might be ashamed of itself, in the choke hold of history, riven still by all it had seen and heard and done. Maybe it was, but it hid that side well, or maybe I hid myself from it. There was a nod to the past just about everywhere—statues of Nelson Mandela, Miriam Makeba songs blasted out over intercoms, memory museums, rows of colorful banners—but apartheid's successor was quite obviously itself. The city's beauty stung my lungs, but its adjacent poverty pierced me too. I had beefed up on South African history and was willing to pour my own sorrows into the ears of the trees—Ireland, our famine, the Troubles—but instead I felt altogether, and a little uncomfortably, at home.

My boutique hotel lay jauntily at the far end of Gordon's Bay. I wore an old T-shirt and torn jeans and walked among the junkies and the backpackers. These were essentially the people from my early twenties, and they reminded me that I had no need to return to my old self. The sea dragged its platter of pebbles to shore. Seagulls careened overhead, dropping shells on the rocks below, splitting them open. In the early morning, the fog came in fast around the mountain and struck a tuning fork in my chest.

I hired a car for a couple of days and drove the coast. The extraordinary wealth of the houses took my breath away. Their long green lawns lay out like rugs. Security booths manned the entrances: it was difficult to see any faces. It was as if nobody existed there at all. Everywhere seemed fenced. Signs for fences. Advertisements for fences. Fences within the fences. The only moving people were gardeners and joggers who quickly disappeared amid the trees and the wires. How had these people locked themselves off for so many years?

At the edge of a wealthy neighborhood, I saw a city dumpster actually rolling by itself down a steep street, set in motion by nothing I could identify, not even a dog or a cat. It started to move in a series of strange loops, clanging along, almost politely avoiding all the parked cars. It bashed off the pavement, hesitated a moment, then tipped over and leaked out a little of its refuse. A gull swooped and pecked at the leavings.

I had no idea that the poverty would sit at such terrible proximity. I turned off the road and there were the disheveled shacks, the potholes, the cracked water pipes, the ghosts wandering along the highways. Men and women pushed shopping trolleys stacked high with whatever little they possessed. The clouds sped away from them. Even the sky seemed segregated.

There were tours of the townships, and the pamphlets advertised them as *ethical,* but I couldn't bring myself to return. I didn't want to be the inconsolable European, walking around in exchange for an ounce of sentiment. I had heard stories of people shot for their dreadlocks. My voyeurism was not going to help. I had to turn around and face myself. Later, when Zanele wrote about the Joe Slovo township in Port Elizabeth, I marveled at the way she described the windblown dust raking the top of the tin roofs and the snap of the aloe leaves when she plucked them from behind the dump: this was the music she said she had grown up to, and it struck me that we all have different soundtracks to go along with our early years. Mine had been the sound of my mother's footsteps at the top of the stairs, retreating to her bedroom, afraid to descend below.

At every traffic light in the city, men and women begged. More often than not, they were strung out and barefoot. The waiting cars clicked on their windscreen wipers and sprayed the air when the beggars approached.

I took a taxi to the city outskirts where the trees hugged the slopes. I didn't want to join the tourists in the cable car, and I struggled my way up Table Mountain on foot, eventually found a quiet perch to look out over the sea. Nothing had prepared me for the wind and the rain and the sunlight that picked at my flesh, got into my bones. I had never seen weather so changeable before, even in the west of Ireland. I had brought a pair of binoculars with me. I trained them back toward the harbor, but it was impossible to see the Georges Lecointe, obscured by a giant white cruise vessel. The fog came in and the temperature plummeted, and I hurried my way down the mountainside, taking the last quarter mile in a darkness that seemed to rise from below. That night I walked the beach and saw a young woman in a long white dress stroll into the water. She was briefly apparitional. I made a slow circle, but when I returned, she was gone. I scanned the horizon: nothing. I half expected to see a group of rescuers leaning down to resuscitate her, but then it occurred to me that she had most likely stepped into the water out of joy or maybe some religious fervor, or else she had drowned. The city didn't feel like it would mourn.

I retreated to my hotel. I had primed myself with a desire to go to sea, if only just to get away from it all, and so I phoned Brussels again. They told me that they would arrange a meeting locally and to expect a call from their chief of mission, John Conway, any day now.

At a certain stage our aloneness loses its allure. I waited for the call.

————

It still astounded me that nearly all our information travels through tiny tubes at the bottom of the ocean. Billions of pulses of light carrying words and images and voices and texts and diagrams and formulas, all shooting along the ocean floor, a flow of pulsating light. In tubes made from glass. In glass made from sand. In sand that has sifted through time.

The whole notion turned me inside out. The depths hum with just about everything imaginable. Moving at an unimaginable speed. In a reinforced tube no bigger than a garden hose. You are here one moment. And then, in a nanosecond, you are somewhere else. I had begun to think that there might be something monumental here. A vague element of the mythical. The velocity of who we are. Every scrap of existence colliding inside the tubes: the weak force, the strong force, the theory of everything. And, of course, every inanity whirling inside there too. All of it tumbling in unison along the seafloor.

It was possible that it would be a matter of weeks before there was a rupture, but on the other hand, it could happen within hours. I had discovered that most of the interruptions came from fishing trawlers close to shore, but that sometimes there were underwater volcanoes and landslides that could cause a breakage and take a cable ship out to sea for a month or more. The prospect didn't frighten me. I was prepared to stay out if necessary. If I wasn't able to write on land, I would write at sea. This new expanse of gray would hold me there—the meeting place of the Atlantic and the Indian Oceans. I could build a thing of simple phrases, like small square blocks, my own ones and zeros, sentences.

The phone finally rang after four days of waiting. Conway was sharp, almost reluctant on the phone. He gave me the address of a hotel that the publicity team had arranged. "See you at five," he said. The line snapped dead.

It was a colonial-era hotel in the shadow of the peaks, at the edge of the Atlantic. Cream-colored. Reminiscent of wedding cake left out a little too long. A row of trees bent in supplication. Dozens of birds perched on the branches like small sentries. The light was snatched inside and served with silver tongs. All the bellhops and waitstaff were Black. It surprised me that they didn't seethe with resentment. The men wore waistcoats and bow ties. The women were in aprons. The place reeked of the past.

Nowhere on earth makes you feel as pale and pasty as Cape Town. It disturbed me. I walked around among the potted palms, embarrassed to be there at all. I wanted to convince myself it was not my legacy: it was, after all, the British and the Dutch who had done this, not me, it was not my fault, I was Irish, and we had been colonized too, we wore the wounds, my place would still be in the kitchen, deferential, taking the peelings from the plates of others. But the truth was there in a glance at the reflection in a pane of glass. I had to admit it. I knew what I was. The men in the chairs all resembled me. I deepened my accent. Still, the bartender called me *sir* and the waiters sauntered around the room in their crisp uniforms.

At the bar I had a Jameson to rebalance myself, but even the giant ice cube was an accusation: all the straight edges, Sykes-Picot in a glass.

Foolishly, I introduced myself to three different men. They were all various forms of me. One of them, a marketing executive, even gave me his card and asked me if I wanted to sit with him until my *companion* arrived. He shook his ice cube in the direction of the bartender to order me a drink. I stammered and shook my head.

In fact, I had already seen Conway in the lobby, but I had discounted him. He was much younger than I'd imagined. In his mid-thirties maybe. Slim, lightly bearded, wearing jeans, wire-rimmed glasses, and a red knit hat. There was something very calm and un-rushed about him. If there was a clock inside him, instructing time, it was ticking slower than the timepieces inside the rest of us. It wasn't that he tamped down the moment, or tightened it, or obscured it. On the contrary, he gave air to it, let it hover, made it new. I would say that he struck me as the kind of man who might be found in a monastery, or a phrontistery, somewhere raw, distant, on the edge. He didn't advertise himself as such, no sandals, no carpenter pants, and he seemed completely unaware that he was standing in the slant of other people's gaze.

I had seen men like him before, troubled and angelic all at once. One evening, on assignment in New York, I had watched Jeff Buckley in a downtown Irish bar leaning into the microphone to sing Leonard Cohen's "Hallelujah." The backspin of memory lands us in the strangest of places. Conway had that secret chord—the sort of man who was there and not there at the same time.

He circled the lobby a couple of times and then walked out again through the French doors into the arc of light. He stood on the patio, looking out at the sea, hand to his eyes, not so much an explorer as a man who wanted to shade himself from the glare. A huge flock of birds flew beyond him, scissoring the sky, a murmuration of starlings.

I texted him but he didn't respond. I thought for a moment that maybe I had gotten the wrong man once more, but he finally pulled out a very old flip phone from his jeans pocket and one word appeared on my screen: *Here*.

I downed my Jameson and walked outside to the patio.

"Conway," he said, and he held out his hand. He was handsome in a way that seemed to puzzle him. His eyes were bottle green, his cheekbones sharp. His face was dark and weather-beaten. The ends of his hair curled out from beneath his knit hat. He was the sort of young and thin I once had been.

"I was just about to leave, to be honest," he said.

"I texted you."

"I don't really like using my phone."

I stifled a laugh. I am not sure what I had expected from a man whose job it was to be in joint command of an internet repair ship, the chief of mission no less, but I certainly thought he would be older, grayer, and at the very least have an aura of the smartphone about him. But here he was, a creature from the unplugged side, or as unplugged as he could get.

"You use a flip phone?"

"Only when I have to."

"Why?"

"Oh," he said, "I like machines that work."

He studied his shoes, but he was smiling, or almost smiling, as if he'd just shared a little joke with the ground beneath him. "Off the boat, it's less cumbersome."

The sunlight was too much for me, and I asked if he minded retiring to a table at the far end of the bar. "I'm happy anywhere," he said, but it was quite obvious to me that he liked the inside of the hotel even less than I did.

I could feel myself being watched, not least by the man at the bar who had referred to him as my companion.

Conway gestured to the chair and waited for me to sit. He mistook me at first for an American. Somehow the publicist, Elisabeth, had neglected to tell him that I was Irish too. He probably thought that I was one of those inescapable bores who immediately try to imitate an accent. His own accent had lost some of its edges and there was a faintly English or mid-Atlantic tinge that I assumed was South African. He mentioned the aberration in the White House as if I myself was responsible for putting him there. I corrected him and he seemed jolted by the notion that I was from Westmeath. I said a word or two in Irish—I was trying to figure out his background—but he dodged me. John Conway was a fairly obvious nationalist name, although it was still nominally possible that he was from a loyalist community. Not that it mattered much anymore. The divides in the North still simmered, but he was long gone from there, and my years of thinking about the Troubles were well behind me.

"Rathlin Island," he said when I asked him where he was from. "Off the coast of Antrim."

His was a childhood of boats, then. An islander. A watcher of storms.

"What brought you to these parts?"

Without answering, he turned the question on me. I have been a listener, for better or for worse, my whole life, but here, now, was Conway initiating a long silence. I had a vague sense that there was some loneliness lodged inside him. I rambled on about Westmeath and London. When I called him John, he insisted on being called Conway. I didn't realize it at the time, but everyone used his last name.

He smiled at a waitress as she passed. She returned and half curtsied, and I could see Conway blush, embarrassed by her deference. When he spoke, she leaned close to him.

"It's amazing, really," he said as the waitress walked back across the bar, "to watch the people who do the actual work of the world."

"Don't you do it yourself?"

"Not really," he said. "I just read a lot of maps. And push buttons."

"Is that it?"

"More or less. It's a big crew. They're the ones who bring the ends together."

"Do you like it?"

"I began as a diver," he said, curiously, and nothing more.

When the waitress returned, he quietly slipped her a banknote. I assumed from her reaction that the tip was large. She lingered. She seemed genuinely drawn in by him. He watched her glide away across the floor.

"There's not much new there," he said.

"What do you mean?"

"These cables have been around for hundreds of years. A hundred and fifty, actually. Not a lot has changed. I mean, it's fiber optics now, but they're all essentially the same. They carry the same thing."

"Which is?"

"News, I suppose. Other times, other places."

I had read a little about the first cables, laid in the nineteenth century by Cyrus Field and his crew of New York entrepreneurs. The steam-powered ships that went back and forth between Ireland and Newfoundland, unspooling the telegraph wire across the Atlantic. The Agamemnon. The Niagara. Passing icebergs along the way. Wrapping their dead in muslin, letting them down into the sea. The relentless tap of the morse code. The men who shortened time and distance with copper and iron wire. The ones who believed in the permanent idea of *faster faster faster.*

"No one cares all that much about the actual cables, really." He twirled his glass and glanced down into it. "I kind of like it that way."

A dread was creeping up on me: maybe he wasn't going to give me access to the story after all. I had negotiated the chance with the publicist, but perhaps Conway was maverick enough to stifle my plans.

"I'd like to spend some time on your boat."

"It's not my boat exactly," he said. "But I can take you down to the jetty tomorrow, show you around. We can spend a day. Walk around on deck. Get you in the engine room. Show you the ropes. Get your hands greasy."

"Actually, I was thinking I'd really like to go out on a run."

"A run?"

"A repair ..."

"There's not going to be any repairs for a while, Mister Fennell. At least I hope not. The Georges is not moving. She's best when she doesn't move."

I did not want to be called *mister*. It was an unusual move on his part—we were from the same country, one north, one south, sure, but we weren't that many years removed from each other. I reached for the ice cube in my water glass, placed it at the back of my neck.

"The publicist said—"

"A run," he said, stopping me short. "A run could take weeks, even months."

"I know that."

The ice water dripped down the hollow of my back.

"I was thinking maybe we could get a shallow-water repair."

"Sorry, I can't just produce a break on demand."

"Of course not."

"Anything could happen at any minute," he said. "Or it could be quiet for ages. Weeks. Months even."

"Well, I'm interested in the waiting."

"Waiting," he repeated, as if the word meant something else.

Beyond the room, the light lay red upon the sea.

"There's another repair vehicle out in Durban," he said finally. "I can get you out on that. It's more likely that something will happen there anyway. The chief of mission is from Angola. And the captain is Argentinian. You'll like him. A good bloke. And this stuff is serious when it happens. I don't like distraction at sea."

He held out his glass to clink as if he had given me a compliment.

The waitress was already back with our second drinks. Conway slipped another bill into her hand. It wasn't brazen, or an act of flirtation, it came naturally, and it seemed to furnish the sense of awayness that hung about him.

She leaned toward him again and thanked him, and her hip grazed the back of his chair. I would have sworn he knew her from somewhere, but when I asked, he seemed genuinely confused. "I would never come here," he said, looking around. "Brussels arranged it."

He seemed relieved that I too hated the hotel, and he mentioned a little hole-in-the-wall bar down in the docklands where he said not a single moment cloned itself. It was an odd thing to say, I thought, but I was taken by it. The bar had a history, he said. It had been a meeting place for activists for decades. "Most bars live by crude repetition," he said. He didn't add anything more. I got the sense that it was an underground spot and that perhaps he knew some of the characters: there was certainly something about Conway that seemed buried away elsewhere.

"We should go there," I said.

"Now?"

"Why not?"

"My partner and kids are getting ready to go to London."

The idea that he had a life outside the ship knocked me a tad off balance. I hadn't thought of Conway as having any sort of settled life. There was, first of all, his apparent youth. And a life at sea wouldn't preclude a family, of course, but he seemed to exist apart from the idea.

"For work," he said.

"What does she do?"

The light grew longer across the hotel floor. Men and women were ghosting through the lobby, dressed for sunset cocktails. Beyond the patio I saw a hawk on the air diving after its mate.

"She's an actress," he said. "She has a gig in England. She's doing Beckett next month."

There were a lot of vectors in what he said.

"I'm in the theater too," I said. "I mean, I've written plays. I'm a journalist, but . . ."

I was panicking, explaining myself too much. But Conway was looking beyond me as if he was figuring out the scattered parts: the hotel, the sky, the birds.

The guests moved in shoals from the elevator banks toward the back patio. They were met by waiters carting trays of long-stemmed drinks. The waiters could have been in their very own production. I felt sorry for them, but then again, I have learned how easy it is to condescend when you don't participate. That seemed to be one of Conway's immediate talents—he could easily have stood up from our table and moved swiftly among them, helping them out, one of the crew.

"You should meet her," he said finally.

"Excuse me?"

"Maybe you could write about her."

"Your partner?"

"Yes," he said. "For your magazine."

I found it faintly amusing that he would think that I would come all the way to South Africa to write about an unknown actress, but he had opened himself to me briefly, and I could see a pathway into my article. I was not about to discount any chance to stay in his orbit.

I asked him which Beckett play she'd be appearing in—I assumed *Not I*, perhaps, or *Footfalls*, or *Happy Days*—but he either didn't hear me or just ignored me. He was obviously animated by his idea. He rose and cupped his hand around his flip phone as he talked to her. It was not, it seemed, an easy sell. He took another step away from the table, drummed his fingers against a white pillar. I was intrigued to see him so quickly flustered. I was about to suggest that it was all just fine, not to worry about it, that I didn't want to take up too much more of his time and would see him again as soon as there was an underwater break, but then he covered the mouthpiece with his hand. "She says to come on over."

At the arched exit, the shadows took him.

———

It was early in the new year, my winter. But the South African summer was in full throat: days of searing heat and crackling storms.

Conway drove by motorbike from the hotel. An old-fashioned Triumph. He weaved ahead of my taxi in the traffic, his shirtsleeves fluttering until he was just a speck in the distance. He had given me the address in Muizenberg: coffee shops, rainbow flags. The taxi took me down a narrow side street. He greeted me with a nod and a half shrug: *This is it.*

The house was a low, unassuming bungalow lined with palm trees. No fences.

It was, by the standards of any conventional life, a conventional house. A tarmacadam driveway. A rolled-up garage door. A lopsided tricycle on the front steps. He beckoned me up the driveway.

The storm door was half-open. The wire meshing was loose and punctured in places. It led to a short, dark hallway festooned with cards strung up with crepe paper. I had forgotten, in the heat, that it was just past Christmas. I had to stop to mop my brow. I was already turned inside out, unbalanced.

Conway led me past a small office, cluttered but neat. The walls were full of underwater photos. Fields of coral. Hypothermal vents. Fissures in the rock. Snippets of color. One of the photos showcased a woman moving upward through the water, in profile, in a wetsuit and a single long black fin, a line of grace and stealth through shafts of silvery light: somehow the water seemed to open itself to her.

We passed down the hallway toward the kitchen.

I had not yet learned his partner's first name, at least it didn't register, or I might have been a little more prepared to meet her. I just assumed she would be Irish, and I was—as I would often be about her, and probably still am—wrong. She was standing, slim-waisted, in the kitchen with her back turned. She was slightly taller than me, and a half head taller than Conway. Her beige pants flared at the ankles. She wore sandals made from car tires, but they were chic and had been threaded with a colorful array of beads. She turned around. She wore no makeup. Her hair was casually pulled back. A small birthmark floated between her eyebrows. Her hands were white with flour and it seemed immediately cinematic, yet she disrupted the image too: her fingernails were chewed down and the cuticles were raw.

"Zanele," she said, extending her hand.

She laughed as she said it, quite possibly a nervous laugh, but it was also the laughter of someone who had seen some things that were entirely incommunicable, and still it felt as if everything wrong ever done could be washed away in her laughter. It occurred to me that she must be the woman in the underwater photo.

"Conway"—she called him Conway too—"told me that you met up in that horrible hotel."

A handmade sign on the wall said, intriguingly, *Rouse your soul to frenzy*. This was the South Africa I had wanted to see, a couple crossing the lines, Black and White, the proof of the times, the ancient conventions dissolving.

She took me by the elbow and sat me down at the low Formica table: the kitchen was appealingly old-fashioned.

"He tells me you're an actress."

"I am, I suppose," she said with a smile, "but it doesn't always get me out of the kitchen."

When she spoke, her voice had a quality of windfall: most of what she said sounded like a piece of unexpectedly good news, relayed against the odds. Her accent held a hint of American. Endearingly, her front tooth was chipped, which gave her a playful aspect.

Conway sat down beside us. He was looking at Zanele as if she was an open window.

I used to presume that I knew a thing or two about love. My sister almost died, quite literally, of a broken heart. She suffered a stress-induced cardiomyopathy caused by a condition known as takotsubo syndrome. Out of the blue, a week after a sweetheart of hers fell from a rooftop while on a peacekeeping mission in Lebanon, her heart stopped functioning properly. She was told at first that it had been a cardiac arrest, but she was informed later by a surgeon that her heart was perfectly normal and that the syndrome was common among women who had suffered a trauma: her heart surrendered. There was a legion of medical literature behind it, *tako tsubo* being the Japanese octopus traps that resemble the pot-like shape of the stricken heart, the sort of thing drawn by countless young lovers in the back of copybooks. My sister recovered, but it was a strange malady that stuck with me. To die of a broken heart. I was fascinated, too, by elderly couples who followed each other in swift succession: I had heard many such stories. I had even attempted to write a play about a publisher in Dublin and his wife who love each other so deeply that he is convinced he will follow her, quickly, death on the heels of death, an inevitable murmuring into the sky of his life, a vesper flight, a graceful upward swing into the outer dark. As she lies dying, he reads to her, not from old books but new ones, stories she has never heard before. For a while I wrote as if my hair was on fire, but the second act frittered away and became something quite unsettling, which in some ways led me, I suppose, to this memoir, or half memoir, unfolding, as it is now, in front of me, in its own vesper flight.

It's what I believe flitted across my mind when I saw Conway with Zanele: I have seldom seen someone so taken by another person. I say *believe* because all memory is, of course, conjecture, a piecing together of the mosaic, and not always to be trusted, but even if it's not exactly what I thought at that moment, it is an honest portrait of how I'm sure I felt: I was in the presence of a couple who were extraordinarily bound to one another.

"She's an amazing actress," he said.

"You've got to excuse Conway. He's ..." She traced the air with her finger, a circle that ended abruptly. "I'm a last-minute idiot who has to have her bags packed, that's what I am."

"When are you leaving?" I asked.

"Day after tomorrow."

"The West End?"

"Oh, no no no," she said, "it's in Brighton. By the sea. Hardly glamorous at all. But we're going to take it by storm anyway."

"She has this idea about adapting it," said Conway.

"It ...?"

"Oh Jesus, Conway, don't bore the poor man."

He went to the fridge and opened two beers. He handed Zanele a bottle of sparkling water.

She was, it seemed, part of a South African theater troupe, Isiqalo, whose members had nearly all grown up in the townships. They had been invited to England by a progressive theater group to perform *Waiting for Godot*, against the wishes of the Beckett estate. Beckett himself had once stated that the roles in the play were specifically not for women, and his estate had prevented actresses from being cast. Years before, I had seen the argument play out in academic circles in Ireland, but smaller theater companies and students were increasingly trying to flout the edict, and female and nonbinary actors were pushing their way into the roles. It was plain to see that Zanele was well aware of the overtones of the ban, and it was also obvious that she thought anyone should be allowed to play whatever they wanted. An old argument. Bygone ideas.

"I'd like to push it elsewhere," she said.

Her idea for the performance was quite simple. She wanted to focus the play around climate change, which was not especially new or edgy as a topic, but it drilled deep for her. There were, she said, so many lines that spoke to what needed to be highlighted these days, and it was, in fact, the great climate play. Beckett, she said, had been writing life in advance, and he hardly would have wanted us to wait around for it all to disappear.

"Let us do something, while we have the chance," she said. It took me a second to realize she was quoting from the play. "There's man all over for you, blaming on his boots the faults of his feet." She leaned forward again. "On the other hand, what's the good of losing heart now, that's what I say."

I suddenly saw her on a minimalist stage, tall and stately, under the shadow of a thin tree, turning a hat on a long single finger.

"It's brilliant," said Conway.

She shrugged. "It is what it is. We'll see how it goes."

"How long will you be in England?" I asked.

"Depends on the run, but we open at the end of the month and we'll be there six weeks, maybe more."

"First time there?"

"Kind of, yes," she said, glancing at Conway. There was a hint of wistfulness in her voice now. "We haven't really spent much time there."

"Your family still on Rathlin Island?"

"Not anymore."

"You don't go back to the North much?"

"It's hard with the twins," he said.

As if on half cue, a small boy about seven years old came into the kitchen trailing a blanket, and he curled straight into Zanele's arms without even so much as glancing at me. The boy put his face against her shoulder, nestled into her. He was dark-skinned, with large eyes. His was a sweet, open face, much like his mother's.

Zanele was a beauty and even more than that: the type of woman who looked like she would continue to grow into her beauty. Later I found out she was thirty-six years old but could easily have been five years either side of that. Her neck was long and striated. Her voice had dips and hollows and musical undertows. Her eyes held an arc of pain. The brows. The birthmark. It was a face to which much had happened, or perhaps I just remember it as that since I now know what sort of life she had led, but I recall thinking, with a gradually dawning sense, that this was a woman who had seen and survived the very worst of things, and that she had somehow transcended them.

It intrigued me that she would dare go to London, or Brighton, alone with her young children, but I presume there was no other way: Conway was contracted to go out to sea and had to remain in Cape Town in case of a cable break.

"Have you ever gone out on the ship?" I asked her.

"The Georges?" she said. "Not me. No. But I do dive."

It seemed like a non sequitur at first, or perhaps it was something metaphorical. "I'm sorry, but you dive where?"

"He didn't tell you?"

"We only met this afternoon, Zee," he said to her.

"Of course, but he tells everyone. That's how we met. Diving."

"Where were you?"

"Where *were* we?"

"I mean, when you met?"

"We were in False Bay last week," she said. "You absolutely have to see the kelp forest."

"With scuba gear?"

"Freediving. Where you hold your breath."

"Like pearl diving?"

"It's unlike anything else."

"I don't suppose I'm cut out for it."

"Anyone can do it," said Conway. "You can actually hear the kelp moving."

"You should take him," said Zanele.

"I really doubt I'd be able to . . ."

"Of course you could."

Zanele leaned back in her kitchen chair. "The disease of our days is that we spend so much time on the surface."

I was momentarily taken aback: it certainly felt like a slight from her, *the disease of our days,* yet there was a balm in her voice, and it soothed me.

"Dumping all we can into the sea. Four billion tons of industrial waste every year. Doesn't make sense, does it?"

It wasn't breaking news to me or anyone else, but the manner in which she said it elevated it. Four billion tons. It unbuckled the mind and became so much more than a statistic.

She clasped her hands over her son's ears and said: "We just don't think beyond it. If this was happening in a fucking sci-fi movie, we'd get it, but we don't. If we had any sense, we would all die of shame."

"I heard that," said the boy. "You said the f-word."

"Well, eff it," she said, nuzzling into him. "But, I mean, seriously, shame on us all. I want to know why in the name of God people accept what's happening to us. You know if the ocean was a bank, they'd have saved it a long time ago. You can tell people this stuff over and over, and they still deny it. It's the dread of too much shit to do."

"You said *shit*," said her son.

"Did I?"

"And the f-word."

She pinched the inside of his knee and he squealed in delight. Then she leaned forward once more, looked at me, and her eyes narrowed and a vertical line appeared between her eyebrows.

"I mean, you can say it with feeling and eloquence and what have you, but you can still never say it well enough for it to be anything more than news from abroad. They just don't listen. One little breath of our history is ruining us forever."

I got the vague sense—which later turned out to be mostly correct—that her career was very much on the upswing and that the world had, in recent years, been opening to her in extraordinary ways: she had always had something to say, but now she was being properly listened to for more or less the first time. She had grown up in a township just as apartheid was being dismantled—if it ever had been dismantled at all—and she had no doubt seen some things that she should not have seen. The seams of her past seemed to burst with the unforgivable, but hers was an open journey now, she was on the edge of success. She was desired for what she could bring to other lives. At an age where she wanted to take the chance, at least one swing at recklessness. A great moment was knocking on the door of her life, and she didn't want to miss it. *What do we do now, now that we are happy?* I had the feeling that the Beckett play and the whole adventure in theater was another form of diving to her.

Zanele leaned down to the child and whispered to him: "You will be so spoiled, won't you, Thami?" She scrunched her knuckles in his modestly Afroed hair, left it dotted with the last bits of flour from her hands.

"Do you have children?" she asked.

To this very day I have no idea why, but I shook my head no: perhaps I thought the truth might get in the way and spoil the moment, or more likely I felt a vague sense of shame that my sloe-eyed son—from a brief but wonderful marriage many years before—was away in Santiago, so far removed from my life.

"You're probably right," she said. "We can hardly congratulate ourselves for the mess we've left them, can we?"

Conway placed two more beers on the table: the bottle caps went spinning.

"You'll forgive me," Zanele said, and she rose from her seat, and the top of her head almost touched the hanging light, so that she was haloed in brightness for a second. "I still have so much to do, and I have to put this big heffalump to bed."

"I'm not a heffalump," the boy said.

"Oh yes you are. And your heffalump sister too. Where has she disappeared to?"

She lifted Thami with ease and kissed his hair, crossed the kitchen floor. She touched her foot against a large seashell that served as a doorstop. "Imka," she called to the young girl, but there was no reply.

Conway watched her. The light followed her out the door.

"Will you do it?" he asked me, and the question flustered me for an instant until I realized that he was actually quite serious about me writing an article about her. I told him that I would, of course, consider it. He thought all the prospect of discovery lay with her. The shine had not worn off him: he had simply refracted it all upon her. I figured that was what Conway was about—his mind went beyond the horizon of himself and landed elsewhere. He was so in love with her that he wanted people to see her, meet her, talk with her, listen to her, be in her presence.

When I went back to my hotel that night, I recalled the feeling I had experienced in the kitchen, and I searched the internet for the term *tako tsubo,* discovering that the exact physiology of the broken heart was still not fully understood.

———

It strikes me that Zanele knew that we are creatures of great change. Not a single atom in our bodies today was there when we were children. Every bit of us has been replaced many times over. We flake away and become new. Whatever we are now, we are not the stuff from which we were originally made. All the people we once were. All the people we had once hoped to be.

Conway took a picture of her in Cape Town Airport just in front of the departure gate on the day she left. In the photo Zanele wears a T-shirt that reads *Unreachable by Machine.* Her body appears loose and limber, but the most striking thing is that she has shaved her hair right down to her scalp. She must have done it the night before she left. She holds Imka's hand, while Thami tugs the hand of another one of the three actresses from the troupe. Their luggage is light. There is no fanfare, but there is a quiet intensity on all their faces, most especially Zanele's.

Not an ounce of beauty was compromised in the shaving of her hair, and later—in London, when her fame began to spread—that shaved look became Zanele's staple.

Conway downloaded the photo and cropped it until it was just a headshot. It was a tiny bit pixelated, but her face could still be clearly made out. He used the photo as his own on his personal email, so that, for a while at least, he must have been sending her messages that could have looked, to an outsider, like messages to herself. She, for her part, used the children as her profile photo. I wonder sometimes about how their communications might have passed one another in the deep, on the ocean floor, in the watery dark, in the days and hours before the cable snapped.

That they had fooled me, and fooled others too, is hardly a surprise. There is not much in our lives that isn't part of a misdirect. Nobody lands on an absolute truth. Most of it is sinewed together with lies. We deceive ourselves. Life unravels. Pressures accumulate. Another world in our world. That silent steam builds up. It seeps into the edges and expands until we crack. Perhaps the manner in which they had behaved in their kitchen, and in the airport, and afterward, when she went to London, and he went to sea, was perfectly normal. It wasn't just that they were putting on a show, or preserving honor, or saving face for the sake of appearance in front of a stranger, or projecting the ease of a well-oiled life, or that they were trying to protect their kids from a decision that wasn't yet final. Maybe they honestly believed that they were going to be able to make it work. Perhaps they thought they might be able to get to the far side unscathed. Zanele was going with their children. Conway was staying behind. She had an acting job. It was short-term. He had a job at sea. All of that was true. And yet there was so much more. They said her journey was for a month or two, but both of them must have had a feeling that it was beyond that. They were rupturing. They were part of the broken things. We all are.

None of this I knew at the time. It all came a good deal later, and perhaps in telling it now I expose my naïveté, my lack of perception, maybe even my inability to shepherd the story properly, but so be it, such is hindsight and the complications of what we choose to call the truth. I have to remind myself that if there's a benefit to hindsight, there's an inherent distortion too. Quite obviously, the present becomes the past. But less obviously, the past is just the beginning of a beginning. Conway is now dead, and all I am left with is the shards of the broken things to put back together again. I still believe that Zanele and Conway did, in fact, love one another. I am, in fact, convinced of it, and it is perhaps the most important thing I can say about them.

I, too, have known those sorts of days when I have put on the Prufrock smile when really all I had was the remnants of a wrecked life.

But I am getting ahead of myself. I was still, at the time, eager to dwell in the story of a repair.

2

Who can say where anything truly begins? The cloud, the raindrop, the original speck of dust around which water collects? We can only ever locate the middle when we get to the end. And then, at the absolute end, what's the point in finding the middle, or even the beginning?

What we do know is that the Congo River had been in flood for weeks. It rained on Kinshasa and it rained on Matadi and it rained on Muanda and it filled up Malebo Pool and beyond. A swell of rain, it shattered all the records. The whole Congo Basin was saturated. The spill triggered mudslides high in the inner forests, ripped up the rocks, sent huge trees and boulders zipping down along the hillsides. The river scooped out the belly of the land, took the thighs of the riverbanks, overflowed its spine. Whole villages were washed away in the storms. Parking lots, dock houses, barges, went floating. Upside-down cars. Ferryboats were flipped over sideways. The torrent took whatever it could, through sluice gates, beyond whirlpools, over waterfalls. It wasn't reported what the full human cost of those floods was, but the toll must have been in the hundreds, maybe even thousands.

I saw a photo of a tiny girl—she looked so much, in fact, like a young Zanele—in a thin pink nightdress, one strap off the shoulder, sitting on a roof, her chin to her knee, pensive as her house took her down the wide flow on the outskirts of Muanda. The photo, published by the Muanda Gazette, haunted me for a long time, and I tried my level best to find out who she was and what might have happened to her, but I couldn't find the photographer and the news desk never returned my calls. The girl, like the water, had moved swiftly along.

The riverbanks spread. The rapids grew. The ferocity was unprecedented. The Congo was so swollen that a Kenyan hydrologist told me that one of the World Trade Center towers could have been sunk in the mouth of the river, where it met the Atlantic, and the building would have been swallowed whole.

Sand and silt and stone and dust. The river gathered the debris from the banks, from the river bottom, from the air itself. Every raindrop, too, had its own weight of dirt inside. The Congo became a malevolence of rushing brown. The boulders tumbled. The rocks somersaulted. More soil was ripped from the bottom and the water became a portrait of the weight it carried. Drowned boats, cars, bicycles, cows, hydraulic jacks, fertilizer bags, spears, pirogues, seeds, insects, birds, old paddle wheels. A heap of bones too, surely, bleached and tumbling now, femur against tibia against rib against mandible against sternum. Day after day, week after week. It was as if the Congo was purging itself, all that history, all that rancor, under the sun, under the swollen stars, a rage of soil heading out into the channel, an underwater canyon that stretched for hundreds of kilometers. The river was flexing its power, wheelbarrowing all it could carry out to the ocean. The current was so strong that it shot a great distance out into the Atlantic, laid the dirt down in layer upon layer of sediment. A sloping shelf, stacked under the sea. And who knew what else lay out there, down there, fathoms upon fathoms below?

Afterward, when I interviewed experts on the submarine canyons of the world—divers who had gone down in submersibles, sonar scientists, geologists, hydrologists—they said it was the closest thing to a living beauty and a possible hell all wrapped together in one, a massive canyon that held many mysteries, the cliffs, the plunges, the depths, the seamounts, the ledges, the ridges, all of it covered in soil as the river swept out toward some final version of itself, to the place where there was no light except that which was throbbing within the cable, carrying, in turn, just about everything.

Conway called me four days after Zanele left for England. I recognized the booze in his voice. I have been there many times myself. It's an acid bath.

He wasn't slurring, he was cool and poised, like drinkers often are. I thought he was going to tell me to get my things packed together, that there was a cable down, and we were ready to head out to sea.

"I'm leaving the Georges."

I knew already that part of the chief of mission's job was to be on board every day, alongside a skeleton crew, just in case anything happened. I assumed he was saying that he was leaving the ship temporarily, maybe going home for a proper night's sleep. But from a distance I could hear that little death rattle—ice in the glass. There must have been a terrible loneliness shunting its way through him.

"I handed in my resignation half an hour ago."

Alcohol as biography. I could hear it kicking in breath by breath. He was at home, most likely, in his empty bungalow, probably padding around the house amid the discarded bicycles and the white kitchen machinery and the shoes that Zanele and his children had left behind.

"Sorry to hear that. I was hoping—"

"Don't you worry, big man," he said. "They'll sort out another chief of mission before you know it, you'll be grand, not a bother on you, trust me." Standing there in the corridor, outside his bedroom, maybe, flicking the hallway light on and off. Serenading the vast emptiness. "They'll have you out on a break in two seconds flat, I can guarantee it, it has to happen, it always happens." In his pajama bottoms, scratching his taut stomach. "Not a doubt about it, big man."

It was not a moniker I liked all that much, *big man*—I had indeed grown a little hefty in recent years—but it was meant, I suppose, as a term of endearment. Still, I was surprised that he had phoned me. An alignment among drinkers. Someone who might understand.

"So, you're going to London?"

"Yeah, heading off in a couple of days. Just got to get my shit together, and I've got to find someone to look after the dog, can't forget about the dog." On my visit I hadn't noticed any dog at all. "Do you want to look after the dog for me?" I wasn't sure what to say, but I told him that I'd certainly help find someone to look after the dog, he could count on me. I began to wonder if he'd been drinking for the whole four days since Zanele and the twins had left.

"Did you hear from her?" I asked.

"'Course I did."

He said nothing more. I thought of him there, drenched in sentiment, looking at a photograph by the bedside or on some mantelpiece, or maybe that photo of her in his office, in her wetsuit and fin, that long single line of desire. I aligned with his operatic sadness—the great brotherhood of alcohol—and I thought to myself that I hadn't had a friend or even an acquaintance like Conway in quite a while. The feeling ratified me, traveled along my backbone, sat neatly in my cranium. The Germans have the best word for it, *schadenfreude,* although the weariness of *weltschmerz* came to mind too.

It was still early in the evening. I suggested that we see each other for a drink—tea or coffee was the code—or maybe we could meet in that activist bar he had suggested the first day I met him, which was not a code at all but a direct invitation to continue to further drench ourselves in booze, which sounded, quite frankly, inviting. South Africa was beginning to open itself to me, and I also had a vague sense that I might, alongside Conway, be able to meet some people who would help me solve that weariness.

But his voice tapered off and now there was someone else on the end of the line, another Conway who didn't seem so interested anymore.

"Come meet me down in Hout Bay tomorrow, we're going to Duiker," he said just before he hung up. "Early, before there's too much of a swell."

———

I had no clue what Duiker was, nor even a swell, but, as it turned out, Conway was referring to a diving site, an island on the western seaboard, by Hout Bay, where the rise and fall of the water could be temperamental. I texted him early in the morning. He replied to say that I was late, he was already there, waiting, but to come along anyway, bring my swimming togs.

I didn't have any to bring, but I wrapped up a towel, took my camera, put it in my leather satchel, went out to the lobby to hail a taxi.

We drove out to the coast, past the necklace of fine houses and, just beyond them, a shantytown. The proximities still shocked me. This country went in all directions. Men lounged by the roundabout, waiting for random work. The taxi driver adjusted his mirror when I sighed. He didn't understand what I didn't understand about it all. "They're just layabouts," he said.

We entered another roundabout. Shreds of clothing waved in the trees. Say nothing, I told myself. I let the sunlight put a hand over my mouth.

The day was already midstride for Conway by the time I arrived. He must have risen very early or else stayed up all night. He had completed a morning of dives and returned to a café on Hout Street with some friends. They sat outside in a semicircle of colorful plastic chairs where they could look out to the docks at the parade of tour boats and fishing vessels. He stood up to greet me with a rather formal handshake.

"Mister Fennell," he said. There was a faint whiff of booze off him, but he certainly didn't look like he'd been down the bottom of a bottle. His eyes were clear and his face wasn't puffy. I implored him never to call me mister again.

I had no intention of diving. Even taking my shirt off was a slight embarrassment. But I wanted to hover for a while in Conway's orbit. He had been joined by a group of freedivers. They wore faded T-shirts and car tire sandals, like the ones Zanele had worn in her kitchen. Togs, which they called *cozzies*. Sunglasses dangled around their necks. I felt soft and pale among them. I wore my camera around my neck and carried everything else in my satchel. "That thing will get ruined out at sea," Conway said, and he lifted it from my neck. He carted the satchel into the café, where he left it behind the counter for safekeeping. He found me a bottle of sunscreen, sat me under a shaded umbrella with his friends.

Conway introduced me as a novelist, and they were briefly intrigued by me when I said that I was writing an article about underwater repair, though clearly disappointed when I made it clear that I had no intention whatsoever to dive for my research.

I had expected surfer types, all beads and white teeth, but his group was made up of a number of young biologists and physicists. I presume it had something to do with the lack of equipment, being bare against the elements, descending into the mystery of the ocean, that great conundrum that holds us together and apart at the same time. They weren't dismissive of the nearby scuba divers, or the boats that zipped in and out of the harbor, or the tourists who were there to watch the seals barking along the shore, but there was a definite sense that they, like Conway, didn't want too much fuss. They were taking a break, they said, since the water was turbulent.

One of the younger divers, Sally, a scientist from Pretoria, launched into a riff on a paper she had recently read on the nature of turbulence. I was largely lost, but the essence of it was that the scientist Werner Heisenberg had written his PhD on water patterns on some river in 1920s Germany. He was asked to mathematically determine the precise transition of a smoothly flowing liquid into a turbulent flow. But the problem was notoriously difficult, she said. Heisenberg had spent months trying to figure it out, and he was only able to give an approximate solution.

"It's all approximate in the end," she said.

"A lot can happen," Conway replied, "in the space between two breaths."

Sally let her hand rest, for a split second, on his thigh. She went on to tell us that when Heisenberg presented his thesis to his professors, he had problems explaining other aspects of physics as well. He tripped up on the simple answers, and so he received the lowest of three passing grades for his doctorate, which embarrassed him so much that he took the midnight train to Göttingen and showed up in the office of his mentor, Max Born, asking sheepishly: *I wonder if you still want to have me.*

I am aware, in telling this now, how pretentious it might sound— Heisenberg, turbulence, mathematics—but at the time I sensed that there was something meaningful about it, even if confusing. I was slightly envious of Conway having such friends and had to wonder about all the years I had spent inside the bottle.

Later—when the actual snap occurred—I would remember another part of Sally's story: after Heisenberg had become famous for his uncertainty principle, he was asked by a colleague what he would eventually inquire of God, and the scientist replied that he would ask two questions. The first would be, *Why relativity?* And the second would be, *Why turbulence?* Heisenberg was quite sure that the first question might get answered in some near future, but most likely the second would go unsolved for a long time.

Fair enough. Most things do.

———

Conway and his friends were not competitive divers. They weren't in it to achieve the greatest depth, or the longest breath hold, but they were looking to visit a different place from the one they were already in. They talked about it almost religiously, and I could sense how Zanele would have fit in among them. *The disease of our days is that we spend so much time on the surface.* It was almost as if in her absence she was more acutely there. It was apparent to me that Conway had seldom been there without her. Her name pinged through his conversations. He had found himself a Beckett line— *can't go on, must go on*—that obviously spoke to him, and he used it frequently, and a little comically, among the crowd when they asked about Zanele and the children.

"They were two days in London and were driven to Brighton," he said. "The kids can't get over how cold it is on the beach."

"She likes it?"

"She's in rehearsals most of the time."

"When is the premiere?" asked a Polish woman who sat beside him. She had a tattoo of a shell on the inside of each wrist.

"Early February, no reviews until then."

"Why don't you go over for it?" asked the woman, who sounded miffed. "Surprise her. Dash in and dash out? Ta-da! Zanele would love that."

She appeared attracted to Conway, but he didn't notice, or he didn't want to notice.

"Someone's got to hold down the fort," he said.

It seemed such an ordinary and old-fashioned thing for Conway to say. He didn't mention his late-night resignation, nor his future on board the Georges Lecointe—in fact, he appeared to have forgotten all about his revelation, and when I brought it up with him, quietly, later in the day, he seemed momentarily disrupted, as if I had invented it, or lied about it, but then he sloughed it off with a wry smile, and never mentioned it again. He had been drunk, of course, and perhaps he'd blacked out, or maybe he was just embarrassed. I didn't doubt that he missed Zanele and his children, but I was beginning to feel, even at that stage, that there was more to it than met the eye. Still, I felt a protective instinct toward him, maybe that of an uncle or a brother.

Shortly after lunch he took my elbow and told me that I was welcome to join them on a boat for a ritual that he and his friends were taking part in. He sensed my reluctance, but he leaned close to me. "Don't worry, you don't have to dive," he said. I noticed for the first time that his eyes had changed color: they had gone from green to a grassy gray.

It was a boat of ten: two young men from Zimbabwe, the Polish woman, and five South Africans, including a woman with long gray dreadlocks who immediately referred to me as a *soutpiel*, which Conway told me was an English redneck. I took umbrage and told her I was Irish, and she said, "Same difference," which I had to privately admit was, these days, probably correct.

I clambered on board somewhat precariously. I was given a life jacket, which I hung casually from my shoulder, until Marci, the woman with the dreads, snapped it shut for me. In the back of the boat was a large bucket with what looked like slabs of rock, tablets, smooth with rounded oval tops. We passed slowly through an area of coral so luminescent it took my breath away. The boat went out beyond a popular pinnacle rock about twenty kilometers from shore to a place they had, apparently, kept largely a secret.

We hovered but didn't drop anchor. Conway and the Zimbabwean diver—Muabi, a young man of no more than twenty-five— sat on either side of the boat: no wetsuits, no masks, no fins. I was astounded to see that the slabs of rock were grave markers, with the carved names of two divers who had died recently in Indonesia. Conway told me that it was a ritual the divers had started a few years before, when a local boy had died at that same spot and they had marked it with a gravestone down in the depths. They began to do it then for other divers. There were apparently up to sixty markers underwater now: all of them placed for freedivers from various parts of the world. The beauty of the gesture was that they were mirroring a diving method akin to that of the ancient Greek divers, using the weight of the stone to take them down to the depths and then depositing it on the ocean floor.

The boat drifted as the Polish woman spoke the coordinates. In the background a radio crackled. I had expected the divers to be on the brazen side, but, if anything, they were laconic and shy, quietly marking the distant dead.

Conway and Muabi got ready. They were all muscle and bone. They took huge gulps of air. Their diaphragms seemed to recede into their bodies. Their rib cages swelled. Wild horses. Then they began taking tiny little sips of air, packing their lungs with more oxygen. A slow sense of control came over them. An eerie calm. They eased off either side of the boat, the stone slabs held out in front of them. Down into the blue prairie of water. I watched them as they became aquatic for the first few meters, their feet shining, their soles pale, until the darkness swallowed them whole and they began their secret correspondence with the bones of the departed. I was amazed what happened with time: it made a *sound* in my ears. An ancient waiting. The drip of a clepsydra. They were diving to a depth of twenty-five meters, where they would find a circular rock formation, and they were going to stack the slabs in such a way that they leaned against one another. It was a spot where shoals of bioluminescent fish gathered, so that even in the incredible dark the divers would be able to see patterns of light.

I found out later that Conway was able, above the surface, to hold his breath for seven, sometimes eight minutes. The dive he took that day was five, which was still enough to rupture my thought patterns. He was able to reach depths that even scuba divers might never know.

"How was it?" I asked when he broke water and circled his fingers in an *okay* signal to the other divers.

He said nothing, just floated on his back in the water, watching a flock of birds on the sled of the breeze. He had stayed down almost a full thirty seconds longer than Muabi, and the exertion had taken it out of him. But he pulled himself up the ladder with ease and sat on the side of the boat while the others took their turns freediving without stones.

With his back to me I could study his form. He was strong and fit in exactly the ways that I had once been.

"So, you got the markers planted?"

"Yeah."

"An underwater graveyard."

"Sort of."

"How dark is it down there?"

"It's blue," he said. "Most everything else gets filtered out except the blue. It's like being in a Miles Davis song."

"What do you think about . . ."

"Very little," he said. "Nothing actually. It's absolute silence. You're free of everything. It's like floating in space. Like outer space, but inner."

He helped another diver back into the boat.

"It's the best place to be because you don't actually think. You can't think."

I knew, too, that it must be punishing: anyone who pushed their body to those limits knew what it meant to overcome pain. But for Conway, it seemed, it was worth exactly as much as it might hurt.

"You just have to deal with the urge to breathe," he said. "After that you have to remind yourself to come up. That's why you never dive alone. It's too seductive. Down there you become something else altogether."

He said nothing more, just sat looking over the side of the boat, tending to the rope. He remained quiet and calm, even when the divers stayed down longer than he thought wise. He had a signaling system with the guideline, a language of gentle tugs, when he wanted them to ascend.

"You and Zanele met diving?"

"I told you, you should write about her, not me."

"I'm just curious, it's not for the article." At the time it was true, and even now, far away, writing this down, I feel that sense of betrayal.

"She was studying theater in Fort Lauderdale. She was on a scholarship, some sort of Tennessee Williams thing. You should ask her about it. It was her first time out of South Africa. She was nineteen. I didn't see her then for a while."

"What were you doing?"

"Me?" he said, tugging ever so slightly on the rope. "I was in Louisiana, working on the oil rigs. Underwater welder. That's how I started out too, but in the North Sea. That was a hell of a job. Scuba work. Wet welding. In the cold. I was in the Middle East for a while too. Then came to Cape Town again. Me and Zee, we met back up."

"When was that?"

"A few years ago now."

"It takes a lot of volume to fill a life."

He glanced at me, slightly puzzled.

"I just mean the chronology of it makes me a bit dizzy."

"It was good money."

"Isn't it dangerous?"

"The deeper you go, the more you get paid."

He was gauging the tension on the rope.

"How does a torch work underwater?"

"Anything works underwater. At the right temperature. We had decompression chambers. The whole nine yards. We could be down there for days. Way beyond the lines of light."

"But. . . . freediving? You're not scared?"

"Why? Your heartbeat goes down to basically nothing. You can get it down to ten beats a minute. Hard to believe, but it's relaxing, man."

"And the dark?"

His shrug seemed, at the time, as good an answer as any, but then he said: "We don't really know the dark until we get there."

He didn't speak anymore as he worked the rope. He had been counting slowly, under his breath, even while talking, and the diver had reached the limits. It was the Polish woman, and she broke the water with a grin, gave the okay sign, then put her lips to one of the tattoos on the inside of her wrist. She swung nimbly on board and pulled herself into a large blue towel, sat herself close to Conway.

I tried to get his attention again. "You were saying?"

"Yes, what were you saying?" asked the Polish woman, extending every vowel.

"I'll tell you later, Fennell," he said, and I was immediately glad to think that he had dropped the *mister,* and that the *big man* moniker might not stick beyond the drunken phone call.

"No," she said, "what were you saying? Go on, Conway."

"We were talking about underwater welding."

"Oh, that," she said. "Everything begins with a Zee."

He seemed to laugh but he made it his cue to dive again. He got himself prepared, took little sips of air, packed his lungs.

"You know he's not a ship captain at all?" she said while he was diving.

"Of course he is," I said. "I've been in touch with his company. We're going to go on a run."

"No, silly, he's a chief of mission—it's an altogether different thing."

She was correct, but it was a nitpick, and it was mean-spirited, and I felt immediately protective of him.

I stayed with the group at the site for the rest of the afternoon.

The force of their backflips took them under. They used a slow frog-work of the legs to bring themselves down through the arcs of light, beyond the refracted beams, bending into the memory of something primordial. It was a sort of ancient theater, the old Greek way, the manner in which divers had gone to the ocean floor to collect sponges centuries ago. They were moving through physical atmospheres, I was told, one atmosphere for every ten meters or so. There was enormous pressure on their lungs at first, and the danger was that they mightn't equalize their ears properly, or that they might stay down too long and, on return, black out close to the surface, where most accidents occurred. But they wanted to search that inner space Conway had talked about.

They were kind with me, tolerant. I summoned the courage to get down to my boxers and get in the water for a swim with a snorkel mask. The Polish woman swam alongside me. Her foot grazed my rib cage. I felt ordained by the moment, and I looked down through the refracted beams to the point where other divers were disappearing, rippling away.

There was the rather obvious thought that I would never get to any proper depth, but it didn't matter, and I wasn't going to let it surround me as metaphor. So, I swam. Salt in my eyes, ears, nose.

I didn't have quite enough power to leverage myself up the side ladder, and Conway simply reached over with one arm and lifted me beneath the armpit, eased me onto the deck. I wrapped myself in a towel and sat in the back of the boat, shivering but strangely happy. I realized with a start that two days before had been my son's sixteenth birthday. I had not seen him for half a decade. Nor had I written to him. *We must try to live,* said Paul Valéry. I am aware how it sounds—the mind makes its flying leaps—but as a young student, I had genuinely liked Valéry and learned much of what he had to say by heart. *The huge air opens and shuts my book.* Valéry had a nervous breakdown in 1892 when a woman he loved rejected his advances, and then he resolved himself to a life of the mind. He wrote a few hours every morning and said that he had earned the rest of the time for what he called his *stupidities.*

The thought returned to me as if on a swing. My son. Far away. I was supposed to catch it, but I misread the arc and it hit me squarely in the solar plexus.

When I got back to the hotel that night, I realized, in the fading light, that I had left behind my leather satchel in the café. I had to return to get it. I was dizzy and out of sorts. The heat had hammered down on the back of my neck all day.

I half expected Conway to still be there at the bar, talking about Zanele and his children, stringing out his new loneliness, but it was only the Polish woman. She told me her name. Petra. It had nothing to do, she said, with the stones that had been planted in the bottom of the ocean. I was confused until she told me that the Greek word for the diving stones was *skandalopetra.* There were a few empty glasses in front of her, but she appeared sober, or perhaps she was just well practiced. I endeavored to catch up. Her eyes were an offshore blue. The memory of her foot touching against my rib cage returned, but I kept a barstool between us. She was Polish, I was Irish, and I wasn't quite twice her age but close enough. I got the sense that her mind was already busy elsewhere.

We shared our melancholy as the moon outside splashed down on the sea. She had a melodic alto voice and a jangling laugh that didn't seem very Polish at all. I had begun to figure that she was in love with Conway, or at the least deeply infatuated.

"They're not even married," she said.

He had used the phrase *partner and kids,* but it didn't bother me one way or the other.

"And they're not his children, you know," she said.

"Oh, I know," I said, though I knew nothing of the sort.

I might have suspected that they were not his biological children, since the boy had been so dark-skinned. There had been a brief sense of dislocation that night I sat in their kitchen, though I didn't know why. I had not seen the twin girl, but I wasn't about to rush to judgment, and who cared if they were his children or not? He had introduced them as his, and Zanele was his partner, if not his wife, and the kids were hers. I didn't want to narrow my own life to the squinting window. And who was I to presume anything anyway?

She turned toward me on the barstool as if to taunt me.

"He has a dark side," she said.

"How so?"

"He has many missing years."

"Don't we all?"

"He's from Belfast."

"He's from Rathlin Island. Besides, who cares if he's from Belfast or Beirut or anywhere else, for that matter?"

"I'm not insinuating anything."

Plainly she was. It is often the resort of the foolish to just mention Belfast as if those who live there and those who depart from it invariably bear all the city's troubles.

"And he was in the Middle East."

"He told me that."

"He aspires downward, you'll see," she said.

At the time I didn't make much of what she was saying: so many of us, indeed, have missing years—even when we try to total them up, the gaps emerge. I can hardly now pinpoint my late twenties, or almost all my thirties. Apart from the joy of my brief marriage, they blur. Her insinuations were tenuous. Conway would have grown up in an era of peace in Ireland. And as for *aspiring downward*, I was hopeful Petra had not meant it with a racial twinge. Surely it was just a way to say that he was more given to silence? I did not suspect her as a racist, or at least I didn't want to, but she certainly had some sharp edges. I didn't push. Conway did not seem like a man who wanted to embrace the rising air anyway. For him *downward* was surely just a journey inward. He was entitled to his privacy, and I had made a promise that I wasn't interested in writing about his personal life, his marriage, or his nonmarriage, or his kids. It was the cables that I wanted to investigate, what happened when they broke, and how it was that he and his crew repaired them. I reminded myself that there were glass tubes thousands of meters below the surface. No human could go that far. It was the glass and its shattering—and what the shattering might shatter—that mattered to me then.

It turned out that Petra had spent one year on a cable ship with him: they had gone on three repair runs together.

"I was in charge of the ROV," she said.

"What's that?"

"Remotely operated vehicle."

"A robot?"

She seemed mildly annoyed. "That's me, yeah," and she leaned away. I had to check my own drunkenness. I felt that I had fallen out of line somehow.

She began talking to the bartender of another journey she had gone on at another time, in Bermuda, in a submersible, to the deepest point she had ever been in her life, thousands of meters beneath the sea, in a specially reinforced underwater craft, of which there were only six in the world. When she got to the ocean floor, she said, she saw the most spectacular things—blind fish, sharks that glowed in the dark, sea anemones with eight-foot tentacles, sea squirts, shrimp, salpae, all manner of undersea beauty—but when she looked out into the narrow beam of murky light that the submersible shone into the depth, near the absolute bottom, she had seen a tiny piece of plastic floating.

"Plastic, can you believe it?"

The bartender seemed to have heard the story before. "Yeah," he said, and he turned up the music.

Petra sighed, gave up on him, sat silent a moment, then finally redirected it at me, the only other person left in the bar.

"There's nowhere we haven't been," she said.

"What do you mean?"

"There's nowhere we haven't fucked up. Every square inch. And now we have to go ahead and shit the ocean floor."

"No kidding."

"As if you care."

"Oh, I care."

She was right, though. If I was to be honest, I didn't really care: it was a piece of plastic, and it floated, and what was I going to do about it? I could pretend, and I could fret, but in the end I had no idea how to respond beyond a nod.

"Just because the truth is ignored," she said, "doesn't mean it's not true."

She sounded exactly like Zanele. Perhaps that was because they were both quite obviously correct. And yet the truth was, I still didn't care. Whatever honor I had was only in the ability to admit that I was, once again, drunk.

Over the stereo, Ted Hawkins sang it for me: *There stands the glass.*

"Are you friends with Zanele?" I asked.

"Oh, everyone's friends with Zanele," she said, and I recalled with a slight start what she had said on the diving boat earlier that day, when she had sounded miffed.

"She thinks she's going to be famous. That's all she wants. She couldn't care less about Conway. She has her missing years too, you know."

I wanted to protest, especially after the bond I thought I had seen in Conway's house, the adoration that seemed to move between them. Instead, I said: "Everything begins with a Zee."

Nothing flatters quite like imitation. Every negotiator and diplomat knows this. Take a key phrase and repeat it. Make it sound new. It will, for the most part, unlock a speaker. They seldom remember having said it earlier. I have been using the trick for years. There is nothing clever or noble in it at all. And certainly not this time. Petra made a gesture that she would soon be leaving, a simple midair twirl of the hand.

I tried to regain my footing, but she smiled in a sort of coiled yawn, glanced at the inside of her wrist—there was no watch there, just her seashell tattoo. She said that she had a phone call to make, which, like so much else in those days, was obviously untrue.

———

Two thousand miles north of us, the Congo swelled. A hypnotic flume. There was no taming it. Huge whirlpools studded the surface. Pirogues were sucked under. Giant barges were sent in a complicated dance. Birds perched on floating timbers. They could travel faster on the river than they could through the air. Down below, the turbulence gathered. The Congo had unrecognized depths. All the things we didn't know. All the things we were doing to ourselves. The manner in which we broke one another.

The riverbed deepened. More soil was swept out to sea. What was it Zanele had said? *One little breath of our history is ruining us forever.* Even the tiniest speck mattered. Shelves of soil and dirt and debris were fired along toward the edge of the underwater canyon. The soil accumulated. Shelf upon shelf. More rain, more sediment, more nutrients, more plants, more trees, more garbage. Millions of tons of accumulation. At the mouth of the river the tide came in and the tide went out. The banks burst again.

Nothing, not even words, can stop the flow of time. Things break. Nobody I talked to ever knew the precise point at which it was triggered. All of it took place so far underwater, and most of the sensors were destroyed in the flood, but it was January, and the enormous slide began, an avalanche, an underwater punch to the back of the brain, rupturing the eardrums of whatever was there to hear it, an eight-hundred-kilometer slide that could have destroyed anything in its path, passing through the underwater gorges, beyond the jagged cliffs, over the drowned ridges, the bluffs, the crags, the caves.

A huge flood then, beneath the sea, and a break in the cable. It was already designed for sway, large loops of it given over to the possibility, but it was stretched to the endpoint, and who knows what it was that the cable was carrying at the time, all the love notes, all the algorithms, all the financial dealings, the solicitations, the prescriptions, the solutions, the insinuations, the theories, the chess games, the sea charts, the histories, the contracts, the divorce papers, the computer hacks, the wild lies, the voices, the terror, the nonsense, the known, the unknown, the promises, the porn, the alphabet of flesh, the singsong of skin, the million wisps of disinformation, the flotsam of our longings, the jetsam of our truths, all of it, all, suspended in a series of wet tubes at the bottom of the ocean floor, and who could tell what was traveling through it at the exact point of snap, say it was you, or say it was me, or say it was Zanele, a thought that began with a neuron in her brain, sparking other neurons, gathering, multiplying, traveling from her cerebral cortex, through her spine, through her finger, through her keyboard, through the circuit board, into electrical pulses, 01001001 00100000 01101100 01101111 01110110 01100101 00100000 01111001 01101111 01110101, and out again, through her building, down a manhole, beneath a street in London, or in Brighton, in pulsating packets of light, to Dorset, or Cornwall, and all the way across the English Channel, codes of light, at billions of times per second, past France, past Spain, past Portugal, past the Canaries, past Cape Verde and Ivory Coast and Ghana and Cameroon and Gabon, until it met the flood, that speck of dust, the thing that tipped it over, and the cable was already wildly stretched, encased by a massive torrent of mud and history, and then suddenly it all just stopped, the cable snapped, and there must have been, at that moment, a tiny leak-out of light into the surrounding darkness, her message to Conway to say *I love you*, or then again, maybe not.

3

On the day of the snap, I took an early walk in the streets around
the hotel. The slanted morning light in Cape Town was tinged with
green. I had been told to be careful, that the streets were dangerous,
even at that hour.

It was not a city built for walkers. The sidewalks were cracked. At
times the pavement just disappeared. At the highway underpass
shopping trolleys were tethered to the ground by rope and chain.
Tents were ranged like mushrooms. A little scarf of smoke came up
from a cooking pot. A lean dog slinked sideways. Gray water leaked
from a rotted length of gutter pipe. Every now and then a shadow
moved among the tents. I had heard that these people had come
from the South African countryside, presumably to look for work,
and ended up living underneath the skittering traffic. Some of them
had built shanties out of scrap wood and boxes. The traffic above
was a constant going, going, going, a death marathon. There were
no children in the small encampments, at least none that I could
see. It was mostly men—tall and thin—and they watched me warily
from the edges of the shade. They didn't ask me for money, although
later I saw some of them walking in the traffic near the mall, peering through the car windows for any kind of contact within: it was
a shock that they weren't hit by the cars.

I passed a group of taxi drivers waiting under the shade of the fever trees. They eyed me up and down. I was only one thing to them, and when they figured out they weren't getting a fare, they went back loudly to themselves. The druggy heat shimmied in the air and insinuated itself into every synapse. A few sad birds sat along the telephone wires.

The mall was a place of safety. It was bright and shiny and harrowing. Security guards patrolled with guns. There were huge lines for the central ATMs: the mall was one of the few places where money could be taken out safely. But the machines were not working. A tinny elevator music sounded out. It was all shine and fluorescence. I could easily have been in a shopping center in Dublin. Perfume stores and watch shops and Christmas stores still open for business. A few teenagers began to appear. They looked confused. There was a hum about them. They ran about, calling each other's names. Ethan! Nelson! Carol! Ogabe! The names went caroming off the walls. I stopped in a coffee shop. Customers with credit cards were being turned away. The stores were only taking cash. I ordered a cappuccino. A young woman with bright blue hair seemed bereft. She looked around wildly. Her cursing was creative. I offered to buy her a coffee. She stared at me as if I had crawled upward from a deep hole. She swung away but came back sheepishly after a few minutes, said she would love a coffee. "Thank you," she said, "you're very kind, you're like my dad." She sat at a table a few feet from me. She looked beyond me. Outside the café the security guards were huddled. Shoppers stared into their phones. Clerks were manning the fronts of their stores, arms crossed, a little bewildered. A powerful moment had eluded me. I turned to the girl with the blue hair. "It's down," she said, "it's all down, everywhere it's down, it's just gone, nobody can get it." It took me a moment to realize that she was referring to the internet. It made sense then, the confusion, the broken systems, the lengthening line at the bank machines. I thought it might have something to do with the electricity, or a storm that was rumored to be coming Cape Town's way.

We were like stunned birds. We had flown into the glass. We had to check ourselves for damage. We stood up. The uncertainty hummed. We tried to brush ourselves off. We were all hitting refresh.

The line at the ATMs grew. The security guards were called. A scuffle broke out. There was something triumphant about having cash in my pocket. I wanted to invite all the shoppers back into the café and gather them around. You're like my dad. I walked into a clothing store. I had the sudden urge to buy something. A linen shirt. A rain jacket. Anything. The teenagers had collected now outside the ice cream store, perplexed. They needed their video games, their power buttons, their squirt of dopamine. No rhapsodies today. I sidled up to them and tried to listen. A rumor was rippling among them that something had happened. A World Trade moment. A hack. An electrical storm. Another catastrophe. They kept checking their phones as if things were about to change at any instant. They didn't have a proper vocabulary. The anxiety got under my skin too. I keyed my phone alive again. It didn't seem real that there was no service at all. And yet the absence connected everyone. We were in it together. For a brief second, we looked at each other and understood we were linked. It was as if something elemental had been taken out of the air and we shared it. Some wonder, some amazement. A steady stream of people moved toward the entrance of a large electronics shop. I presumed at first they were inquiring about their mobile service. But when I went inside, they were gathered around the huge bank of television sets. It was like we were searching for some solemn scrap of meaning and we would only find it on the screen. I discovered myself at the back of the crowd. I tried to worm my way through. How was there an image on the television when there was no service on our phones? Someone said that the local cells would be back soon. Something had happened to the radio towers when the internet went down. Confusion all around. The televisions were tuned to several different channels. As if one of them might reveal the secret. A soccer game. A talk show. A quiz. I pushed forward some more. A bit of news was filtering through the crowd. A problem with communications, someone said. Officials were confident. They were confident of what? Excuse me? Confident of what? Suddenly all the televisions were switched to a single channel. A news program. I slid my way to the front of the crowd. The whole of western South Africa was experiencing a slowdown. Mobile service was interrupted. Some places had no internet at all. It hit me then with the force of the obvious, a quick blood rush: it was possible that one of Conway's cables was down. There were other possibilities—an outage on land, a breakdown in the landing stations—but something told me that it was coming up from the water, from somewhere we didn't quite know, somewhere deep and dark and impossible. I immediately tried to call Conway. There was, of course, no signal.

———

In the hotel I was unable to check out. The clerk seemed unconcerned. She had no access to the web. I stood in front of her with my one giant suitcase. The sweat made perfect ovals on my light blue shirt.

"There's no manager on today, sir."

"How can there be no manager?"

"I just told you, sir."

I had learned, in the couple of weeks I had been in South Africa, to detest the word *sir*. It had all the quality of a very agile slur. A gesture of deference and an accusation all at once. A sly word, used repeatedly, with great precision.

"But that's absurd."

"I understand, sir, but there's nothing I can do about it."

She was looking at a space behind me. The lobby was full. Ghosts, all of them. I might have found my ex-wife and son there. Most everyone was looking at their phones. A few of them had unfurled their laptops.

A faint signal had returned. It could still well be that there was a break aboveground, not in the sea at all. I had read enough to know that the internet was self-healing. The data would be rerouted. Another cable would begin to fill, or half fill, the void. I presumed there were engineers at that very moment, their hair lit in digital blue, in London, or Portugal, or Lagos, trying to figure out exactly what was going on.

It didn't prevent me from dialing Conway again. I was of the mindset that if I tried often enough, I would surely get through. Turn the phone on, turn the phone off. I attempted a message from my laptop to the publicist in Belgium. The silence mocked me.

A loud African man in the corner announced that he had a full signal. He walked around the room, hefty and tall, spilling his self-importance from his button-down shirt. He was talking of stocks, of bonds, of futures. I was convinced it was a ruse. A woman stalked his shadow. "I have to call my daughter in Joburg," she announced. "Please, please, please, can I borrow your phone?" He ignored her, then announced that he had lost the signal. She seemed to disappear into the floor. "Can you just give me a hot spot for a second?" He turned in the other direction. "Does anyone have a working signal, please?" she said, holding her phone aloft. It appeared to me as if she—like all of us—was part of the inner workings of our devices, the circuit board, the battery, the liquid crystal display.

There was a slight edge of war about it all, as if the news of an enemy engagement had just been announced.

I went back to the front desk. "Can't you just take down my credit card number and bill me later? I really have to go."

"We're not allowed to do that," she said, and paused. "Sir."

"I'm involved in the repair," I said.

"Excuse me?"

"There's a line down at sea. I'm a fiber-optic guy. I've got to get out to sea."

A confusion washed over her face. Who could blame her? I too had, until recently, thought that the information we got just flew through the air around us, that it was satellites that carried all our lives, our messages, our signals to one another. Most of us never thought of information coming through cold, wet wires under the sea.

"Do you have a pen and paper?" I asked.

"Excuse me?"

"A writing instrument."

"We're not living in the Neolithic Age, sir," she said, and abruptly, in that one moment, I liked her.

She must also have felt some of the affection leak from me be-cause she reached across and—still without smiling—got me a pen and a piece of stationery stenciled with a butterfly. It was not the type of hotel that might have its own stationery, and at the top of the page it said *From the Desk of Chantal.* I wrote down the details of my credit card, my address, my passport number, and slid the page toward her.

"I'll take care of it."

"Thank you, Chantal."

"Oh, I'm not Chantal," she said. "Chantal's the manager."

Hers was a long and beautiful laugh, it had many elsewheres in it. I would remember it months down the road, the way it just seemed to rise up from the lobby and trill through the air where none of the other signals bounced.

"Good luck, sir," she said.

I wanted to dwell with her for a moment longer, take a deep breath, go back to pen and paper, remain there. The man in the lobby began his charade again. People followed him around. He had the air of a medieval piper.

Outside, the heat assaulted me. There were no waiting cars. I had to walk past the highway underpass to get to the taxi rank. I dragged my suitcase, one wheel of which was broken, so that it made a celebratory cackle.

At the underpass, by the traffic lights, a woman moved, bent and misshapen, between the cars. She wore a yellow dress and a bright blue headscarf. She held a bundle at her chest. The cars kept their windows rolled up.

She spotted a white van toward the rear of the waiting cars. Its wipers moved and a small mist of water sprayed up. Some car horns beeped. She didn't change her pace. The van inched forward. I thought that it might plow her down, but it stopped abruptly. She limped to the driver's window. The driver reached out with a handful of coins. The woman went to place them in her bundle. A few fell and scattered on the ground. The van went on. The woman bent down to pick up the fallen coins. Another car had pulled up behind her. I fully expected the car to start beeping but it didn't. Instead, the woman patiently picked up the coins, stood and smiled and leaned against the bonnet. The car moved a little and lifted her a little in the air. I was convinced that I would be witness to a terrible hit-and-run. But the woman righted herself on the car and sat upright, the yellow of her dress vibrant against the paintwork. There was no traffic in front of them. The driver eased up the speed and brought her to the front of the traffic lights once again. She slid with a certain panache off the bonnet, landed on her feet, grinned, and bowed. The other cars pulled up behind them. She began walking back through the traffic once again.

I recognized in a humbling flash that she was not connected. No phone. She was the least affected person of us all. I attributed to her a slice of joy. The display had caught the eyes of the other drivers, and they, too, had opened their windows. She walked along, tucking all that she got into the bundle at her chest. She tried to repeat the trick with another car at the back of the line, but the driver panicked when she leaned against the car, and instead of going forward, he reversed. She stumbled. He drove around her. A faintly terrifying squeal of the tires. She walked back up through the traffic with her arm outstretched. Her yellow dress was dirty. She came toward me. Her eyes were large and tender. She was missing a bottom tooth. She said something to me in a language that I didn't understand, though perhaps it was English. I fumbled in my pocket. I peeled several bills off the roll and handed them to her. She looked at the money as if I had made a mistake, then turned away sharply in case I changed my mind.

She bent down into the bundle at her chest and kissed the head of what I can only assume was a sleeping child.

———

I took a taxi to the port. The driver was ecstatic to have a disruption in his day. He drove quickly but took a quite obvious roundabout way toward the jetty. The fare ticked steadily upward. The Georges Lecointe lay in wait at the front end of the jetty, behind two layers of security fencing. Already there was traffic backed up at the gate.

The driver asked for a tip. I responded that it might be a good idea to go the correct way next time. "Very funny," he said, but I handed him a hundred rand anyway. He beeped his horn merrily as he went off.

Now that I was about to leave it, I had begun to like South Africa, but at a certain point there is no turning back. My shadow eased away from me. I walked along the row of twenty or more cars, dragging my loud suitcase.

The cars were queuing up to get beyond the gate. I took solace in the fact that beyond the gate, parked on the jetty, was Conway's motorbike. I felt a sort of privilege of knowing. I had anticipated this. There was a breakdown somewhere. I was privy to it.

"You need to wait here, boss," said the security guard.

I stood in the liquid pulse of the sun.

"I'm here to see John Conway. He's chief of mission. I'm traveling with him."

"I know who Conway is."

"Can you radio him?"

"I'm going to need your passport and your documentation."

I handed him my passport. He glanced at me again. "And your documents? From head office. Brussels."

"I didn't download them."

"I need your authorization."

"My phone is out."

"No shit, Sherlock, everyone's phone is out."

"Conway has all the details," I said.

"You can wait in the shade there," he said, pointing to a small canvas canopy inside the gate. "Just take a seat, I'll see what I can do."

The Georges Lecointe sat in the water off the jetty, no more than a hundred yards away. It was, I suppose, an unexceptional boat at first sight: boxy, busy, but simple too. The length of a football field, no more than that. Off-white, with the coiled purple insignia of the Belgian owners. To the untutored eye, the boat stood about three stories high. Steam rose from her highest funnel. On the decks were an array of masts and hoists and containers and satellite dishes and things I hoped I would eventually understand.

I checked again: the local service had returned, but no internet. So, the radio towers were back. I tried Conway. No answer.

The Georges tilted against its mooring ropes. It was elderly but looked as if it was smartly kept, except for a long rust stain near the front of her bow. The stain was about six feet in length, like an erasable scar. There was a flag—I couldn't tell from what country—flying from the back, snapping in the wind.

Some quick and darkening clouds hemmed it in, a roily gray. The heat was pouring down. A storm was more than a rumor now. The wind coming off the water smelled like wet metal.

Cars were being waved in and out of the port gate. Trucks came and went among the orange cones. The men—it was all men, no women—scampered about. Food was being delivered. Machinery too. Four harbor police cars had their sirens spinning. They were looking for the ship's purser. From my seat under the canopy, I could see figures moving on the decks of the boat. I tried in vain to see if I could spot Conway. They were all just quick silhouettes. A foghorn went off at regular intervals. Several more police cars arrived. I repeated that I needed to speak with Conway urgently. The guard waved me away again. I could feel the damp creeping at my back. Each noise from the guard's radio was surely a message for me.

Some seals barked just beyond my range of vision: they sounded at first like children. After an hour the guard came across and gave me a cold bottle of water. The small mercies. He had left messages with the chief mate and the purser and with Conway himself. "Someone'll be with you soon, boss."

Time ticked inside time. The birds quarreled on the air. They landed on the mooring ropes and then took off again.

I had never been on a proper boat except for a ferry ride to Holyhead as a young man when I was trying to run away from myself, but I had liked the wild, pitching feeling of that trip in my early twenties. In London I had chased the literary life. Readings in cafés were a popular thing at the time, and I paraded around, hair askew, shirt ambitiously undone, waiting for the wine to be uncorked. Afterward, in my notes, I wrote: *The music of mediocrity. A choral piece for the empty glass.* I had spent a few months trying to blow my heart out with cocaine, then gave it up just as quickly. On the page, the voices eluded me. Now here I was, sitting, waiting for another boat to take me elsewhere. So much of who we are is who we cannot be. We flatter ourselves when we think we can become something entirely new.

It was early afternoon before Conway broke the trance of waiting. He descended the gangplank. I stood up to wave at him, but he wasn't coming down to meet me at all, he just caught sight of me from the corner of his eye. He was dressed in jeans, a collarless shirt open to the third button, his knit cap tight across his skull, the curl of hair emerging.

"Oh, Mister Fennell," he said, "I forgot about you."

I attempted a smile. I had no comeback. "What's the story?"

"Give me five minutes?" he said. "I'll get you sorted."

He stepped across the jetty to a waiting car. The occupant of the passenger seat got out: a woman in her early thirties with startlingly blond hair, the only woman I had seen on the jetty so far. She had a clipboard with a number of pages attached. She was animated, maybe even angry. Conway had to sign every single one of the pages. I could sense her impatience from far away, just as much as I could sense the opposite from him. He was all calmness as if making his way to the seafloor on one of his dives.

The jetty buzzed with more deliveries. Bags of flour. Trays of avocados. Ink cartridges. Boxes of paper. Six large missile-size tanks—oxygen or nitrogen, I couldn't tell from the markings.

Conway signed off on the last of the documents. The woman tugged his sleeve. She seemed to be imploring him to do something. He nodded. It all rolled off him.

When he turned again, he seemed surprised to see me once more. He strode across and stood above me in the chair. There were no shadows anymore, the sky was too dark.

"Well, you got your cable break," he said.

"Where?"

"Not entirely sure, but it's somewhere off the coast of the DRC right now."

"The Congo?"

"In and around there."

"What happened?"

"No clue yet. Looks like there could be a second break too. In another cable. A separate one. Off Gabon maybe."

"How far away is the Congo?"

"Six days' sail up the coast. All things being equal."

Joseph Conrad rang in my head. *Heart of Darkness* had had its day for me. I had read it when I was hospitalized as a child. In Ireland it had served as a perfect colonial portrait of the British—the horror had always been theirs, not ours.

"When do we leave?"

"There's a lot of shit to do—"

"Anthony."

He nodded. "Anthony."

The woman's car pulled up alongside us. She rolled down her window. "Are you goddamned sure you can't get out before the storm, Conway?"

"You talk to God, arrange it, then I'll make it happen," he said.

She raised her eyes, buzzed her window up aggressively, and the car crawled off. He watched her go. "I don't think she's ever met anyone she likes better than herself," he said.

"Who is she?"

"One of the clients."

He removed the knit hat, rubbed his arm across his hairline, blew air into the cap, shook it, and put it back on.

"She's got ten million dissatisfied customers and they can't even email her."

There was a certain amount of pleasure in how he said it. I thought about his flip phone: it would not be working either. But a radio buzzed at his hip. And I noticed then that he also had a smartphone in his belt. Conway was not a man without complications. I was about to ask him about it when he leaned into me with a perfectly distant whisper.

"You should head along, there's no point in waiting. Go back to your hotel."

"Can't I go on board?"

"No point, Fennell. We're not setting off for at least twenty-four hours, probably forty-eight, to be honest. We have to figure out the right cable. Then load it. That's a half day's work. Supplies too. We need a tug to pull us out. And this storm. We might be hunkered in here for days, you never know."

I worried that he was trying to ditch me.

"Can't I just, maybe, observe?"

"I don't have a cabin for you yet."

"I don't need much, I can sit anywhere."

"I was going to put you in with the officers," he said.

"No need."

"The cabins are tiny, you know that, right?"

"I've no problem with that."

"They've got storms out there. They can be two hundred miles wide."

"I understand."

"Waves coming at you, six floors high." He paused. "Once you're on, you're on. Your passport gets stamped. Your exit visa. And then you're at sea. You're out there, you see nothing but water, and, trust me, you can't give anyone directions to rescue you."

"I get it. Hotel California."

"We can't wait to get out. And then we can't wait to get home."

"And then you can't wait to get out again?"

He glanced sideways, said nothing.

"Conway? What happens if you can't fix the cable?"

"It's not a question."

"But if it was?"

"The whole country slows."

"And then?"

"If another one breaks, on the east coast, Africa breaks. I mean, it all shuts down. Everything. Screeching halt. Then everywhere else begins to slow down too."

A gull teetered along the mooring ropes.

"There are four hundred working cables, Fennell. Not even fifty boats to fix them. Do the maths. Take out a few strategic cables, we're well and truly fucked. I mean it. It's catastrophic."

"No pressure, then?"

"Not a bother."

"Turbulence," I said.

He gave a wry smile. The gull soared off.

"Do you think anyone beyond Africa gives a shite?" I asked.

He stood there, nodding, not in any affirmative but more in a knowing way, like his physicist friends who were well aware that you could not locate the speed and the position simultaneously, and that the only good answer is the uncertain one.

I felt vaguely triumphant when he spoke sharply into his hand-held radio and called for his deputy to bring me to my cabin with my suitcase.

"Oh, hey," I said. "Your dog."

"What dog?"

"Didn't you need someone to look after your dog?"

"There's no dog, man."

"I thought you had a dog."

"Oh," he said, "Zanele took care of her before she left."

It was a small detail and it fell in line with his announcement of his resignation, but it still gave me pause. I knew the feeling. Blackout.

There would be no alcohol on board the ship: he had already told me that. I welcomed the notion. It was time for an extended drying out, not only for Conway but for me too. The booze had slowed me down, crawled into my cranium, pulled a curtain across my perception. The bottle does a good job of drinking the mind.

Conway's deputy took my bag without introducing himself. He

seemed like a man trying not to panic. I was led upward along the gangplank. The ship was abuzz. Other officers and crewmen strode briskly about. All in civilian clothes. No uniforms, no hats.

We negotiated the maze of staircases, a series of doors. The smell of fried cooking singed with engine oil. I was led onto D deck, which, as it turned out, was where the officers' cabins were. Conway must have been mistaken, I thought. A room had been prepared for me, after all.

The deputy heaved my suitcase into the cabin and onto the small single bed. A porthole window, rectangular, not round. A sink, a mirror, a tiny bathroom with a standing shower. A lumpy pillow that had seen better days. The only thing on the wall was a map of the inside of the ship and an evacuation plan. Apart from the rectangular window, it was much the same as I thought it might be.

"Samkelo," he said, extending his hand to me. "You're welcome on board. Just so you know, we're locked in. There's no way we're getting out of port for a couple of days. The gale's shaping up to be thirty-plus knots. You might feel a little ill."

"I'm sure I'll be fine."

"You ever been on a docked boat before, sir? In a storm?"

"Not really, no."

"This is a black sou'easter."

"No idea what that means."

He looked at me without sympathy. "Anything you need, the ship hospital is on main deck. Starboard. I double as chief medic. We've all got two jobs."

"And Conway?"

"He used to dive. Not anymore."

"Why not?"

"He's boss. He sticks with the ship. No matter what. The captain and him."

He nodded and turned to go.

"And what about the internet?"

"What about it?"

"How do I get on?"

"Conway's got to sign off on that."

"But where's it coming from? When we're out at sea?"

"We've got satellite," he said, peering through me. "It's expensive. We have to limit it. And it's slow. The chief has to sign you on for full access. Johnnie, the Aussie, will hook you up. He's the tech bloke. Tall. Blond. Tattoos."

The wind whipped and rain smacked against the pane.

"Good luck," said Samkelo.

The door closed behind him.

The initial mystery of any journey is not so much where you will end up, but how you got to the starting point at all. There were my books, and there were my failures, and there were my losses. There was my youth, there was my pride, and there was my ongoing silence. There were all the lights that I had blown out in my life. All the times that I'd been the stage actor in the wrong play. I had come now to the very tail end of the African continent, at the meeting point of two great oceans. The break was thousands of kilometers north of us.

We were looking at the best part of a month or more at sea, in a cabin that felt like it was perched at the known edge of the world: for me, at least, there was little else out there.

———

As a child, I was used to small rooms. At the age of ten I came down with a case of spinal tuberculosis. I spent months on end in a tiny room in hospital in Dublin. Books were a companion. The library trolley rattled around twice a week. *To the Lighthouse. Brave New World. Guests of the Nation.*

At home, during recovery, I had a view to a small green field and a hedgerow. I used to see my mother standing, frozen at the top of the stairs, her hand on the banister, unable to make a step downward. She gazed into the distance. She had long, beautiful hands, but when she was nervous, she could hold nothing in them, not even rosary beads. Her mouth quivered ever so slightly as if trying to remember a prayer. She had, like many Irishwomen of her generation, become reliant on prescription pills that were handed out freely by doctors at the time, long before we had our stories of Big Pharma. She was cited for depression, I suppose, but the pills poisoned her with a silence that was not something that had belonged to her when she was young. In later years I asked my father what exactly happened, and he said to me abruptly: "That's water under the bridge." It quietened me but left me in doubt for the rest of my life.

Very few children escape an episode of major sadness, and the loss of my mother was mine. I was so young at the time that I didn't really know what was happening. It is often ourselves we blame for such losses. We do not know that we can be burned by an adult truth. It is the first of the small oblivions we have to learn. I do recall that she retreated very quickly, or at least it seemed that way to me, and the shine went out of her, the light disappeared, and all of a sudden she was upstairs the whole time, little more than a shape beneath the covers. She would come out of her bedroom and stand on the landing in her dressing gown. Sometimes her foot would tremble as she was about to make the step down beyond some invisible threshold, but she never did. My father came up, commanding his shadow, carrying trays of food to her, soup and tea and bread, and guided her back to bed. He was sleeping in a separate room—something I only came to ponder years later—but one night, shortly before she died, I stood at the door to my mother's room, listening, trying to see inside. I could glimpse their image in the glass of the bedroom window. He was holding her. I think he might have been brushing her hair. He appeared so much bigger than she was. She was softly crying and he was trying to appease her, stroking her long gray locks and whispering something I couldn't quite hear, almost a chant, *there there* or *now now now*. He held her like that for a long time and, without even turning his head in my direction, said with a startling sharpness, "Get you to bed, young man." Moments later I heard the door click, and a little rhomboid of light on the grass outside went dark as he clicked off the light in her room.

The next afternoon he came into my room to tell me that my mother had passed away. It is always a shock for a child to see a parent cry. We somehow think that they are far beyond feeling, though of course they never really are.

———

My first three days on the Georges Lecointe—when we were still docked in the port in Cape Town—went by in a haze. We were hemmed in by the storm, a Category 4 with a fierce gale off the sea. It blew heavy and then feigned calm. The slanted rain rifled hard off my porthole window, ended abruptly and then began again. Conway called it a jazz storm.

He was perfectly prepared to try to brave it and bring his team out to sea, but he was restrained by the harbormasters. There were rules to follow, apparently. No boats could leave port if the winds were over thirty knots. They wouldn't even allow the Georges to move from the dock to load up the necessary cable. We stayed put, under the gaze of the mountain. It hardly mattered to me at the time.

On the second morning, as the storm grew, I felt ill. Even at dock, the pitching of the boat reached inside me. I found it difficult to lie down and impossible to stand up. I tried to lean against the corner of the wall with a view to the porthole window but couldn't keep my balance. I was given medicine for seasickness. It didn't work. The cabin reeked.

A petty officer, Hercules, brought bread and water.

"See if these are interested in you," he said.

They weren't.

"Maybe it's food poisoning," he said.

There was a slight mockery in his tone.

"Try to get some sleep, bud," he said as he closed the door.

I lay down again. My stomach heaved. Night came. No release. The rain. The wind. The smell of sickness. I tried to wash the pillowcase. My feet slipped in the vomit.

Hercules came and gathered up my bedding, slopped the cabin out, hosed it down. I was allowed a neighboring cabin for a while, but that had to be hosed down too. I shut the small porthole curtain against the storm. My brain ran rudderless. I wasn't at all sure of the time. I hunkered in my tiny shower, all my clothes off, curled up tight. It felt better to have the shower water pouring down upon me, rain within rain.

I didn't even flinch when Conway came into the cabin. I thought he might stand at the door and address me from around the edge of the doorway, but he leaned up against the sink, his back to the mirror. I couldn't even muster the strength to pull the shower curtain across.

It was, I'm sure, quite the sight, my naked carcass curled up in the tiny space. Conway must have thought he had found a rare specimen to bring out to sea, but he talked to me plainly, as if across an ordinary space. It wasn't unusual, he said, and it often happened to first-timers, even here in the port. But I had to be careful. Dehydration was a severe risk. There were certain people who could be prone to constant seasickness. He could let me off the ship now if I wanted, but there would be no way that he could allow me on board again. He was quite sure that I'd feel better once we were properly out on the water. It was a simple matter of adjustment, but I had to make a decision right away.

"Once out there, I can't come back in," he said. "Nobody gets that. Not even the captain or me. You've got to work with us. We caulk the long seam."

I had no idea what he meant, and I felt vaguely schooled, but I said, "I hear you," which was true and untrue at the exact same time.

"Any evacuation you will have to pay for yourself."

"Right."

"We have no landing pad, no luxuries, nothing."

"Fair enough."

"And when I'm out there, I'm out there. It's all that exists for me. There's nothing else. You understand?"

I nodded.

"What do you think?"

"I've come this far."

"That's good," he said. He turned and washed his hands in the sink. "You've got to understand the nature of a boat, Fennell. You make the most of what she can do, and you never ask her to do something she cannot."

"I get it."

As he stepped over the lip in the doorway, he said wistfully: "I'm happy that you met Zanele."

The door snapped shut. I crawled from the shower. Two large jugs of water sealed with cellophane had been placed by my bedside. A small plate of lemons. Some rehydration tablets. Some salted crackers. My bedding had been cleaned again.

I lay down and turned my face to the wall. I began to heave once more. That evening, I was even sicker than before. More than once I thought about crawling off the boat and leaving the assignment behind. Who was I kidding anyway? The idea of an actual repair was the sort of soul-destroying bullshit that I needed to strenuously avoid.

The rain rained upon itself.

On the fourth morning I was surprised upon waking to be able to wake at all. I wasn't at all sure where I was. Then the cabin came into focus, and the porthole window. When I stepped to it, gingerly, I was even more surprised that there was a landscape of open sea in

front of me, a corduroy of moving waves, and a shelf of early red-
ness in the sky.

During the night, while I slept, they had loaded the giant tanks
with hundreds of miles of coiled cable and we had been taken out
into the hallways of the sea by tugboat. We were in the channel
now, beyond the turning basin, with Table Mountain in the distance.

We passed in the shadow of a huge gray container ship and out
into the brightness once more. The horizon dipped as the prow rose
and fell.

Small countries of light and dark poured across the sea.

4

I suppose we go out to sea because we want, eventually, to come home. I know this now, but it was new to me then. The best way to experience home is to lose it for a while. Then, when it is gone, you can know what it is. You can yearn to return to it. It is a form of wounding. You welcome the scar so it will remind you of where you once were.

We go to sea, too, because there are rules out there to obey. Simple determinations. You have a job. A cable is broken. The ship leaves port. It travels to the break. You find the cable, lift it up, splice it, put new cable in. Return to port. Go home with the story intact.

That's not what happened, but that's what you want.

———

Fifty-three men. We steamed out of Cape Town, running a wide course. I watched Table Mountain become a thin ledge. It faded. No land.

It suddenly didn't smell like the sea anymore. Or, rather, I had never properly smelled the open sea before. A vast, waking freshness. Conway walked the ship with me, introduced me to the men. It was clear they adored him. He knew their nicknames, their hometowns, their family members. He spoke several greetings in short bursts—French, Arabic, Zulu.

"I've a few words here and there," he said.

"Where d'you get the Arabic?"

"You've got time at sea. When the job's done."

"Really?"

"Most good things happen on the way back."

There seemed to be something innocent about the intent: just make the repair and return. On the top deck he spread his arms out and said: "All yours, Fennell."

I was the idler on the ship, the only one with nothing to do. I walked the innards and out up onto the deck, down to the engine room and up again.

The Georges asked to be explored. Maps on the walls. Navigation charts. Evacuation routes. Arrowed strips on the gray floor. Always another corner and another set of stairs. No space wasted. There was never a long run of emptiness, even up on deck. A lifeboat here. A storage room there. I walked down the metal stairs, along the corridors, out on the platforms above the giant cable tanks. There were two huge tanks, each twelve meters deep, filled with cable. The wire lay neatly coiled in vast celtic circles beneath me. Odd to think that the wire could all soon be at the bottom of the sea.

I circled around. In the mess a few men were gathered. I slid into the seat opposite Hercules. He was, rather humorously, a small, lithe man, a little isthmus of hair on his forehead.

"She's a working boat," Hercules said. "She gets a lot of respect."

"She's a she?"

"Of course she's a she. She couldn't be anything else."

"The men like her?"

"Mother lover wife daughter."

"There's a regimen on board?"

"What d'you mean?"

"I mean, is there a hierarchy?"

He stirred his coffee with a swizzle stick, took another look at me, sized me up. "Is this shit going in your book?"

"I'm not here to write a book, just an article."

"For what?"

"An online mag."

"Are you going to quote me?"

"Only if you want me to."

"Where's your tape recorder?"

I pulled my phone from my pocket, keyed it alive.

"Damn," he said, "you've got full service."

"They hooked me up yesterday."

"Most of the guys on here don't have access."

"Why?"

"Drains the satellite."

"What do they use?"

"There's a computer down below. You've got twenty minutes. Facebook and Twitter, all that shit."

"Do you have access?"

He didn't reply.

"You can use my phone if you need to."

"I don't need to," he said, "but thanks, man. Where were we?"

"Hierarchy."

He considered his coffee and poured a little sachet of powdered milk into it. "You got two separate crews, see. Boat crew and cable crew. Abdul's the captain. And Conway's the chief. Abdul calls the shipping shots. And Conway calls the repair. They're the boss men."

"Abdul's from?"

"Algeria. Or Morocco. One of those."

"And the others?"

"They're from everywhere. Most of us from South Africa. A few from Zim. We got three from Madagascar, two from Benin. Danny, the cook, he's from Bosnia. And there's Matt the Scot. He's the cable engineer. He don't talk to nobody. Except Conway. When he has to."

"And who does Conway talk to?"

"Everyone, man." He glanced down at my phone. "Petrus is going to make you laugh. Johnnie is going to say something he thinks is smart, but sure as shit isn't. Omar, the prep chef, he's just crazy. But Conway's the one. Everyone talks to him."

The boat pitched high and his coffee pitched with it, but Hercules stalled it with one finger.

"Never a fight?"

"Bit of handbags, maybe. None of the usual shit talk, though. The captain's Black. The chief is Irish. You're in a Stevie Wonder song, man." He seemed pleased with himself. "Write that down, man. It's family here—"

"Plenty of families have shit talk, though."

"You know what I mean," he said. "We don't get into it. We've a job to do. Some guys are Christian. Some guys, Muslim. Matt the Scot's a Jew. What about you?"

"Nothing really. Sort of in between."

"I figured."

How he figured, or what he figured, I wasn't sure.

"What d'you spend your time on?"

"This and that. We don't have much time."

"And money?"

"The money's good, man. There's no bar here. No shop. No fashion show. You save it all. No gambling. They don't like you gambling. You can get shit for gambling. They can fine you."

"What're you going to gamble on out here?"

"Seriously? Try the breakfast menu. The next wave."

"You got a family?"

"Sure," he said, nothing more.

"Hercules?"

"Yeah?"

"There's no women on board."

"You noticed?" He sized me up again, squinted, and tapped the table in front of my phone. "Doesn't make for any weird fuckery, if that's what you're asking."

It wasn't what I was asking, but it was a good enough answer, and as it turned out, it was true. There was no fuckery going on among the men on the Georges, or none that I heard of, anyway, not that I would have cared, since I have long since given up the idea that someone else's fumblings mattered anyway.

Hercules rose to leave. He suddenly seemed pensive. I was pretty sure he didn't want any more questions, but he lingered a moment.

"There's daily prayer sessions if you want them. Some of the guys, we get together ..."

"Sounds good."

He knew full well that it didn't sound good to me at all and he turned, then stopped at the mess door. "We got some AA meetings here too, you know."

It bothered me that he had intuited something. Alcohol as biography indeed.

"Yeah," I said. "I'll wait a little while."

My stomach had settled down after my wretched illness. I walked down to the engine room to take some photographs. Bokamoso, Petrus, and Nizaam were there in the hellbox of heat and roar. In their orange jumpsuits and black rubber boots. Walkie-talkies at their hips. They moved among the propulsion engines, the water pipes, the boilers, the generator, the filters, the fuel strainers. There was something human about it too: the mysterious workings of the viscera, the liver, the kidneys, the heart.

"It's the magazine man," said Petrus. He lowered his eyes when he saw the camera around my neck. His forearms were thick. His hair was cut tight. "I'm too pretty," he said. "I might break that thing."

They went from metal platform to metal platform, up and down small flights of stairs, through the throbbing maze. The closest I had ever come to it before was at a newspaper in Dublin, the smell of the ink from the printing press, the words tumbling on the rolls, the papers churning down the chute. It was hard to fathom how the men squeezed in behind, under, and even inside the machines, but they were well choreographed, a working ballet, all muscle and ratchet. The air smelled—almost tasted—of thick oil. It went into the gaps between my teeth.

"She's a healthy old horse," said Nizaam. He slapped the side of the oil container. "She could stay out six months if she wanted."

"How long've you ever stayed out?"

"Most I ever been, ten weeks. Up in France."

"Ever any problems?"

"Froze my ass off. Whatever they tell you about France is a lie."

"Old Royce," said Petrus, "dropped a denture off the side once."

"No pirates?"

"Not since last month."

"Who'd be dumb enough to rob a cable ship anyway?"

"Same idiot dumb enough to go to France," said Petrus. "Fell in love with a girl from Brest. That's his problem."

Nizaam laughed and threw him a spanner.

"Nothing much happens here, man."

"All we got is a roll of wire."

None of the men were interested in having their photographs taken. They couldn't fathom why it might be remotely interesting.

"Try the cable guys," said Nizaam. "They're engineers. Pretty boys. They like to be reminded how they look. We're just looking in one direction."

"Which one?"

"Home."

"Storm knocked us back a few days." Petrus cleaned the oil from his hands on a small red cloth. "But we're getting there, yeah."

I took a clandestine photo. Later I zoomed in on his large dark hands, the scars, the very white of his cuticles, the smear of oil along the ridge of the cloth. They were the sort of hands that had surely been on boats since boats began. Some things never change. Melville was among my childhood authors when I was laid up in hospital. *My body is but the lees of my better being.* His maps, the true places.

On the main deck, in a glassed-off room, I sat with the engineers, Samuel, Bogani, and Ndlovu. It was the cleanest room on the ship. No oil. No dust. They were constantly cleaning, wiping, adjusting, preparing.

"You can get your photos later," said Ndlovu. "When it matters."

Two small black boxes sat in the center of the room. Fusion machines. They would bring the ends of the glass fibers together. The tiny world linked to the epic. I studied the inside of a slice of cable. I had somehow thought the wires would twist around one another. They lay, instead, in perfect, neat concentric rings. Like the inner workings of a tree, except there were no markings of time. If all of this was miraculous, it was deeply practical too. At the very inner core, protected by several layers, lay the glass tubes. The conduits of the light. The xylem, the phloem. All of that which we were saying to one another. Carried by that which we could never precisely locate.

Up near the bridge I watched Abdul, the captain, take his prayer mat out and set it up on the aft deck. Worship at sea. No minarets, no steeples. The middle of nowhere was not nowhere after all. He was a handsome man—Algerian, it turned out—in his early sixties, gray hair tightly cut, lean and fit. He wore crisp yellow shirts and Lacoste sweaters, and a pair of glasses hung around his neck: the two ends snapped together with a magnet. He spread out the small carpet, bent to his knees, and faced Mecca.

In the corridors the men moved fluidly among and around one another, well used to the ebb and flow. Down the stairs. Through the narrow passages. They stopped and allowed the officers first access, with priority up and down the steep stairwells. I, too, was learning how to negotiate the corridors, figuring out a way that my body didn't stick too far out from my brain. To my embarrassment, I was considered high up in the pecking order. It made me anxious, but there was little I could do about it: even though I was the idler, the crewmen stood back and let me pass.

Still, I had an early sense that the ship was opening up to me. It was a boat, a small boat, an older boat, not much more than the length of a couple of blue whales, and there was one intention, the story immemorial: to survive the harpoon, skip the vortex, complete the job, and get back to where we came from.

———

In the colonial hotel, Conway had told me that he didn't like distractions out at sea, but he invited me to the control room to sit alongside him and his deputies, Samkelo and Ron. The room was on a lower deck, small and windowless. Marine maps on the walls. Photos of severed cables. A tray of rope knots in a glass case. His instructions were clear. Observe patiently. Not too many questions. No video. Stay off the Wi-Fi until late at night. The bandwidth from the satellite was narrow and slow and it couldn't be compromised. No drinks or food anywhere near the equipment. One phone line was a permanent satellite link to Brussels, punctuated by talks with engineers and geologists and hydrologists. The second, the personal smartphone, was clipped to his belt. Clients were calling from South Africa, the Democratic Republic, Sierra Leone. They wanted timelines and answers. Conway used a radio to link with Abdul upstairs on the bridge. *There's a small front coming Wednesday. Make sure those channels are moving. We need those charts from London. We can't fix it telepathically, you know.*

The phone calls came in fast and furious from Brussels. They seemed to have an expensive ringtone. There were slowdowns all along West Africa, they said. Cacuaco, Libreville, Douala, Lagos, Cotonou, Accra, Abidjan. They were worried too about the load on the eastern cable that ran, on the other side of the continent, all the way down to Madagascar. If that cable broke, it would be a global disaster. Every day that Conway didn't get the western break repaired was another day for things to fall apart.

I didn't know at the time about his turbulence with Zanele, but in retrospect Conway seemed to have buried it all in his work.

"Want to know where hell is?" He put the phone down on the maps in front of him, so that all that we heard was muffled anger on the far end, which I presumed was Brussels.

I couldn't quite understand the language flitting around us: *cross slope, shunt fault, double feeding, holding drive, dynamic positioning.* The Wild West of telecommunications. The room hummed with intent. Conway seemed to have a code of nods and numbers going with Samkelo, who, in turn, relayed it to Ron.

Samkelo was tall and thin, with perfectly creased shirts. Ron, third in command on the cable team, was a tight, compact man from Virginia, the only American on board. He was elaborately, if predictably, tattooed—a grappling hook and a series of rope tattoos high on his arms.

On each of their desks sat three computer screens: nine in all. On one long table, an extensive row of marine maps. At the end of the table, a globe, the earth turned inside out, the countries blue, the seas green.

The only time Conway left the control room was to go to the head. Pissing at the bow, he called it. While he was gone, I sat in his chair, tried to decode his computer, but it was all hieroglyphics to me.

"You'll get used to it," said Samkelo.

"No you won't," said Ron to me. "It's rocket science."

It was an admirable insult, and I laughed.

"Don't listen to him, man," said Samkelo. "We're just chasing a line."

"Is that all it is?" I asked Conway when he came back in. "Are you guys just chasing a line?"

"That's about the shape of it," he said. "Except this one goes downward, not up."

I was reminded of the notion that he liked simple machines. I had spent a good deal of my early undergraduate years infatuated with the plight of the mill workers in England more than two hundred years ago. Their gray caps, their gray lungs, their gray skies. The pitched battles on the outskirts of their gray factories.

"A bit of a Luddite, are you?"

"I'm not sure what that means, Fennell."

I began to launch into an elaborate man-over-machine history, but Conway cut me off. He already knew a lot more about it than he let on.

"They only took the hammer to the looms because the looms were being used to exploit them."

"Meaning?"

"Meaning we're just fixing wires, man. Not the internet. I'm not responsible for the shit that happens out there. That's someone else's job."

"So you just fix it and move on?"

"I do the hardware. And I'm not a Luddite, man. No way. If I was a proper Luddite, I'd be swimming home."

The phone rang again. He may not have been in full opposition to the technical, but I was convinced, watching him, that he was listening more to the sea than to the voices on the other end of the line.

He sank into the work. It amused him that his swivel chair had a slight hydraulic leak. It lost pressure slowly as he studied the maps, and after it had fallen an inch or two, he stood abruptly, touched the low ceiling, and readjusted the handle. Every now and then he would rise out of the chair and stretch. His muscles tautened. It was as if he wanted to dive again, and I suppose that chasing the depths was close enough to diving: the mystery, the darkness, the exquisite unknown.

To me, the idea that there was a cable lying so far beneath the ocean still seemed otherworldly in itself. Conway showed me a computer visualization. The canyon walls were alarmingly steep, even in their vaguely cartoonish form. Putting a cable across the canyon was unavoidable. There was no way to skirt around it. The cable could not be suspended in mid-ocean: it would most likely drift and snap in the currents. It had to fall into the canyon, cross the floor, then rise again.

Conway navigated the computer cursor across the screen. "This is the world as it is," he said. "Impossible. And fucking beautiful."

He wanted to create a repair that would last. He needed to navigate the knickpoints and the bottlenecks in the canyon. He was trying to calculate how much slack they needed on the new cable, or if they needed slack at all. He had been in touch with hydrologists about the effects of any new turbulent current. Woods Hole. Bermuda. Johannesburg. Conway had to figure out the break, then decide where to make the new cable fall. If he got it right, there might not be another break for a decade, but if he got it wrong, it could snap again with the next flood.

The men were still a tad wary of me, but on my way to the officers' mess, Ron and Samkelo caught up with me. Dinnertime. The mess wasn't much different from the one next door. Tablecloths and glassware, that was about all. Our food was served: beef burgers, creamed spinach, and scalloped potatoes. Land food. It almost made me laugh.

"Fresh fish comes later," said Samkelo. "When we slow down."

"At the break?"

"After the fix."

"How long will that take?"

"Some of these landslides can last a week," Ron said. "They're hundreds of kilometers long. The canyon walls collapse. It's like a huge train of dirt. On land it would wipe out whole city blocks, take down buildings. We've no idea what sort of havoc we're heading into."

"What will the slide carry?"

"All sorts of stuff. Mostly dirt, but you never know. We could lift up something human, something from way up the Congo."

"Four hundred kilometers out to sea?"

"I've seen teakettles," said Samkelo.

"You think we'll find the break?"

I worried that it was a stupid question, but they didn't take it as such, and I felt justified when Samkelo said that they weren't sure if the exact fault could be pinpointed. "Not in the absolute, anyway," he said. "It depends on what the underwater slump had done."

The wire could be buried under sediment, or spliced in different places, or the ends might have been swept way off course from one another. The canyon we saw on the maps might not be the canyon we would be getting at all. The unbuckled world.

"Needle in a haystack," said Ron.

My doubt was nagging me. "But what happens if you can't find it at all?"

"We go backward and forward until we can."

"But if you can't?"

"It's not a question."

"I mean, what's the answer?"

"You're not going to lay a whole new cable," said Samkelo. "Unless you've got a couple of billion dollars."

The essence was that Conway and his team had to pinpoint the problem, get the ship in place, then figure out a way to lift the cable from the canyon, then mend it and return it to the seafloor. There was, of course, no way any human could dive to that depth. And the remote-controlled vehicle—the one Petra had been in charge of on previous journeys—could only go down two kilometers. At four, it would be crushed like a tin can. The only way they would be able to get the cable up from the ocean floor was the old-fashioned one: to lift it with a grappling hook. A trip to Hades armed with a piece of steel.

"Just like the old days," said Samkelo.

"Conway seems calm enough."

"He's always calm," said Samkelo. "I've been with him three tours."

"Someone told me he has some missing years."

"I don't know what that means, Mister Fennell."

The sudden formality silenced me. It was a form of loyalty. Conway protected them. And so they protected him.

In the control room Conway was still deep in his calculations. Without looking up, he nodded. "Have a gander at this." He pulled over a chair for me, pointed to a spot on the screen hundreds of kilometers out from the mouth of the Congo, isolated in the ocean. He zoomed in on it. "Now we just go down."

"Sorry?"

"And down again."

The cursor plunged.

"It's not just dark down here, Fennell. It's way beyond that. The purest dark you can imagine. You can't get darker anywhere, not in outer space, nowhere. And nobody has ever been down there. Not a soul."

It seemed to me like a confusion of mathematical lines. To him, it was a place to be.

"Nothing living down there, is there?"

He swiveled his chair.

"More life on the bottom of the ocean than anywhere else, Fennell. In the vents. The layers. The currents. Things down there betray all the categories, man. Creatures we haven't even seen, let alone named. Bacteria. Vertebrates. Marine snow. It's all there. That's where we came from. The original place. Only a couple of hundred people on earth can even dream of what goes on down there."

It wasn't a lecture, but it certainly felt as if he was talking somewhere beyond me.

"We all think it's empty but there's no such thing. The ocean is a sort of solid, man. We've got to move through it. It's a *thing,* Fennell. It's not some vast emptiness. Not a void. In your article, don't call it a void. It's a medium. It brings us somewhere else. We just don't know how to think about it. We've forgotten. We crawled out of there hundreds of millions of years ago. And we still know next to nothing about it."

He zoomed in on a graph of the canyon floor. The layers. The texture of the abyss.

"And our cable runs at the bottom of it all," said Samkelo from across the room.

———

All that traffic on the floor of the unknown. I went up on deck and stood at the railings.

Still, for me, there was the visible world. I liked watching the waves even more than the sky. White horses, I had called them as a child. The raw edge of the roll. They shied or reared, lowered their heads, charged, and galloped on. A sort of hypnotic dance. They clashed, intermingled, overtook, passed through one another. I could watch their complications for hours on end. From starboard the waves gestured toward the land, keen on arrival, moving in a regimented way. Their latticework seemed more purposeful to me, probably because they moved toward a destination. It was the more nostalgic side of the boat. They knew where they were going. They would eventually get there. From portside, however, it appeared to me that the nostalgia was gone. The geometry was lost. It seemed wilder, more chaotic, a fantastic jaggery of lines, hitting each other at all angles, violent, careless, spraying in every direction. Smaller waves imposed themselves on the bigger ones. On one side, the rumor of land. On the other, a plentiful nowhere.

The evening sun dropped down into the gray bakery of the sea. I was joined on deck by some of the crew for sunset. Samkelo, Tahlana, Espère, Romário, Adam, Ron, Léon, Hercules. Their cigarettes flickered like streetlights at the aft mooring station. They extinguished them in a giant paint bucket, then hurried back to the kitchen or the engine room or the bridge, where there was work to do.

For the first few days I patrolled the deck, alerted the crew if there was anything new to see. Another boat in the distance; the gray fluke of a whale; a floating tree trunk; a swordfish that jabbed a needle mark in the sky; a mummering bait ball of mackerel just beneath the surface of the water. The ocean teemed. The birds were fewer now, but more glorious for their scarcity. Terns, storm petrels, shearwaters, frigate birds. They swung with the wind, skated, sloped, soared. An albatross followed us and settled on the stern. Other birds perched high on the satellite masts. The vee of water spread in the distance behind us, a channel of churn. All was white and chaotic until it met the fast-moving darkness of the water's ridge.

An old school poem came back to me. *Gash gold-vermillion.* I felt that I had begun to discover color. There were patches of yellow and green to be found in the gray. The widening wake gave new colors too: magentas, a rutilant line of gold at the edge of the waves. The sky itself was enough to hold me steady for a long time: *blue-bleak embers.* The further north we got, the warmer the days became. I wore a wide-brimmed hat and sunscreen. Still, the sun cracked open my skull. With cargo shorts and high-top running shoes, I could have stepped out of just about anywhere—most likely, I must admit, the mall—but even that didn't matter: what was being chased here was different from anything I had sought before.

The albatross took off huge in the air and disappeared. No ancient mariner, I didn't look for it, or take it as any sign, good or bad.

Night fell. I was dazed by the phosphorescence on the water's surface. Lines of light were breaking other lines of light, moving on, reappearing, forming shapes that opened and reopened. A moon insisted itself through the clouds. The clouds parted themselves to a star shower. A meteor seemed to go backward. Even the satellites had a sort of fascination for me, moving brightly amid the constellations, intruding on the old myths. Fish flew out of the water, whole schools of them in the dark. They flashed silver and then bowed back down. An underwater sheet of squid. A stretch of krill.

We were traveling at about twelve knots. It was, by all accounts, a good speed against the prevailing wind. The weather was clear. There was no storm on the horizon. We were making headway. The Georges had a confidence about her. She was ready to take on whatever came her way.

I was hooked on the plot of the waves. The hours passed as hours pass: they were sweeter hours than had passed me by for quite a while.

I could feel a pulse of life returning.

My ex-wife, Irenea, was a Chilean choreographer so simultaneously happy and sad that I thought, at times, she might burst into flames.

We met—fittingly, it now seems—in an emergency room on Dublin's southside. She had come to the hospital with a high fever and aches. I limped in on a routine stupidity while cleaning the gutters. "I presume you were dancing," she said when she saw my hobble. Her accent caught me off guard. We remained on a row of hard chairs as other patients came and went. She knew exactly what to do. Go home. Ice, elevation, ibuprofen, a tight compression bandage. Get crutches for two weeks. Don't be an idiot. Stay away from gutters.

I am often shy in the presence of beauty, but I thanked her and wrote her number in ballpoint pen on the inside of my wrist. For a full four days there was no answer to my calls. My temple pounded witlessly. On the fifth day I went out to St. Vincent's and asked for her name at the front desk. She was in isolation. She had collapsed. She was being monitored. Only family members were allowed to see her, but none had come, and the staff was trying to make contact. I came back when the shift had changed, told the new receptionist I was her fiancé and that I had been away. I was distraught. Where was she, where was she? The receptionist gave me the room number. I justified my actions as the extension of a possible fiction.

I began the routine of visiting every day. The staff wasn't able to pinpoint the cause of her infection, and any visitor had to dress up in gown, gloves, face mask. A doctor asked dismissively if I really was her fiancé. The next day I produced a ring. I was worried there would already be one on her finger because I hadn't actually looked—I hadn't been with a woman in quite a while, and I wasn't used to thinking in that direction. I sat by her bedside. She was morphined out and didn't quite know who I was at first. I read to her from *Lady Windermere's Fan* in my desire to get to the rather obvious line that all of us are in the gutter but some of us are looking at the stars.

For the first weeks I knew her, she only saw me in hospital getup. When I took her out of the hospital, guiding her wheelchair into the Dublin rain, she burst into tears and said she had never been treated so kindly before. When we reached her small apartment in Rathgar, she said she intended to keep the ring, she was grateful for it. She had six months of antibiotics for osteomyelitis through a drip in her arm. Together we nursed her back to health. I was saturated with a simple sense of joy. It didn't matter to me how long it might last. She whispered my name and she sounded like the first person ever to say it. We were married in the church opposite the hospital. She was eight months pregnant by then, her body a rich series of curves. Her parents, brothers, and sisters all arrived from Chile and Argentina, all sharply and beautifully dressed. They were quite obviously disappointed that she hadn't been swept off her feet by *a real Irishman*—their actual words—but she balanced her champagne glass on her stomach and quoted a Neruda poem about beauty and sorrow, and it salved my tired heart. I felt myself floating toward the shadow of the dreamer I once had been. I wanted to unscrew all the locks from the doors, throw open the windows. I was sure we had discovered a newness that nobody else knew about. A sleepy laziness followed our lovemaking. There was tenderness between us that I would give all the world to be able to revisit. She taught me the Portuguese word *saudade*. I thought I had never heard anything so exquisitely sad in my life. We learned to be together without speaking.

Back then I didn't bank the happiness. I wish now that I had. Stupid to think our wine will never turn.

Irenea left when my son, Joli, was a year and a half old. She left a note quoting Larkin's line about the good not done, the love not given, and the time torn off unused. I discovered later that she had been diagnosed with depression. It makes perfect sense now—part of our human warmth is the darkness we don't show to each other. She left behind a box of clothes, including those of the boy who had once breathed on my chest. Their departure brought on a flood of tears such as I had never experienced before. I still recall the time with crushing clarity. I had blown it. Flubbed my lines. Forgotten what I was supposed to say. Or never knew in the first place. Then it was the bottle. Out of character and into character. The unhappy mind takes a morbid delight in solitary grief. I soaked my toothbrush in whiskey so that each morning I would get a taste of what was about to come.

Over the next few years I went to Santiago several times to try to rescue things, but Irenea had found herself a charming house among the fragrant suburban lawns of Bellavista. She was a choreographer once again, working at the university. She had found a stabilizing medicine for her depression, and she was even performing small roles that gladdened her. Another man's shoes sat in the closet and my son was happy to call him Papaíto.

I learned early in life to break away easily from intimacy. No matter what pain there was, I did not fight back. It roiled me, but what could I do? Those were *her* brown eyes in my son's head, and they were aligned with her life. I had seen the Christmas photographs of gaudily overlit couples trying so hard to appear content, and I didn't want to be the man in that particular portrait. I moved down the driveway toward some peaceful and distant performance of fatherhood.

There are ways of seeing and there are ways of return.

———

One morning, far off the coast, I saw Conway standing on the starboard side of the upper deck, his hands on the rail. It was one of the first times I had seen him fully alone, out of the control room. Distant and slightly forlorn.

A surge of comradeship rose up in me and I wanted to prolong the moment, if even just for a minute or two. I recognized that unapproachable loneliness. There was nothing for Conway to see, as far as I could tell anyway, no land, no light, no lost birds, no awful floe of plastic bottles, but it is often the unseen that most deeply stirs the imagination. He must have remained still for about twenty minutes. There was no telling what he could have been thinking, or what he might have been missing. All of those things that are hidden. The hadal zone. The trenches. The surprise eruption from the floor of the dark.

The wind quartered around him. He pulled down his knit cap, then simply turned and made his way back toward the bridge as the sun came up. He caught my eye—I was standing near the bow, looking up—and we nodded to each other, but that was all, and he was gone, a footprint on the damp deck.

I looked east again but there was nothing but the ocean and the ocean and the ocean.

5

Early dawn, three-quarters of the way toward the break, Petrus appeared at the stern of the Georges Lecointe. His shape alone gave him away. The powerful shoulders. The square cut of his hair. The air of a blacksmith.

Gradually the light rose, and more color emerged: his orange jumpsuit, the small red towel lolling from his pocket. It was odd to see Petrus away from the engine room. He held the satellite phone to his ear, listening but not talking.

The waves came sideways at the ship and broke hard. Petrus stood, soaked in spray, then moved to the mooring station for shelter. He gently rubbed the bulky phone against the thigh of his jumpsuit, dried it, then held it to his ear again.

After a quarter hour, Conway emerged from the bridge. He stood in front of Petrus. They nodded. The waves broke harder still. Conway put his hand on Petrus's shoulder, took the satellite phone from him. Petrus left quietly through the fog of spray.

At noon the photograph of Petrus's mother was printed out and put on the bulletin board. She had died in Maputo. Of pneumonia. She was a small, stout woman, not unlike a version of my own mother.

The Georges halted for an hour and a service was held on the top deck. Omar read the prayers. Boninga sang an old Xhosa funeral song. It was strangely celebratory. The crew clapped and Petrus sang along, then bowed his head. After a moment, his chest began to heave. Petrus seemed far too old to still have a mother, and far too much a working man to weep in public, but sometimes we forget that we have blood inside us until it emerges.

After the ceremony, he went straight back down to the engine room. Later that evening I saw him hunkered on the metal floor with Conway as they serviced the freshwater generator tank. They opened the drain valve, cleaned out the filters. There was no reason for Conway to be there except the obvious one. Men everywhere know it.

I still have the photograph on my phone: Conway's boots and Petrus's boots sticking out from behind the metal container as they worked on the ejector pump, the small red cloth passing between them.

———

For eighteen years I had waged war with myself, and I hankered for a drink, but I had not brought anything, not even an emergency bottle. Before South Africa, I had gotten to the stage where it was two bottles of wine a day at least, sometimes three, even four. There were whole weeks that I could not recall.

In Dublin I had been a keen recycler simply because I didn't want the bottles to pile up. I drove to the bottle bank every day. An artful language: *the bank*. I made a deposit. I got rid of the accusation. The glass toppled into the void and smashed. It was all so horribly musical. And then I drove to the supermarket to load up again. I used to think that I drank myself to pieces in order to recover my senses, but really it was just an avalanche of tedium. You can fool your head and your heart but you can't fool your liver. It still hurt to touch it. I didn't know if time was with or against me. But I had forced a truce with the idea that I could go dry.

Without drink, time seemed to expand. Out of the bottle, the hours got breathing room.

I clicked online. A privilege. Conway had given me full access to all my devices. But my inbox was tired: mostly spam and discount updates from wine shops. Unsubscribing was part of the cleanse. A single text from my editor, Sachini, asked me how it was going. *Spent a few days sick as a dog, but out at sea now, and on our way to the break. Sometimes I feel like I'm traveling slowly to a five-alarm fire. The break is in a canyon. Four km down, the perfect underwater shitshow. Weather fine now. No wine, no booze at all. Food ok. The chief of mission's a mystery. Looks like he fronts Nirvana. Crew is solid. We stopped for a funeral service. They sang and went straight back to work.* She sent me a link to an article in a Cape Town newspaper. It was nothing, really. A cable down, businesses in danger, a ship out at sea, a repair expected within the next two weeks. I was pretty sure that there would be an online chat somewhere, charting the progress of the Georges, but I couldn't find one. Sachini sent another text: *No danger of pirates I hope :-) I heard they are off the coast of Somalia.* I was tempted to write back and give her a geography lesson. How quickly we go from being the ignoramus to, at the very least, the substitute teacher. For the first time, I imitated her emojis. *Not likely, we're in the middle of nowhere, too far out from the west coast, maybe a surveillance plane could find us, but I'm keeping that for my spy novel :-) So far out there are no more birds.* She wanted to see if I would figure out who manufactured the cables—the where and the how—but I brought her back around to the original intention: the fire at sea, the brigade on its way, Conway at the helm. She relented and our texts fell away. I was hardly her priority anyway.

I cast around online, checked the news sites, the football scores, the headlines. Migrant boats capsizing. Bloodshed in Venezuela. The damp white loaf with his State of the Union address.

Here we were, under the leaking roof of the world. What would happen if we were to leave the cable alone? If we didn't fuse the lines? If there was no repair at all? If we just allowed ourselves to drift? The rains, the floods, the underwater earthquakes, the landslides. The revenge of the host.

After more than a week on the boat, and time away from the booze, it was beginning to feel as if a sort of clarity was coming to me. I was able to press two fingers against my liver without a stab of acute pain. A small stalactite of hope. The curtain was being drawn open across my mind. A fledgling brightness. I was in a small room, in a small ship, and the task at hand was to knit at least some distant parts of myself anew.

I began composing a handwritten note to my son in Santiago. Perhaps a letter would break through to him. Writing it by hand would require deliberation. I could think about what I truly wanted to say. No deletion. No easy cut and paste. It occurred to me that I hadn't bought a stamp in many years and didn't know what country the letter would eventually be posted from. Perhaps the DRC. Or back in South Africa. Maybe even Ireland. Home. If such a thing still existed. Maybe we found home in those we left behind. Sentimental, but no less true. Get it done. The only begrudger was, in fact, me. Nobody else was stopping me. Forty-eight years old. A third of the glass remaining. There it stands. I didn't know if a handwritten note, no matter how earnest, would just aggravate the wound for Joli. He was at a tender age. The imposition of the father. On the other hand, if I said nothing, it was ammunition for him to feel abandoned—fair enough, his mother had been the one to actually leave, but it certainly felt that I had propelled her. The other elemental question was, How exactly did I feel? It is generally supposed that a father, like a writer, says what he knows and knows well. But perhaps it is not so. Perhaps a father's subject, like that of the writer, is to articulate that which he longs for. It had been many years since I had seen Joli. He had been polite to me but distant. I had stayed one afternoon in Irenea's house over coffee and cakes, and Joli had spent most of the time on his phone. He glanced up at me every now and then as if surprised that he could ever have come from what sat in front of him. He said to me that he liked drawing and was interested in being a sculptor, but he also had an interest in the writing life. He had written stories in Spanish, which Irenea had shown me. Though I couldn't really read them properly, I had enough of a language inkling to think that he had a bit of talent, and I had glimpsed, in his bedroom, a copy of my first novel, which had both gratified and terrified me. I doubt he had read it, and why should he? It was even tough for me to recall just exactly what I had written in those pages.

The words of my own father returned to me again on that constant swing: *All the truth but none of the honesty.* I have always believed in a general algebraic integrity—you take from one side and you add to the other, and you let the scales sway until they finally settle. I would give the letter as much time and craft as I could. If it didn't seem worthy in the end, I could keep it, or destroy it, so be it.

I wrote it in switchbacks, went through a half pad of paper. *Dear Joli. M'ijo. Son.* He was sixteen years old now. There wasn't much of me in him at all. He looked like his mother apart from a fading sprinkle of freckles across his nose. I wanted to try to tell him that I was beginning to see the world in different ways. All the fracture. All the loss. All the life at the bottom of the oceans. All the brokenness. There had to be something we could do about it. I was interested, I told him, in Gramsci's notion of a pessimist of the intellect, an optimist of the will. The world was shitty and dark, yes, there was no doubt about it, but so what? That was no great revelation. Maybe something could come about from the people who were interested in repair, even someone from his own generation, or even especially him, my own son? I paused and tore it up. Wrote myself a separate note: *The old palliatives. This daily plate of shit I try to feed myself.* Who was I fooling? What was I doing there? What was I looking for? What manner of falsehood was I engaging in? The sulk existed for a reason. Perhaps I had overdosed on the cure? Maybe I actually needed a stiff drink? An old friend had once told me that the only path toward anything good was to risk sentiment, but now that sounded like a cheaply parsed wisdom. Maybe the truth was that very little at all was being risked. Perhaps it was simply a job for Conway. A way to get by. A paycheck. Nothing much honorable about it beyond the time spent at sea. Maybe he and the crew did it because that's all they could do. They could have been anywhere else as much as they were here. As absent as they were present. The same for me. Absent and present, present and absent, a writer who wasn't writing. I was a journalist and the story might pay the Glasnevin bills, or it might not. What did it matter? Of course, it could have been both these things at once: the daily plate of shit *and* some sort of meaningful repair tangled up together. I wanted to join the two ends, but perhaps my own cables had ruptured. I balled up another sheet of paper.

Maybe I should just text him? Wasn't that how fathers got in touch with their sons now anyway? Out there, traveling mostly on the ocean floor, in a series of cold, wet tubes, all our longings, all our desires, who knows how fast how deep how jumbled, from our bare bedrooms, out to the black boxes behind our apartments, under the streets, *Hi Joli, hope u had a good birthday,* into a landing station along the coast, out into the shallows, pulsed through with electricity, *Sorry I missed it,* further still, in a rock bed trench, down a slope, deeper again, shot onward by the repeaters, *I feel terrible,* beyond the cliffs and the plunges, the seamounts, the ridges, the ledges, the abysses, the hydrothermal vents, *I swear it wont happen again,* out into the middle of the ocean, fracted and refracted, this tiny shot of sorrow pulsing in the dark, *I'd really like to see u soon,* landing along the coast, in a deepwater harbor, *If u can get your mother to send me a picture great,* into the landing station, down into other fiber-optic tubes, following the highways or the railway lines, to finally— within a fraction of a second—find him there, in his small suburban house in Santiago, two bedrooms, three TVs, one double bed, one single bed, another father, so unlike me, *Tell everyone I said hello,* and for Joli to glance at the text, and not to know anything of my terror, the sheer gut-wrenching fear of how to sign off with a son I had more or less abandoned, should I say *Cheers,* or should I say *Best wishes,* or should I dial it up with *I love you,* or an exclamation mark, or seal it with three small *x*'s in a little row, or tell the proper truth, the whole truth, nothing but the truth, and the honesty too, *I'm so sorry I failed you, son,* which would no doubt feel especially pathetic in a text, one which probably would not get read or even opened at all.

⸻

"Room service."

Conway knocked on my door. It was a tolerant rap, halfway apologetic. He had spent most of the travel days in the control room and upstairs on the bridge. I wasn't sure he ever got much sleep. But there were few signs of tiredness. No baggy eyes, no slouch. The extent of his stamina surprised me. The exhaustion must have toppled over into energy. The desire to get to the area of the break.

"Pull on your jacket," he said. "Let's go for a jog."

Together we moved up the stairs. I was beginning to understand the geography of the ship. For the first couple of days, it had been a series of funhouse mirrors, but I was starting to know its turns.

On deck, the sea spray woke me.

"We've a third break," Conway said.

"Where?"

"A feeder cable coming off the main one. Up north. Ghana. Close to shore. Some fishing vessel ripped it up. That'll be our last job."

"Unless we get another one, I suppose."

"Yeah, we'll be out another week or so, maybe two."

"That's fine by me."

"You've no one to go back to, Fennell?"

"They're not exactly tying yellow ribbons around Dublin, no."

In fact, the prospect of another week, or two weeks, buoyed me. More time at sea was simply that: more time at sea. I had a letter to write. A third break would be interesting, especially one that might be close to shore. Maybe we would need the remotely operated vehicle or even a diver.

"Listen," he said, with a tinge of apology in his voice. "I've been asked to ask you something."

We stopped at the edge of the railing, the spray fresh in our faces.

"Fire away."

"There's a news story coming out in the *Times*."

"The *Times*?"

"Yeah."

"Which one?"

"No clue."

"Who told you?"

"Brussels."

"What's it about?"

"I don't know. You can use my sat phone."

He handed me the bulky machine.

"I like machines that work," I said, but he either didn't hear me or didn't remember.

"Who's this?" I asked, but he stepped away. The number was already programmed. It was answered on the first ring. It was the first female voice I'd heard in a while—Elisabeth, the publicist I had talked to over a month ago. It felt odd to realize that there was still another world out there.

I watched as Conway moved further along the deck, where a few of the technicians were standing at the aft mooring station, their cigarette smoke drifting out to sea.

"Monsieur Fennell," Elisabeth said. "How are you?"

"Good, yeah—"

"How are they treating you on board?"

"Grand."

"I just wanted to fill you in on a few things," she said through the static.

Her voice was a controlled skid. It soon became clear to me that there was negative chatter about the storm and the four-day initial delay. The company, it seemed, was getting flak. The suggestion was that the Georges Lecointe was moving too slowly and that the repairs would take much longer than originally thought, jeopardizing the economies along the western seaboard of Africa.

It didn't surprise me that the story had caught another cog: in fact, it surprised me that there hadn't been more. The internet traffic had been redirected to the cables on the eastern coast, but there was still a massive slowdown. In stock markets. In trading exchanges. In businesses. Worse than that, there were parts of the west coast— Ghana, Nigeria, Angola—where the connection was out altogether. Hospitals without internet, governments without phone service, mobile firms hemorrhaging assets.

"Well, monsieur," she said, and then proceeded to rattle on at a fierce pace. Publicists seldom think too far beyond the initial malodor that has been slid under their noses. She said that some reporter from the *Financial Times* had been calling the head office and that perhaps I might want a scoop.

I clenched the phone. At least it was the *Financial Times,* not the London *Times,* or *The New York Times.* And if others had an interest in the story, it validated and deepened my own.

"So you want me to write a news story?"

"Well, not exactly," she said carefully, "but I think, the people, they need to know. The broad strokes. The boat's on time. No need for panic. A reassurance. That sort of thing."

Truth was, she wanted me to preempt the story and neutralize it. She would help me place it as an *exclusive.* She had contacts in France, Belgium, England, Germany. I wanted to tell her that I wasn't that type of journalist and that, in fact, I was hardly a journalist at all. I wanted to assert the privilege of the serious writer, the great unsung chronicler of our times: I wasn't in pursuit of a hard angle, I was there to go deeper than all of that, and she could try whatever grapnel she might like with me, but I wasn't prepared to sacrifice my principles. All horseshit, of course, since it flattered me to even think that I might get a story anywhere near one of those papers.

There was a time delay on the phone. She seemed vaguely disappointed when I said yes so easily, and that I would try to send her something by early the next morning. It had all been too facile for her, and I tried to put some backspin on my foul shot, but I knew I would attempt to write a glossed-up news story for the mighty Belgian telecommunications conglomerate, and fuck the consequences, even my own integrity.

It all churned a little in my stomach, and I wondered how my editor might feel about it. We were heading toward the Congo canyon after all. The river had spilled out and taken its toll.

I stepped along the deck and handed Conway back the phone, told him that I had agreed to her request.

"Grand job," he said.

He sipped the air like he did when he was preparing to dive.

"Just don't quote me."

It galled me a little that he didn't want to be quoted, as if he was not part of the story, but then it occurred to me that he wasn't able to avoid it, now or ever. Even if he went unquoted, he would always be responsible in some way or the other for what happened on the Georges.

Zanele suddenly flashed across my mind. The T-shirt she wore when she left the airport. *Unreachable by Machine.* He was turning away with the satellite phone when I asked him: "How's Zanele? The kids?"

He was taken a little off guard, as if he didn't remember that I had visited their home, sat with them in the kitchen, followed her laughter out the door. Or maybe it just wasn't something that we were able to talk about out at sea. It was, after all, a personal question, and I had vowed not to write anything intimate. And yet I had seen what had arced between them—or what I thought had arced between them—and his adoration for her. He had even proclaimed drunkenly that he was going to resign, move to London, to be with her. Perhaps, I thought, there was another part of him that didn't want to eat around the bruised edges of his life: he'd had a blackout after all.

"I can't afford to think about these things, Fennell. I'm out here with a job to do."

The Irish way. *Whatever you say, say nothing.* Maybe his silence was preserving Zanele and the family. The only thing Conway could control was the possible repair. It was, as far as I was concerned at the time, one of the more admirable things I had come across in quite a while.

I retreated to my room. I wanted to file the story with the publicist that same evening. It wasn't an easy piece to write, even after some earlier years at a news desk. Who what where when how and why. The boat. The break. Off the coast of Africa. Now. The repair. But still the *why* eluded me. But perhaps that was always the way. Nothing in the story lent itself to any essential drama. Nobody would care about a boat that was actually on schedule and doing its job. It would be far better to write about the struggles of the Georges Lecointe at sea if there were any, but essentially there were none, or none that were of newsworthy consequence anyway. *Boat at Sea Under Blue Sky.* It wasn't much more than *Dog Bites Man.* I wrote and rewrote. Finally, after a few hours, I finished something passable. The story took ages to load. It spun its little wheel as if it were protesting its own existence. I felt melancholy when it was gone. I had given something false away.

Almost immediately Elisabeth came back to tell me that, apologies, apologies, monsieur, there was no need for the story, she had

contacted the reporter for the *Financial Times,* and she had man-
aged to set him straight about the timeline, the financial implica-
tions, the African economy, and everything else. So much for broad
strokes.

I wrote to Joli and said that it was no great surprise that the
world felt as if it were in chains since they actually trawled the
ocean floor and tied us up in easy knots.

———

In the middle of the evening of the sixth night at sea—I had by
then, with the storm delay, been almost ten days on the boat—
Samkelo rapped on the door of my cabin. "Just checking in," he
said.

We were due, within twenty-four hours, to get to our area of the
break. We were closing on the Congo channel. Three hundred and
fifty kilometers off the coast. We were in mild water, but there was
another small storm coming our way.

"Waves will be up around two or two and a half meters, sir," he
said. "You might want to have a word with your stomach."

"How much can the ship take?"

"She's got a high freeboard. She can take just about anything.
She can go right up until Sea State six."

"What's Sea State six?"

"What's coming in is just a little tickle. Sea State six is more like
a riot. A three-story building coming right at you. We missed out
on that down south. You should be fine."

He turned at the door and I saw him glance at the sheet of handwritten paper in front of me.

"Writing to my son," I said.

"Good."

It was an odd thing for him to say, but he hovered there, and I
figured he wanted to talk.

"Do you have children, Samkelo?"

"Oh, yes," he said. "Nearly all of us have children."

He stayed silent, then closed the door and stepped along the corridor. Few of the stories we have inside ourselves ever get properly spoken.

The wind gathered. Droplets of rain blew against the porthole. It seemed quite a while ago that I had been in Conway's house and Zanele had asked me if I had children and I had denied my son.

I would continue to write the letter to Joli. And I would write to Irenea too. There was so much that needed to be said. It was not, as my father had said about my mother, water under the bridge. All things reemerge.

I rode out the storm. I was mildly disappointed that we might have passed the equator and Conway had not made a ritual of it for me, but it turned out we were still south of the line. Life remained counterclockwise. The waves climbed to seven feet. More than a tickle, as Samkelo had said, but I didn't get sick, and I didn't have to strap myself in. It wasn't comfortable by any means, but there was a beauty in it, the shatterwork of the lightning where the silver seemed to pull itself up from the ocean itself. And then there was the distant noise of the thunder, the elongated cracks and their contrapuntal echo around the ship, as if it had been designed only for us, which, in a way, it was. Thunder at sea can help you believe all the myths.

6

I almost want to draw a picture of where we were. It would be quite simple, along the lines of the ones I saw Zanele's children had drawn when, years later, I went to visit her in London.

A child's rendering. The boat near the top of the frame. On the rim of the ocean. Incredibly tiny. Alone. Just recognizable by its shape. Like a paper boat. Perhaps the suggestion of a flag fluttering from its stern. With a small yellow sun in the top right-hand corner. Beneath it would be a huge swath of blue, getting gradually bluer and darker, until it turns pitch-black, so that the whole sketch would seem to be just a portrait of a toy boat bobbing on a slight portion of sky. There would be a silver line extending from the boat down through the darkness. It would fall straight at first, but after a while, the line would begin to descend in a jagged manner, hitting off unseen canyon walls, until, toward the bottom, the drawing would show a crude, oversize grappling hook and, beneath it again, the thinnest of thin lines, a wire from which there is a burst of light.

All of this is maybe not, on reflection, so much a child's painting as it is a version of what I tried to understand as I stood on board the Georges Lecointe that early February, watching the crewmen begin to search for the cable. We were dropping a fishhook into the depths in the hope of catching something that might make us whole. They worked in unison, the bridge and the deck crews. Well

103

drilled. Efficient. They positioned the boat and lowered the grapnel off the bow. The metal grapnel was about one meter long. In the shape of a flatfish. It looked relatively primitive. But the men treated it with reverence. One mistake could be fatal. If technology was about magic, it was also about brutal reality. The grapnel had to be lowered by chain and rope. A snapped chain could take a man's head off. A slip could be disastrous. Everything had to be carefully calibrated. All the directives were clear. The men remained on the one radio channel. Grapnel down. It hardly made a splash. Ten meters. Slowly it uncoiled on the winch. Fifty. One hundred. Past the twilight zone where no upper light could ever go. Two hundred. They followed the descent on the screens in the control room. They had mapped the currents. One kilometer. Two kilometers. It took an hour or more to descend through the waters. Three kilometers. Grappling in the dark. Four. What it grazed nobody could know: whales or squid or any manner of marine life, sea trees and floating grasses and rock ledges, the shape of which could only be imagined.

When it hit the bottom of the ocean—and Conway had established that it was truly the bottom—the boat began its slow journey dragging the metal hook across the floor, or what, at least, our crew thought was the floor. It might hit a rock or it might snag on a root system. It might find itself caught on a tree branch that had been swept along in the Congo avalanche, or a car muffler, swept that far out in the ocean, all the remnants of the continent, the dislodged things, the shit, the grime, the everyday torments. Most likely the cable was buried in sediment, or vegetal debris, and Conway couldn't know how deep it was, or how the grapnel could actually snag it. The debris could be a meter or more thick. The grapnel had to find the place where the cable emerged from the sediment. It would grab the wire, trigger the cutting blade using tension, sever the line, and then be brought up, the cable in its claw.

The boat moved at a snail's pace, little more than a knot. Sometimes it did not feel as if we were moving at all. The blue sky, the black sky, the realms of intermediary purples and reds. The men were tense. The deck was tense. Even Conway was at the edge of tense. We were waiting for the moment of pull.

It was vaguely possible, too, that we would drag up an ancient cable, not ours. The old cables followed the colonial routes. Out on these waters, the slave ships had crossed. I was reminded how, once, my father's tractor had dragged up a rib cage. He was plowing the field, the famine bones brown with soil. Time within time. The past rattled around. Cyrus Field patrolling the deck, his hands behind his back, his coattails flowing behind him. The ancient ships meeting in the middle of the Atlantic. White flags at the mizzen. Every atom belonging to them. Pulling our hopes along the ocean floor. Joining two places together. The binary of morse. Our ones and zeros. The telegraph men. Their acoustic strikes. The hook descending to find the broken ends. History within history. Men and women belowdeck, chains around their necks. A wave of water. The shipwrecks. Warships along the coast. New cables. Transatlantic calls. My son waiting. Rain on the tributaries. The Congo flooding. A young girl swept away. Fiber optics. A tree trunk hammering along the river bottom. My father stepping off the tractor. He shook the grass from the rib cage and threw the bones beyond the plowed edges of the field.

Conway brought the empty grapnel up.

———

There are birds that switch off half their brains and sleep as they fly. How Conway kept from falling down with exhaustion I will never know. Each sweep of the ocean floor took almost fifteen hours. He halved his time between the control room and the bridge. There was no quit in him. He might have dozed off in his chair, but that's about it. There was an incredible boredom and a simultaneous promise about it all. He remained cool and so, therefore, did every-one around him. I waited for a short blast on the foghorn: that would be the signal for when the cable was caught.

The first two days and nights of searching went by without much incident. Every time the grapnel emerged from the water, Conway was there to collect the sediment that had lodged inside the flukes. Mud and deep-sea grasses clung to the sides of the blades. He scraped off the residue carefully and put it in containers.

"A memento for you," he said, handing a container to me. "You won't ever touch anything coming from anywhere deeper than that. Keep it."

"It's mud."

"It'll eventually harden and become rock."

"I can give it to my boy."

He looked at me, confused. Perhaps he remembered my denial, back in Cape Town, I wasn't sure. But I could tell something sharp had whipped across his mind, and he was looking at me differently, and he recognized a newness, and he did what men do, just a gentle punch to the shoulder, an acknowledgment of some deficit, some loss.

The most casual things can, after all, twist our tired hearts. Mud from the bottom of the ocean. I placed the container on the tiny writing desk in my cabin as a paperweight.

The grapnel went down again. Slowly we crawled. Ndlovu and Matt the Scot had set up fishing lines to run from the stern. It was earlier than I had been told, but already, it seemed, the men were ready for some form of return. Out from the sea came bluefish, flounder, Atlantic blue marlins, and, on the second morning of the grapnel hunt, a huge swordfish that thrashed around on the rear deck. It was hung in the air and a chain saw was used to remove its bill. I wanted a photograph, but the pool of blood was too slippery on deck, and the moment disappeared.

At lunch and dinner, the fish were cooked and set out on trays.

The offerings of the sea. It was odd to think that these specimens had been in the water just above the cable we could not find.

The grapnel brought up a swirled nest of plastic. A part of a rope was entwined too, along with a piece of styrofoam. We had no idea if it came from the ocean bottom or if it had been floating mid-water and just latched onto the flukes on the way up. Hercules took his knife to the mess and slowly untangled it. He handed pieces of plastic off to Conway, who examined them. There was a cracked sheet of hard plastic entwined inside it all and a small piece of cellophane wrapper from what looked like a cigarette pack. He was moody, aloof, pensive. I guess he was recalling Zanele's words about all that shit floating in our oceans. I had to admit the truth in what she had said. Petra too. *There's nowhere we haven't fucked up.* The words returned to me on that ancient swing. *Just because the truth is ignored doesn't mean it's not true.*

The grapnel was dropped again. Another sweep came up empty. Conway gathered the crew on deck. He had printed out a huge map of the underwater canyon and placed it on an easel. There was the air of a conductor about him. The orchestra hummed.

"We're driving the grapnel west to east, perpendicular to the route, here. When we splice it back together again, we're going to lay it well away from the knickpoints."

He had to be mindful of the distance of cable he wanted to replace. There was, he reminded them, a second break that they would have to take care of, and then a third. He had loaded enough spare cable, he wasn't scared of that, but he also had to be aware of how many repeaters they would have to use. The repeaters were spaced every eighty kilometers or so, to recalibrate the electricity shooting through the wires. I stood on deck and listened. I had found my own part in the orchestra: a grudging admiration for the difficulty they faced.

"Straight to hell, boys," Conway said as he left the crew.

On the fourth night of sweeping, the grapnel was hauled up with a small, translucent octopus smushed in between the flukes. It was predawn. A chill in the air. I heard the commotion and pulled on my waterproof jacket, joined them on deck. A squall of rain murmured across the sea. The droplets stunned my cheeks. A circle of men hovered over the strange creature.

The creature was no more than a foot across. It was crushed inside the blade. Part of its translucent body was covered in mud.

"Gather that up and take a sample in formalin," said Conway to Ndlovu. "Put the rest in the freezer."

"How did that get there?"

I had to ask Conway twice before he answered.

"No clue," he said, but I could tell that he and the rest of the crew were intrigued. "It's probably nothing."

"You mind if I go along with Ndlovu?"

"Fire away."

Ndlovu used a pair of rubber gloves and an improvised tray to load the creature. The rest of the mud was carefully scraped into another container. He was tall and thin with wire-rimmed spectacles, mostly given to silence. His onboard job was to look after the remote vehicles, but he was also one of the resident fishermen.

"It's an octopus?"

"Looks like it. But there was mud on it, see? That's odd. Because that means it was at the bottom of the sea. Unless the grapnel dragged on another ledge. And it's more translucent than anything I've ever seen before. We'll take a sample, freeze the rest, see if science folk want it when we get to shore."

We descended to the kitchen, where the chef and the two young cooks were preparing breakfast. The Bosnian, Danny, gave the octopus the once-over.

"Nothing, man," he said. "I've seen them all the time in Vietnam."

"This isn't Vietnam," said Ndlovu.

"That's what you think."

The cooks took pictures of the octopus on the tray, selfies that were stranger-looking than the octopus itself. They made faces as they clicked their phones. Ndlovu went ahead and dissected a piece of the octopus, dropped it in a jar.

The next afternoon I strayed down to the room where the computers were kept. It was a simple affair, near the canteen, beyond the television room. Two computers were set up on one desk. Instructions on the wall reminded the crew of the twenty-minute limit.

Both the young cooks startled when I walked in. It was their free time between lunch and dinner. The younger, Phileas, swung his screen away from me, but the other, Omar, had the selfie displayed on his screen. I asked him if I could take a photo. They exchanged a few words in a language I didn't understand—I thought I heard the word *magazine*—and then Phileas swung his chair around and gave me a thumbs-up.

It was all quite pedestrian, not one of those moments that might strike a chord, until I stepped back across the room for a wider angle and got a glimpse of Phileas's screen. A photo of Zanele. He clicked out of the screen, and again a volley of language went across the room.

"That was Zanele?"

It was, I was sure, the photo of her from the airport: her head shaved. She had a poise and an ease about her.

"Oh, that? Yeah," said Phileas, embarrassed.

"Is there news?"

"News?"

"About her performance?"

"I don't know nothing about no performance, man."

"In Brighton?"

They shot a few more words back and forth, obviously not designed for me, and then clicked out of their screens.

"Are you seeing the chief?" asked Phileas.

"Yeah."

"Do us a favor, man. We're only supposed to be on WhatsApp."

"No worries," I said.

They were stretching the limits of their online access, but the picture made me curious. In my cabin, I opened my browser, dove down into the net. It surprised me to see that she had a good measure of fame, especially among younger South African men. Her roles in a couple of very small indie films had put her in a narrow spotlight. A horror film, *Shab,* shot in a shanty shebeen, had been an underground punk hit. A celebrated short, *Ousie,* where she had played a nineteenth-century maid on a farm in Stellenbosch, had won indie awards. Her later work was more arty, touching on racism and climate change. There was a great deal of praise for her, but so much of it centered on her beauty, which she seemed to want to shy away from. She had done a couple of mostly humdrum interviews saying that she wasn't interested in peddling herself, and her desire was to lean toward theater rather than film. There were several pictures of her with a South African actor, Aubrey Mmodi, with whom she had founded the theater group. No photos with Conway.

I asked him about her again in the early evening, on the bridge, after dinner. His relative silence had not been a standout thing in all the cramped maleness of the ship, but still it intrigued me.

"She's grand," he said.

"And the kids?"

"Not a bother. They're used to me being away."

"When's the premiere?"

"Coming up."

"Is she nervous?"

"Nerves are good for you, that's what Zee says. She likes it that way. I just don't think about it all that much, Fennell. I'm just out here. Getting the work done. I don't think of much else. I've got fifty people to look after."

He glanced at me as if I might be a part of the deadweight. I tend to smile when wounded: it is a bizarre tic, admittedly, one of my more awkward responses.

A moment dolphined up: Only once had I ever seen my parents show outright affection. It was at my sister's wedding when they were both slightly tipsy, and embarrassed by themselves, doing a waltz, in the middle of the Imperial Hotel in Westmeath. My father danced with his suit jacket off. His waistcoat was too tight. My mother appeared in a patterned dress the like of which she very seldom wore. They both looked old and stout. As they danced, my mother's hip touched the edge of one of the circular tables and knocked a glass onto the floor. The glass smashed and my father bent down to pick up the pieces, and then they went back to waltzing stiffly. But in the middle of the floor, my mother looked down at her dress and saw a small smudge of blood on her hip. My father hadn't realized that he had cut his finger. Without thinking, my mother lifted his hand and put it to her mouth and sucked at the wound. When she drew away again, she delicately picked what must have been a tiny sliver of glass from her tongue. My father wrapped the splinter in a handkerchief and put it in his pocket. They continued their dance. When the music stopped, he leaned down and kissed her full on the mouth. Decades might have gone by as they sauntered back over to their table.

The nostalgia knocked me sideways: I hadn't thought about them like that for quite a while. I was surprised to see Conway still sitting in front of me. He knew I'd gone somewhere else.

"I just concentrate on what I have to do," he said finally. "It's easier that way. We have a line to catch. See, here." He pointed down to the map. "The seventh circle."

He was convinced he had found the proper line of sweep now. He had put most of the elements of the jigsaw together. The outlying factor, he said, was the appearance of the new sediment in the canyon, the additional layers that had appeared since the moment of landslide, the unknown stuff, as he called it. He had to drag the grapnel at the correct depth. If he was wrong, he would have to double back and try a whole new set of tactics, which could take days, even a week.

"It's all about timing now," he said.

"What are we looking at?"

"We're going to skirt the edge of the canyon here. And here."

"And after that?"

"All bets are off."

It was clear that nothing more was to be said about Zanele or the children. He had closed off those questions.

"Don't forget we're down in the canyon," he said.

I wasn't quite sure what he meant, except maybe to warn me of the length of time it might take to retrieve the cable. It was easy, looking out, to think of it as endless emptiness, a relatively safe zone of undulating gray. But there was a wildness beneath us, canyon walls, caves, crevices, crags. If the water were to dry up, it would be thirteen thousand feet of endless free fall.

———

It was late at night in my cabin—close, in fact, to morning—when I heard the foghorn go. It meant only one thing. I scrambled into my jumpsuit and pulled on a pair of boots. Several crew members emerged from their cabins, wiping the sleep from their eyes. They pulled their helmets on as they climbed the stairs. I fell in with them. I could, for the first time, take the stairs without being winded.

It was a clear, sharp night. The stars lay in a deep scatter. The unending blackness stretched behind them. The foghorn went off once again: this time a long, loud whistle. I wish I had recorded it. It was, in my memory, very beautiful, not unlike a whale sound from the hidden deep.

The grapnel was hauled on board under a row of fluourescent lights. The men shone in the bath of dark. Conway moved with them. They wore their safety gear: rubber boots, gloves, neon jackets. The grapnel had been ratcheted up through the water. In its claw lay one end of the actual cable. It was secured and locked down. Petrus thumped Omar's shoulder as the cable was lifted. Matt the Scot took his camera out. Samkelo was laughing. Music split the night. *Purple Rain* slid over the loudspeakers. Conway was silhouetted against the wakening sky. I got the sense that the men could repeat this moment over and over again. The cable itself was such a paltry thing—an inch and a half wide, a roll of metal and plastic and glass—but it didn't matter: this was exactly what they had been searching for. They had left their homes for it.

"There she is," Conway said to me when I wandered across the deck and stood beside him. He took me by the elbow and led me through the small crowd. The cable looked like it had spent some time being ripped apart. It was still streaked with mud, and the outer casing was frayed. How did it ever carry what it carried?

"What happens now?"

"We cut the bad end. Then we buoy the cable. We pull up the second end. Cut that too. And then we join them together."

"Simple as that?"

"Yeah, just like that."

It was not beyond me that he had said *There she is,* and that he had been waiting quite a while for this moment, in his ongoing silence about Zanele. The cable, after all, went between London and Cape Town. It reached from where she had been to where she now was. A rope of time and distance. Beyond the uncertain. He had, I thought, delayed talking about her and the children on purpose. He wanted to find the end of the cable first and then initiate the repair. *There she is.* He had been waiting all that time to connect.

All stories are love stories. I still maintain it despite what I know now. I write this, in longhand, in a place not too distant from where my son lives. I could drive four days from the Atacama Desert and be on his doorstep.

We are all, indeed—you, me, us—shards in the smash-up.

PART TWO

1

It is, I suppose, the job of the teller to rearrange the scattered pieces of a story so that they conform to some sort of coherence. Between fact and fiction lie memory and imagination. Within memory and imagination lies our desire to capture at least some essence of the truth, which is, at best, messy.

Zanele was attacked three nights after her premiere. She survived it, went to hospital, was released early on, recovered quickly, and soon turned it around. But these bare essentials don't do the story any real justice. Nor do the online reports. Nor does the camera footage that was posted on various sites. Or the rumor mill, which went into full operation almost straightaway. Even when I met her later, it was still not fully possible to separate the wheat from the chaff. If this were a fiction, I would scold myself for telling too much, and at the wrong time, and in the wrong order. A breathless *and and and*. Unable to handle so many spinning plates, I would cap my pen and begin again. The story would unfold in a simpler way, with clarified motives and a neat chronology, a logic of time and distance, and not the wild crunch of coincidence that it truly was.

The particulars appear fully formed now, but, at the time, the way they unfolded was one fluid shock tangled inside another.

Zanele had already been in rehearsal for weeks. She had written in a blog that the days were long on work but short on light. Brighton was a pleasant town, she said, and her kids were settling in. She and her fellow actors were all staying in a large house on the banks of the Hove River. They were helping her to homeschool the twins, Thami and Imka. The biggest problem was getting used to the dark falling at five in the afternoon. The rest of the time was spent in rehearsal. Her version of *Godot*, as she had said, was a simple enough metaphor for climate change. She didn't have to populate the stage with anything too obvious, but she did want to give a sense of the rising seas, and the floating patches of garbage, and the disappearing ocean meadows, and indeed the human hope that remains a rumor and doesn't, in the end, appear. It was what she had talked about in the kitchen in Cape Town. One of the opening reviews suggested that the design was perhaps a bit obvious, but that didn't appear to bother her. She threw light around Beckett's words, and that light, a blueness gradually dimming into dark, was her way of speaking the truth that the play itself spoke. *Let us do something, while we have the chance! We should have thought of it a million years ago. Have you not done tormenting me with your accursed time!* The rippled rear curtain evoked a vaguely underwater territory. The stage tree was, in fact, made of coral. The color drained gradually from it as the light dimmed.

The play took place in a small theater in an old deconsecrated church in a part of Brighton that was rapidly gentrifying. Everything about the theater felt, by all accounts, primed for a previous era, and perhaps that was part of the magic of it. Zanele was taking an old classic and reappropriating it for the now, the time that *was* stepping inside the time that *is*. She had done an interview with a local website, the Hove, and a couple of *bossies*, as she called them, had demanded a boycott on the basis that the production was not respecting the artist's wishes. She was trampling on copyright, but Zanele was using the ban to make her exact point: some stories were just not being told. Besides, she was quite sure Beckett would, in this day and age, approve of what she was doing. She defended him to the hilt. She only wished the sage could return and sling a few lines at the living. He would undoubtedly be capable of finishing the unfinishedness he had left for us. She found *Godot* profoundly funny and absurd and moving all at the same time, she said, but the main reason she had chosen to direct it was that it spoke to the only emergency that really mattered: the climate and our unwillingness to show up on our own stage.

On the fourth night, the theater was a little more than three-quarters full, and according to reports that were later filed, both in the police station and online, the audience was appreciative, if a little tentative. Zanele was playing the smaller role of Lucky, the slave, who had one monologue about God loving us dearly with some exceptions for reasons unknown.

She remained mute for the second act, which is when a young man quietly stood up toward the rear of the audience. Those who witnessed it said it happened in a sort of slow motion. He was pale and thin, dressed not unlike the character of Pozzo, in a bowler hat and waistcoat. Several people had to stand to let him pass along the pew. Rather than going to the side of the church, which was quiet and dark, he went toward the middle aisle. He turned in the direction of the stage instead of the bathrooms at the rear of the church. As he moved forward, some in the audience began to watch him rather than the show. It was just prior to the exit of Pozzo and Lucky. Pozzo—played by Zanele's friend Miriam—had just said the line *Don't count on me to enlighten you,* before the infamous line *Up pig!,* which Miriam never got to say because by now the attention of the audience was on the young man as he silently approached. Some in the audience, not familiar with *Godot,* thought for a brief second that it was part of the performance. In his hand the young man held a glass jar, which witnesses afterward said they mistook for a drink. Zanele, in character, was on the floor, but she rose to her feet as he approached, which later gave rise to speculation that she knew him or had at least been warned about what he was going to do. The young man unscrewed the lid from the jar as he stepped up on the low stage and moved deliberately toward Zanele. She threw up her arms and turned her face just as the liquid was flung through the air.

Hydrochloric acid. In a pure form. Designed to burn.

The jar fell and shattered on the ground, and the attacker simply sat back down in an empty chair in the front row, crossed one leg over his knee, and waited. Within seconds, a number of audience members had approached him from behind and pinned him to the seat. He didn't writhe or try to break free, just sat there without saying a single word. There was, by all accounts, an eerie calm, and the phone footage that was later posted on the internet shows very little except a group gathered around Zanele on the stage. The camera swings toward the young attacker, who seems to ask for his hat, which is then, rather bizarrely, placed on his head by one of the audience members.

Other footage shows the police and the ambulance arriving. The police get there first, and they run to the stage, which, by that time, is puddled with water. Zanele is naked from the waist up, having torn her own acid-riddled clothes off in panic, and she is sitting, her head thrown back at an angle, while water is being poured on the side of her face from a watering can. The puddle blooms on the stage around her. Her blouse, or her shirt, is kicked off to the side, later to be photographed and posted online, a very distinct hole in the shoulder, and the collar half-eaten away.

The paramedic, a tall, young, redheaded woman, directs the proceedings. She can be heard telling Zanele to keep her head tilted back in order to prevent the runoff from her eyes. She uses a towel to dab the side of Zanele's face, and then the footage stops, presumably out of some sense of decorum, while she is being loaded onto a stretcher.

———

I still find it stunning that our first repair was completed at almost the exact same time as the attack on Zanele occurred, and yet—improbable as it may seem—it was. The sun descends as the curtain is opened. The suicide occurs before the love letter arrives. The guitar strikes precisely at midnight.

I saw Conway as the message came through on his phone. We were on deck, waiting for the final test on the repaired cable. The structure of his face changed, not in a calamitous way, but in a slow, descending manner, as if the tracks of his tomorrows were coming down the line and positioning themselves at his feet.

He walked between the bridge and the control room and then up to the top deck, pacing back and forth with the satellite phone. He still moved like a person who had no spill. All calm, all control. I should have recalled the notion of turbulence. He was at the core of it, the inner point around which everything else churned.

He was joined by Abdul. They stood at a short distance from one another. I couldn't imagine what was being said between them.

I remained at the aft mooring station, with Ron and Samkelo.

"So, when does he leave?" I asked.

"He doesn't."

"What do you mean, he doesn't?"

"Can't get a helicopter. We're too far out. No landing pad anyway. And it's a two-day sail to the coast. It would take ages to get to London. The airports here are a nightmare."

"Can't you have another boat pick him up? A faster one?"

"Even then."

"Besides," said Ron, "there's Brussels."

"Brussels?"

"Policy."

"Seriously?"

"You saw Petrus."

There was nothing callous about it. It was simply matter of fact. We were out in the middle of the ocean. We had just completed our first repair. It would still take ten days for us to get to Brighton by ship. A message made it in a fraction of a second. This was the miracle, and it was also the curse.

"And if someone's dying?"

"Of course, if there's any imminent danger, we go in."

Abdul returned to the bridge. The buttons were lit up on Conway's satellite phone. He closed it, and came toward us, asked Ron for a cigarette. I'd never seen Conway smoke before. He cupped his hand around the flame, leaned his head back, blew a stream of smoke from his throat.

I was waiting for something profound to be said, but he simply glanced in my direction. "I'd prefer if you didn't write about this, Fennell."

I stammered something about how he could trust me, I wasn't interested in anything sensational.

"She's out of hospital," Conway finally said, holding the cigarette in front of his face, a foot away, turning it around and around, watching its glow.

"And the kids?"

"They're being looked after, yeah. It's going to be fine. I got it covered."

"You're going to stay on the boat?"

"We'll get the job finished."

"I'm sure Brussels will be happy."

He stared at me. "Fuck Brussels," he said. "This has nothing to do with Brussels."

I was out of line. And I knew it. And Conway had called me on it.

A small wave hit the hull. Another. And another. He stamped

out the cigarette, looked at Samkelo. "Let's get the cable tested one last time."

"Yes, sir."

I had never before heard Conway addressed as *sir* by any of his crew.

"And let's get out of here now."

By morning, the ship was crawling north. Conway gathered the men on deck—I was not invited—to tell them that he had been in touch with Zanele, and it was good news, or relatively good news, in the circumstances, and that, yes, she had been attacked, and, yes, she was in shock, it had happened out of the blue, nobody could figure it out, but she herself was out of danger, and there was no immediate cause for alarm, and no lasting damage, and he was grateful for their concern, and Zanele sent her thanks for their good wishes, she and the children would be fine, all she wanted was to finish the production of the play and get home. They needed to proceed to the second and third breaks, he said, and fix them as soon as possible so that everyone could return safely in one piece, not least Zanele herself.

I only heard about the meeting from Omar at dinnertime. It stung me to be left out of the loop, but I was the idler, and Conway had driven that home. I had been in my own cabin, trying desperately to figure out what was going on. My satellite connection was extraordinarily slow and there was, at first, very little official news of the attack. But after just one night, the rumors had begun to collect, like those malignant rain clouds that had caused our snap in the first place. We were all in the Congo now, flying headlong with the current.

———

One hundred and sixty kilometers. Almost a full day. The second break. All open sea. The wide blue sky.

Conway had announced that the canyon here would be steeper. There were some tricky knickpoints. The drop-offs were extreme. The grappling hook could easily snag. We had to get the boat settled and the maps established. It was no time for a fuckup. He wanted everyone on full alert. The boat would make the sweep near where London and Cape Town had pinged it, and he hoped that we would get it right. He needed some luck, especially if the cable was submerged in silt, or snagged on a cliff. A foot to the left or right could make all the difference.

He didn't mention Zanele, but the turbulence had begun to envelop her too. The photos of her ticked in, layer by layer. It had made the front page of the British tabloids the following day. *Acid Trip*. The tweets and the chatter immediately followed. It was all there—race, art, climate change, celebrity—and the fires were impossible to put out. The rumors on the internet spread quickly— Zanele was scarred for life, or had been attacked by a fellow actor, or had organized it all herself. It was bizarre and it fed upon itself. There was the photograph of her walking along the beach weeks before, a publicity still, posted alongside a picture of her on the stretcher with her breasts bared—pixelated out in some of the papers, but zoomed in on several websites. In the photo there was a look of anguish on the paramedic's face, and the shot was beautifully balanced, these two women who seemed to know what the exposure, or the exposures, might eventually mean.

Our boat moved slowly in the nowhere. Conway had gambled on a line of search, but it just wasn't working. We crossed the canyon in long sweeps. We were clanging against rock and plant and sand and stone and whatever else the ocean gave us. It was the first time ever I had seen him truly agitated. His body looked like it was set on springs. He paced between the control room and his cabin. He took a pen from behind his ear and scribbled in a small moleskine notebook.

I walked the narrow corridors. Bulkhead to bulkhead. A small light sneaked out from under Conway's door. He wasn't sleeping. I listened from around the corner. He was muffled, serious, intent. I couldn't quite make out what he was saying, but I'm sure he was talking with Zanele.

The days swung into nights, nights into days.

My head pounded. At least the deck was somewhere to go. The ocean sent its spray over me, but I wasn't exactly being anointed. There were no birds out this far. The boat was so slow it was as if it wasn't moving at all. It was all a great surround sound of uncertainty.

Maybe that's why sailors went mad at sea. Once you figured it out, there was nowhere to be. On a boat you were locked to its limits. We were yearning for more than the boat could give.

Without booze, my sleep was different. Drinkers don't dream. Or at least we don't remember our dreams. Now they woke me. My son galloping with horses in a yellow field. A piece of bleached coral whipping through the air. My father's tractor hauling up new bones. I didn't want to interpret them. Analysis can char us beyond recognition.

I heard Conway's cabin door banging shut behind him. I was sure he had caught me trying to listen, but he ghosted past my room, back up on deck, where he scribbled in his notebook. I tried his door. It was locked shut. What in the world was I trying to do? I was a surprise even to myself. I tried the handle again. As if it would somehow unlock itself.

The days were wearing thin. We both wanted out. Time wasn't ticking inside time anymore. It hovered above me. For Conway, he was elsewhere, and I presumed the elsewhere was her.

There was still no sign of the wire. We were a slow ship skimming the surface of the sea, trailing a piece of iron deep beneath us. It was possible that we had made a mistake at the beginning of our search and now we were drifting further and further from the actual break.

He called a meeting shortly after the storm, gathered us on deck in a circle. I felt gratified that he had at least included me. He looked a little haggard. A darkness about the eyes. We had been five days searching for the second break.

It was personal now.

He was running against the cable. The wire was eluding him. It was smarter than him in its lostness.

Still, the way Conway spoke was plain and old-fashioned, and the men liked him for it. He knew their fears. He was able to blink open the moment. He pushed his fingers in under the rim of his knit hat and scratched his head, as if acknowledging their confusion. He had not gathered them to hear old news, he said. He was going to try another angle of search. He was quite sure it would work, but if he had to, he would retreat and double back. Trust me, he said, it won't be much more than a couple of days. The last repair would be easy enough. A feeder cable. Off Ghana. Close to shore. The purpose now was to catch what we had there in front of us. Focus. Patience. Before you know it, he said, we'll be home. Are there any questions? A hand went up. Alonso, the young steward. Just something about computer time, he said. I felt my face flush. It was slow, said Alonso. There was hardly time to send messages. We need to know what's going on with our families. At home. With our mates too. We want to stay in touch. Conway nodded. He wished there could be access for everyone, he said. If anybody ever needed more time, they should come to him. He would allow them access to his personal account. And he had his sat phone. It could be used for emergencies. All right, then. We're going to catch this thing tomorrow. Any more questions? How's Zanele? She's doing well. They found Godot. How's that? Caught him with a grapnel. Laughter rippled through us. Any bets on breakfast? Just one more thing, Chief? Sure. Food here sucks, said Omar the cook. Laughter again. The men were looser. Conway had helped open them. Before you know it, he said, you'll be back in Camps Bay. Now, let's go fix this fucking thing.

In my cabin, I allowed myself to descend again into the rabbit hole of the web, a tumble into the worst part of ourselves. It was true that Zanele was in the clear and recovering. She had, quite publicly, said *Fuck it,* and returned almost immediately to the stage, which had filled the house. The Beckett estate had relented for fear of what the publicity might do. It had allowed a short run so long as the money was going to charity. Isiqalo was a nonprofit. The doors stayed open. During the first few shows Zanele wore a bandage over her ear, an iconic echo, but for all other purposes she didn't draw any attention to what had happened. Still, the amount of publicity around the show was stunning, with police outside, and reporters with cameras, and bag searches, even a temporary metal detector installed at the church door. Tickets were being scalped. The hype had kicked in. The tabloids had begun to follow her.

These sorts of things, of course, happen all over the world, in places far away, every day, and we hear nothing of them, but every now and then one of them reaches into the back of our brains and lands a concussive blow. The tiny theater was packed. It was a *show for the ages,* one magazine said. A *talkback to the times.* But the acid was burning through to a different place. Zanele was the Woman Who Had Been Attacked. She was a celebrity. It was nasty and it was crude—the rumors of her organizing the attack herself, the suggestion that she had been in cahoots for the publicity, the whisper of an affair, the intolerable chatter about breast surgery and her supposed scars. There were the usual put-downs, the epithets, the names. On the deeper edges of the web, the poison dripped. The idea was that she had somehow crawled her way out of the township and made an opportunistic name for herself. There was a 4chan board, mostly out of South Africa, where she was mentioned in the most glaring of terms: a *pekkie* and a *loslappie,* with a ream of laughing emojis. She was also called a *coconut,* as if to say she was dark on the outside, white inside. The n-word was also tucked away in obscure corners. Shock and awe. It was filthy and it was wrong and, like everyone else, I was consuming it willingly.

There were a few photographs of Zanele from her college days. She was mostly in the background. She carried herself with a certain surprise as if to say that she was wondering what she was doing there at all. She had, in the past, taken part in several productions, including Samuel Beckett's *Not I,* which I figured was perhaps where her interest in the playwright had begun. There were one or two other notices about her student work, but after that there was a sudden drop-off. These must have been the missing years that Petra had mentioned.

It was only as I went down further into the rabbit hole that Conway appeared in the outer reaches of a Facebook account. It was an old photograph of him and Zanele on a beach somewhere in Florida. He wore a billowy white shirt and wide white pants, and she was in a bikini with a towel wrapped around her head. She held herself modestly. She was taller than him in real life, but in this photograph considerably so. Neither of them seemed bothered by appearance of any sort. You got the sense that they were looking at the photographer and not at the camera and might even have been hoping that there was something more interesting in the distance behind them so that the camera would leave them alone. But the thing that jolted me the most—and gave me immediate pause— was the assertion, in a caption, that Conway's name was not John at all, but Alistair. There was no second name, but it was almost certainly him: the roguish glance, the same curl of hair, the lively eyes. There was no other mention of Alistair that I could find in Zanele's orbit. No amount of googling or sophisticated research could reveal anything more. It was a British-sounding name, and he was from Northern Ireland, so it made sense, and why should it matter anyway? Maybe he was a Loyalist, or maybe he was a Republican, but who cared anymore? All those troubles seemed so far in the past. How many worlds do we need to live inside anyway?

I sent an email to Petra asking about the missing years. I did not expect a reply. I fell asleep with my laptop tumbling off my tiny bed in a high-sea night, and I feared for a moment that it had broken altogether. The screen was cracked but it was intact.

In the control room the next day, I mentioned to Conway that I had been checking out Zanele's reviews online and that I had seen a picture of him and he had been mislabeled as Alistair.

"That was my middle name. I used it for a while."

He picked up his coffee, swirled it around, drank it, pushed the cup away sharply.

"We've got to get this done. Eye on the prize, Fennell. None of us go anywhere until we get the job finished."

"And then it's straight back to Cape Town?"

"That's about the shape of it."

"Zee will join you there?"

He waited a moment. "Zanele," he said. "Of course she will."

His radio crackled.

"You don't want to go to London?"

"London's not my gig really."

"You could go up north. Didn't you say—?"

The radio announced itself again. A call from Abdul.

Conway poured the last of his coffee into a paper cup and stood to go. "Problem is," he said, "you can't leap through time."

Yet it seemed to me that leaping through time was precisely what Conway wanted to do. He needed to finish the job for several reasons, not least that he was watching his partner's life unfold, maybe even dissolve, from afar. He had been unable to be there when the acid was thrown. The line between gossip and celebration had wrapped itself around her. She was being courted and distorted at the same time. Fame. Her life was suddenly different. And his was too. A certain amount of calmness was ebbing from him. He wasn't able to locate the broken cable. We were drifting above the Congo canyon. He had to get the ship back to Cape Town in one piece. He had once had another name. The world could easily throw another break at him. He could be kept out to sea another month or more. So much was out of his control.

I could sense Conway tightening as he walked away. On the table he had left a bunch of crumpled napkins.

———

That evening, in my cabin, my phone and computer greeted me with the spinning wheel of death. I felt like I was back in the mall on the day of the snap. Stare into the abyss long enough, it will stare back at you. I had a sudden recollection of the woman in Cape Town who had shunted herself up on the bonnet of the car and taken a small trip through the traffic, her yellow dress fluttering a little in the breeze. And then there was Chantal, from the hotel on the day of the snap, or rather the woman at the front desk who was not Chantal. We're not living in the Neolithic Age, sir.

Out the window a scatter of red slouched on the sea. The ancient rhyme suggested that the light was a delight. I fell asleep and woke in a high sea, felt a measure of pride that I was able to tumble around bed without banging my head off the wall. A spider had nested at the foot of my bed. There were a number of small, translucent eggs in the flimsy web. I thought about flushing them out or bringing the whole web up on deck, releasing it, but what was the point, it brought no harm, I would be off the ship soon, I should leave it be.

I joined Conway on the bridge shortly after breakfast. He was deep in some mathematical equation, sketching a line on the computer from one side of the canyon to the next.

"Satellite's out?" I asked.

"No," he said, "but you can use the computers up here."

"My phone's not working."

"I know that."

I was taken aback. "What's going on?"

"We had to limit access."

"Why?"

"I've got to be fair to everyone, Fennell. You heard Alonso. They all have to call their families. We're using a lot of data. Johnnie has been reconfiguring things. You can use the computers on the bridge. And the ones down beyond. They're available too. All yours."

I knew full well that I wouldn't be able to get any prolonged access through the computers on the bridge. They were in constant use by Conway and his team.

He was still sketching, moving the line across the screen. "Sorry, man."

"Seriously?"

"Listen," he said, "there's really nothing I can do about it, Fennell."

He didn't say it in a sinister way, but there was a distance in him. Perhaps he didn't want me inquiring about Zanele. Or I had touched a deep nerve when I had asked him about the mislabeling of his name. Or maybe he was, in fact, named Alistair, or someone else altogether, a man who had disguised himself into something entirely new. Maybe Conway was not Conway at all. Nothing was beyond the realm of the possible.

I still had the same access to the onboard computers as all the other men, but my unfettered access was gone. No portable phone. No internet in my cabin. The idea of censorship wasn't far from my mind. So much for my grand admiration of the ship's democracy and my desire for men not to call me *sir*.

"And if I have to make a call?"

"You can use my sat phone, Fennell. Anytime. It's yours. You want it now? You can have it. Here."

Whenever angry, I grow silent. The petulant boy in the farmhouse. I knew that distant child quite well. The trembling red lip. The retreat to the barn. The stare over the shoulder.

"So I don't have my own access?"

He nodded.

"I do or I don't, Conway?"

"You don't."

There's a position, or rather a condition, in chess called *zugzwang*. It is the compulsion to move to a place where you don't want to move, but you must, and the only way to survive would be to skip your turn, which is impossible.

———

I had lost a number of pounds over the previous few weeks, but I had not yet breached the gym. My anger steered me there. It was a small room with only seven machines. The men glanced up, surprised. Ron. Matt the Scot. Omar. Alonso. They were younger than me, all of them. Their music was younger. Their bodies, younger. Their reflections, younger. The mirror told me all this, but I took a secret satisfaction in not having to pluck my T-shirt away from my stomach as I had done a month before. I stuck to the stationary bicycle. Cycling at sea. Another delicious irony. I closed my eyes and willed myself elsewhere. I hadn't seen land in quite a while. I raced against Conway. Fuck him. He had taken my access away. Sweat dripping down on the handlebars. Rap music in the background. I clicked on the machine's controls, climbed another hill. He was not who he said he was. A liar. An impostor. The mind whirled. The proverbial dust. What sort of wreckage had he been part of?

The men in the gym were antsy. They seldom had to search this long for a cable break. Another day passed. Another followed. Conway had begun to patrol the deck. He had made a mistake. He was not the sort of man to do so. Maybe he would have to start the search all over again. The hours had acquired a thickness. Matt the Scot broke his silence with me. There had been one tour in the Atlantic where, in the wild weather, it had taken four and a half months to fix the cable. Another one, in Indonesia, took six months. It was the life you signed up for. You finished the job no matter what. You belonged to the break, he said. It owned you. There was no escape.

I wanted newness. I contemplated shaving off my hair, which had taken on a shaggy aspect at sea. But the change I desired wasn't so much about my appearance as it was getting away from the ocean, finding some form of firmness beneath my feet.

I kept myself away from Conway. Watched him from afar. Every time the winch brought the grapnel in, he studied the mud carefully. The hook was unfurled again. He watched it disappear down into the water. There was something he was hiding. It lay at some depth. He had cut off my access. What was going through his mind? I descended the stairs to the computer room. A line of men waiting. Twenty minutes. It was hardly enough time to even check email. I ran a search on his name. There were no Conways on Rathlin Island. No photographs. In the newer articles on Zanele, there was no mention of him. It was as if he had been crafted out of the story. There was mention of Aubrey Mmodi and how he and Zanele had formed Isiqalo together. Mmodi had left the troupe and moved to London, where he had become a well-known actor, mostly in Shakespearean roles. The timer went off. I had to go to the back of the queue. It was obsessive and stupid and I knew it. Instead of trawling her name, I disappeared again to the gym. Another day. Another emptiness. The pounds were disappearing. If anything, I would just shed myself. It seemed to me like a form of drinking. My breathless abyss.

There were several times I saw him on the deck. He remained looking portside. I wanted to blindside him. Forgive me, Conway, but I know you are lying. Your silence. Your cover-up.

The cable was beginning to gnaw at us all. How vast, how tiny. How easy, how impossible.

And then, as if sounding just for me, the foghorn went off: a long, loud whistle. Omar, on the bike beside me, let out a small cheer and high-fived me. I wasn't sure what to do. The other men quietly shut down their machines, gathered up their towels, left the gym. For a moment I was alone. I climbed off the bike, stood in the middle of the floor. I removed my shirt and looked at myself half-naked in the mirror. It was the first time I had done so in the best part of a decade. The mirror was freckled with age too. Young, I had wanted to be old, and old now, young.

The ship slowed. I felt her halt and move into a theatrical pirouette. I quickly slipped on my shirt again.

I walked along the corridor and up to the joining deck, where the crew was already gathered. Conway was holding the end of the cable, inspecting the break. It looked as if the cable had been frayed. His hands were covered in muck. He scraped it off the end of the grapnel and pressed the muck into a ball. He gathered the men closer. He held out the ball of muck on his hands. I couldn't quite hear what he was saying, but I could see the electricity move through them, the foot shuffle, the hum of proximity, the nodding heads.

He caught my eye as I approached. He gave me one of those nods that men give each other at certain times: it was halfway between *I know you* and *Don't fuck with me*. Perhaps I was overthinking it all and it was just the cramped space of the ship that was toying with my mind.

—

The second end of the cable was lifted after a few hours. I watched the joiners put the tiny tubes together. The fresh cable was called up from the holding tank. It spun out of its coil. Up it came from the belly of the boat. To the glassed-off room on the main deck. The Hospital Room.

The joiners stripped, cleaved, and cleaned the fibers. There could not be a single blemish. The ends were brought together. The old and the new. The fibers were matched in the fusion machine. The coupling, they called it. The arc of the electrical pulse had to be perfect, like a lightning bolt that knew exactly where it wanted to go. The joiners, Bogani and Samuel and Ndlovu, were precision men. Jewelers. They wore gloves and safety glasses and lab aprons. Booties over their shoes. Masks. They tested and retested. Optical. Electrical.

The boat was positioned. Our coordinates were mapped. The descent of the cable would have to be carefully monitored. The currents were determined, the canyon bottlenecks identified.

The last of the tests were pinging along from London and Cape Town, meeting on the deck of the Georges Lecointe.

Ndlovu handed me a long, thin piece of fiber-optic tubing. He placed it on my palm. "Look at it," he told me. "Closely. Put it to your eye." It was thinner than an eyelash. The glass itself, he said, was so pure that if you stacked it up, layer upon layer, you would be able to peer hundreds of feet down into the water and it would all still be crystal clear.

The foghorn blasted. The cable was ready.

Down it went.

To hell indeed.

———

The next morning I knocked on Conway's door. We were on our way to the final break. I wanted to see if I could negotiate my own brokenness with him.

He was sitting behind his desk. There was no chair in front of it, only a couch at the rear of the room. He didn't gesture toward it. I stood with my hands behind my back. There was a row of ink drawings on the wall behind his desk. The Agamemnon and the Niagara in high waters a century and a half ago. A marine map showing the route of the first cable. A pencil drawing of a fiddler standing on the capstan of an ancient cable boat.

"I just wanted to figure some stuff out," I said.

"Fair enough."

"My access. You know. I just thought—" The resentment shivered along my forearms. "Maybe it was a little convenient?"

"Convenient how, Fennell?"

So much of our courage stems from a sense of shame. "I mean, you took away my access when I asked you about your name."

"I don't know what you're getting at."

"I'm just wondering exactly who you are."

He laughed in a way that wasn't laughter at all. He turned a pen up and down in his hand. On the desk in front of him, his moleskine notebook.

"Your friend Petra told me that there are missing years."

"Is that so?" He lifted his wire-rimmed glasses onto his forehead. "Petra's an interesting person."

"Are you and her—are you . . . ?"

"No," he said, and he half laughed. "None of your business, anyway, but no."

"She mentioned Belfast."

"They all mention Belfast."

"I wonder why."

I had walked myself into the trap I had seen so many others set for themselves. As if he was wounded, as if he was on the run, as if he was in disguise: it was all bullshit, convenient to certainty, and I knew it.

"You want to know the great mystery, Fennell?"

He gestured then to the couch behind the coffee table. He remained sitting behind his desk.

"I left the North when I was eighteen. And I never went back.

And I never will. Fuck that place. That's the extent of it, Fennell. There's your mystery."

"And your name?"

"I changed my name, yeah."

"Why?"

"It doesn't matter. I went to the States, Fennell. To Louisiana. And I was a diver. I told you already. In the oil fields. Are we off the record?"

"Yeah."

"I was illegal. I don't want you writing about this shit. I've a ship to run. A repair to do."

"You have my word."

"It's simple. I had no green card. I met a girl. I wanted to stay. So I changed my name. There you go. Life and times. She left. She had to leave. She was only meant to study there a couple of months. We were kids. We fell in love."

"Why couldn't she stay?"

"Do you know what it's like, man, to try to get a visa?"

"And you?"

"I stayed. She left. Then I went and found her again. A couple of times. I went back and forth. Cape Town. To Louisiana. Florida. To Port Elizabeth. We were so young. We had no idea what we were doing."

"And Petra's missing years?"

"They weren't missing to me, man."

"The Middle East?"

"I was a diver, Fennell."

"Where?"

"I worked in Yemen and places. Nobody's business but mine."

"Who'd you work for?"

"I was a combat engineer."

"What's that mean?"

"Ordnance."

"Bombs?"

"No, I mean ordnance. Explosives. It was a long time ago, Fennell."

"Those were tough years," I said.

I tried to coax it with silence. I waited, but he said nothing. More and more Conway was looking like a man who was careful not to glance too far backward. He would have been operating as a diver in the years after 9/11, and I wondered what sort of trauma might have come his way.

"So you joined up?"

"It's never going to make the six o'clock news, Fennell. Nothing to tell you."

"Why the name change?"

"I just didn't want to be illegal anymore."

It seemed so simple and obvious that it had to be true. He hadn't changed his name to disguise himself at all, but to become the person he felt he was. He joined up. An ordnance unit. Underwater. It was work he had done before in the oil fields.

"And after that?"

"I went to South Africa. Permanently this time."

"For her?"

"If you can't shake something free, you go back and you grasp it. I couldn't forget her."

"And the kids?"

"They're not mine, but they're mine."

It was as close to the flip side of my own experience as I might get.

"And your name was?"

"Doesn't matter, Fennell. Why does it matter?"

He turned the pen in his fingers, glanced away, popped the cap, wrote something on the page in front of him.

"Banks. Alistair Banks."

"From where?"

"Wherever."

"She's from the townships."

"Is that a question?"

I wondered if it was all true: he had grown up on a small northern island, he had gone to the States as a young man, he worked on the rigs of Louisiana, he met Zanele when she was on scholarship in Florida, they fell in love, she moved back to South Africa, he joined up, he went off to war, he suffered whatever he had suffered, and then he followed her, found a job, and he worked on the ship while she went into the theater, and all he needed to do now was to get the repair done so he could go be with her again because he loved her. Simple as that, if anything can be simple at all.

"The acid?"

"What about it?"

"Did you have any idea . . . ?"

"Jesus, man," he said. "Of course not."

There was something so wounded about him. I regretted the doubt that I'd harbored. I stood up from the couch, thanked him, made to excuse myself. I was quite sure that he was prepared to say nothing more.

The boat rocked a little and I stopped myself at the edge of his bookshelves. For a moment I wished I could stay, examine the titles, see what it was that he read. It was something that never occurred to me before: What did Conway actually read?

"You know what I think, Fennell?" he said.

He gestured me back to his desk, slid the phone across the table. I leaned over. A photo of Zanele. At a party. With two men and another woman. Her head thrown back. Her laughter. Her joy. The curve of her neck. The shelf of her clavicle. Conway flicked through other photographs. A tall, thin man repeated himself in several of them. Aubrey Mmodi. He had a confident air, intelligent, knowing. Conway clicked off the phone. It was obvious that Zanele's life was caught in a whirl. She had touched a nerve and it zipped along through every other nerve it encountered. The body electric. The curse of fame in the exponential age. It had all happened so quickly. She had captured something of the zeitgeist, or something of the zeitgeist had been captured in her, and it wasn't going to let her go. Whether it was against her wishes or not, she was just about everywhere. And so was Mmodi. She had probably sought refuge there. A degree of safety.

It struck me then—as the easiest of things often do—that Mmodi must be the father of her children. So much made sense, in that moment, about her trip to London, the manner in which she had left Cape Town, the aura that had surrounded them in those final days.

"Funny thing is that I'm out here repairing this shit. You want to know why?"

"Tell me."

"Because I keep thinking that someday it's going to matter."

A small join in the tedium. Maybe that was what Conway wanted. Things broke, he went to sea, he attempted the repairs, and, like the rest of us, he didn't quite know what to make of it. He had told me that he wasn't responsible for what happened on the internet and all that truly concerned him was the actual cable. But that gulf had been blurred. He had attempted to fix something. The hopeless, eternal question: To what end?

"You know what Cyrus Field and the rest of them said about the cables?" he asked. "Vail? Morse? Ellsworth?"

The ink drawings of the old boats hung on the wall, right over his shoulder, masterful, intricate, evocative. They seemed not just of another era, but of another creature altogether. A different humankind. And yet they were not different at all.

"Faster faster faster," I said.

"And," he said, looking out the porthole window, "*What hath God wrought.*"

"As a question?"

"You know what Zee wanted to do?" he said. "She just wanted to go out there and say some things about the shit that we're in. That's all."

"And you're here—"

"And we're just putting the ends together so people can ruin one another. What we wrought . . ."

He recapped the pen with a snap.

"Everything gets fixed," he said, "and we all stay broken."

Out the window, the cloudy half-light of morning. I started to say that maybe it wasn't too late, that he could still join her, there was still time for some of the harm to be undone. He swung his chair toward the porthole and his face was caught in the light. His laughter wasn't derisory or designed to condescend, but there was an exhaustion about him, and I wondered how much of it was about jealousy, or her being betrayed by fame, or a dread that she had returned to someone she had once loved, or loved again, or some other deep fear that I had no ability to understand, either then or now.

Conway had come to some edge. He was out there hunting, and maybe he was just hunting himself.

He rose from his chair, placed his hands on the edge of the desk, said he needed to go join the others, there was still one more break to complete, we had to get north, off the coast of Ghana.

"Let's just go fix this fucking thing," he said.

It was the second time he'd said it, and it didn't mean all that much at that particular moment—everyone wanted to go fix everything, of course, everything had to be fixed at some time, his colleagues had already explained it, there was no other choice, the fix was as inevitable as the break, and even if it made the ruin possible, he still had to go ahead with the work. Later I learned to never forget what he said and how he said it: there was a resolve inside it, and a loss too, the like of which I don't think I will ever hear again.

2

I saw *Apocalypse Now* when I was twenty-one years old. In a cinema in London. My memory muddles it, so I can hardly remember what happened beforehand, or where I went afterward, but I had developed that literary feeling that young men often get, I wanted to be at the raw edge of everything, and the idea of a film about apocalypse had a gravitational pull.

It was a cinema in Camden Town, and I was taken aback by the opening of the film, not just the helicopters coming in with their yellow bath of napalm, and the fire in the trees, and the downpour of musical doom, but the moment when Benjamin Willard, played by Martin Sheen, waits in a hotel room for news of his war mission. He stands half-naked at the window and hard shafts of light cross his face through the venetian blinds, and then he stares up at the ceiling fan while he contemplates his life. *Saigon. Shit, I'm still only in Saigon. Every minute I stay in this room, I get weaker.* I came back the next day for the early screening, and later I searched out everything I could about the scene.

I was in a storm of cocaine at the time, and I suppose I aligned myself with Sheen's character in some needy way. I thought he spoke to something in all of us, maybe even more than Kurtz and his horrors. In any case, I soon came to find out that the scene with Sheen's character was as much truth as it was fiction. Sheen lies in the bed with an automatic pistol beside him. He drinks. He smokes. He burns a cigarette hole in his wife's photo. *I hardly said a word to my wife until I said yes to a divorce.* The ceiling fan whirls in a helicopter echo. He begins to roam the room, crossing back and forth in a rhythmic dance, jabbing the air with short punches. *Each time I looked around, the walls moved in a little tighter.* In the lamplight, he strips to his underwear. The music kicks in. A quick cutaway to the napalm. Huge blossoms of orange fire over the trees. Back in the room, Sheen goes to the mirror and jabs another punch at his reflection. He hits the glass and his hand retreats. The glass shatters. When Sheen draws back from the mirror, his hand is bleeding.

Over the years, with the appearance of *Apocalypse Now Redux*, along with the uncut version, I began to discover that the scene, shot in the Philippines, was mostly unscripted. Two cameras were being used, and as they rolled, Sheen, drunk and high, pleaded with the director, Francis Ford Coppola, to let him continue with the meltdown. Sheen was dealing with his own inner demons. Coppola wanted to get the most out of the actor, and so he taunted him when he stood at the vanity: You think you're so handsome, look at you, what's your mission, Willard, what the fuck, look at yourself, man, confess. He liked the idea of Sheen jabbing at the mirror, but he didn't have any clue the actor would lash out and smash it into pieces. The jab was short and sharp. The glass flew and crashed to the floor. When the blood appeared, Coppola wasn't sure he should keep the cameras rolling, but Sheen, still in character, fell across the hotel bed in a half roll, so that blood necklaced the white sheets, a small row of jeweled stains. He stood and stared at his hand, then began to smear the blood across his face and forehead. He took off his underwear and sat on the floor, naked, weeping. The cameras rolled until everyone was exhausted. The crew was stunned into panic, but a medic was called, and everyone got out of the scene alive.

I watched it over and over in my early twenties, in that grotty little art-house cinema in Camden Town, and later on tape and DVD and Blu-ray, and I read as much as I could about how that moment had been constructed.

It returned to me—no, it didn't just return, it sideswiped me, it eviscerated me—when I was in my hotel room in Accra, wondering what had happened to Conway after he disappeared from the Georges.

———

We had crawled into Accra on the edge of the gloaming. We had, without me realizing it, crossed the equator. There were no rituals, no foghorns, no announcements. The ocean was itself, but a part of me could tell that we were already spinning in another direction.

Somehow Conway didn't appear all that much different than he had most of the journey. There was a slight tiredness about him, yes, and a patch of darkness under the eyes, but mostly he had held himself together, maintained his calm around the men, kept the center stable. He gathered everyone on deck and talked us through the approach.

The landing station was on the Ghanaian coast, south of Accra. We would approach close to shore, to be guided in by the coast guard, and we would spend the evening in the bay. In the morning we would locate the break. It had been a fishing accident, by all accounts. The wire had been ripped up by a trawler. It was probably a clean break. We knew the wire came straight out from the landing station on the shore, just behind the beach. Conway had already studied the geography of it all. From the marine maps it looked like it was in shallow water, and most likely it would be retrieved by a diver rather than using the ROV. There might be a little digging to bury the cable again, and we might have to use a trench digger, but either way, the turnaround would be quick. He didn't think it would take any more than three or four days to fix. And then it would be eight days maximum to get back to Cape Town. Unless, of course, there was another break. He was proud of the crew, he said. They'd done a fine job. They'd beaten the canyon. They'd soon be on their way home.

He caught my gaze, gave me a half nod, as if to say we were back on track. *Let's just go fix this fucking thing.*

Conway went to the bridge. I stood on the open deck. I couldn't yet see land, but there was the faint flicker of distant lights. They lay low and static, like exhausted stars. The radios crackled. The coast guard. The port police. The engineers in the landing station. Coordinates rang out. Marine chatter. Talk of permits. Approach patterns.

A shout came from the front of the boat: "Dolphin."

Not just one, but a dozen of them, and then more, several dozen, as if they were multiplying in front of our eyes, arcing out of the nightwater, bow riding, surfing, little strips of white and gray cresting the waves, propelling themselves forward alongside the force of our thrust. It was a magnificent sight. The surprise exalted me, imprinted itself on my retina.

I looked around for Conway but he wasn't there. The boat slowed, and just as quickly as they had appeared, the dolphins were gone.

In the distance now, an outline of the land. It was the first time I had seen it in six weeks. Most of Accra lay in darkness. The city had been in slowdown since the snap. Our broken cable was the only feeder. They had relied on satellite all that time. The hospitals had little or no internet. The government. The TV stations. It was almost as if you could feel the brokenness. I had craved the shore for weeks. Now it was within touching distance. A tide wind had turned. A smell of fire drifted out from the coastline, a whiff of burning tires.

Two well-lit boats approached. Smaller than us, but they felt imposing, regimental. Their shapes wavered and then were clarified. Patrol boats. Gunmetal gray. They created a rill of phosphorescence and in their approach they whispered war. Two uniformed men stood at the prow of the lead boat. Glints of light came from their epaulets. Their guns were unstrapped. Some radio communication went back and forth. A foghorn split the night and the coast guard guided us south of the city, in the direction of the landing station.

We moved on at no more than a walking pace. Shallow water. Wooden dhows in blues and reds and yellows. They bobbed, empty, on the oily surface. Two separate searchlights shone on us. Voices crackled. Copy that. Slow your approach. Requesting permission. A pirogue was returning in the dark, lit by a single lantern. The fishermen stared at us. Gaunt and exhausted. Their late-night catch glistened on the floorboards of their boat.

Another crackle came from the radio. Depth soundings. Coordinates. We drifted south of the city. There were some fires burning in barrels along the shore. Shadows quivered along the beach among the palm trees. It was odd to see human figures beyond the boat after so long at sea.

The Georges was guided into safe water. I retreated to my cabin. I wrote up some notes and penned a few lines for my son. *Hey Joli, I am in touching distance of the world again.*

I slept and woke to a thin reef of light. In the corridor Samkelo and Abdul were conferring at Conway's door. They looked intent, but I thought little of it. I went toward the stairs. In the mess I poured myself a cup of coffee and then climbed up on deck.

The heat was already gathering. I could feel it sizzle at the edge of the day. The city in the distance. The palm trees along the shore. A flock of seabirds fretting above. The beach. The landing station— where the cable came in from the sea—lay just beyond the shoreline. It was a small flat-roofed house, fenced in, but largely inconspicuous. Some boys were playing soccer, using the fence as a goal. The ball thwacked against the wire.

The end of the journey. I wanted to remain a moment and breathe it all in, but a crowd was gathering by the aft mooring station, and the voices were hushed, and some of the watchers were pointing toward the water, and others were looking at the shore, and I thought for a moment that they had seen the dolphins again, or that they had noticed something odd floating near the boat, or that the break had been relocated, but when I stepped along the deck and joined them, they closed ranks. Petrus, Samkelo, Omar, Ron, Matt the Scot. The whole boat had been searched. No missing jackets. No scuba gear taken. Everything intact. It had to be a simple mistake. The sat phone was still in his cabin. No messages had been left. It took me a moment to realize they were talking about Conway. I tried to interrupt them. Has someone jumped ship? Matt the Scot turned his back to me. Are you recording this? Put your fucking phone away, dude. I'm not recording anything. Everyone chill, okay. People don't jump ship, man. Hey, did we try the sick bay? Maybe he had a dizzy spell. Might have fallen, hit his head. We might have to dive. Have you called the local police? There's no way he's OB. Coast guard are on their way, man. Anyone check with the landing station? The harbormaster? Anything's possible, man. All the scuba stuff's there? The rope ladder? The flares? He'd never do that. We should kit up, take a dive. Just in case. I'm fucking telling you, man, no way. Maybe he just dove, got himself in trouble. Come on, man. We've got to look at everything. He knows better than that. What's Abdul saying? We've been on three tours, the chief doesn't do shit like that. Anyone call his wife? Here's the coast guard, maybe they heard something. Nobody in the sick bay, man. What about Brussels? Not a thing.

———

What struck me most, as time went on—and Conway didn't appear, not in days, not in weeks, not until well over a year afterward—was that there were at least two very clear realities to be gleaned from the Coppola film.

The first was the opening scene's sequence itself, the supposedly fictional one, where Sheen, as Willard, awaits his orders. He goes mad in his room, drinks himself into oblivion, punches the mirror, smears himself with blood, pushes himself toward breakdown. It is filmed and edited and becomes a work of art. Even though fictional, and even though Sheen loses a wristwatch for a split second in the footage—a mistake in either the editing or the staging—we believe in it as a coherent whole. It becomes a portrayal not just of what might have happened but of what possibly *did* happen in Vietnam, Cambodia, Laos, all those years ago. Willard's mirror punch marks an era. It lodges itself in a part of our minds, so that whenever we think of war, or a war movie, we think of Willard, or indeed Kurtz. *The horror, the horror.* The shots are beautifully crafted and timed to the music—"The End," sung by Jim Morrison, ironically placed at the beginning of the film—and the sequence becomes real, at least in our minds, perhaps even an intimate portrait of who we were, and maybe still are. *This is the end, my only friend, the end.*

The second sequence is the one that actually unfolded in the room, in the Philippines, with Sheen drunk and out of control, and the cameras rolling, and Coppola not sure if he should let his actor continue, and the accident of the mirror punch, and the splash of blood across the sheets, and the cleaning of the wound, and the question of whether to shout *Cut!* and abandon the scene, and the eventual complete breakdown of Sheen a couple of weeks later, a heart attack that almost killed him.

And although this second sequence is what actually did happen—a firmer reality, if you will—it is not the moment that gets remembered.

One sequence, the invented, gets shot down the tube. The other, the real, gets lost in the haze.

—

For the first two days I walked the city. I was sure that I would find evidence of Conway somewhere. The appearance of a knit cap would turn my world inside out. If I saw a figure that looked even vaguely like him, I followed.

Through fruit markets. Clothing markets. Loud electronics stores. Along the waterfront, beyond the harbor, down the roadside beaches. I took a taxi to the airport and asked about him at the airline counters. I waved my passport about as if it might help. Nobody had seen him. The police had already scoured the passenger manifests. Nothing. I tried the bus station. I waited in the lobbies of hotels. The tourists, I learned, were there to seek out their original roots. Accra was the place of no return. So many had been forced from here centuries ago. Now their descendants were coming back. The new ghosts. Time. Distance. Longing. I walked through the searing heat of the city and drifted through the bars. I didn't drink. I wanted to be sober when I found him. Unlike Cape Town, it was not a place where I felt at home. My head spun. The nights were volcanic. I walked through the white archways, past the fine ancient homes, the tall gardens. Piano music drifted out from open windows. Laughter rang from the balconies. I continued down the middle of traffic lanes. Along the broken sidewalks. Through the vast new buildings of the city center. It was a city that smelled of promise. Of secrets. Of confusion too. People bumped into me. I didn't turn. I'm sure I seemed possessed. I wasn't sure what bothered me the most, the fact that Conway had left, or that he just hadn't said anything to me or anyone else.

In my hotel room the internet was completely out. My phone didn't work. The cybercafes were shuttered. I ordered room service. My air conditioner chugged to a halt. The bottles on the sideboard sweated. The water seeped down into the carpet.

The Georges was still in the bay. The crew had searched for Conway in the waters. They had sent in specialist divers. Scoured the seafloor. Not a shoe, not a shirt, nothing. The coast guard had done extensive sweeps of the coastline. Phone calls had been made to Zanele in London, but she had not heard from him at all. She was, by all accounts, distraught. Her handlers wanted to contain the story. A message was sent back to Cape Town to see if Conway had somehow returned to his small bungalow. Petra went out in a taxi. Nothing. The house was locked and undisturbed. Conway had vanished completely. I called the publicist in Brussels on the hotel phone. The answering machine taunted me. I checked at the front desk to see if she had returned my call. The man on reception was surly and curt. Excuse me, sir, I said. Thank you, sir. He didn't respond. *Sir* had no currency here. The clock hands on the wall circled as if they wanted to dig themselves into the plaster, create a hole, burrow away, escape.

I was called to the naval police station for an interview. In a trailer at the back end of the docks. A fan whirled noisily. The floor was bubbled by the heat. The Missing posters were on the wall. Conway was not among them.

The detective was young, compact, braceleted. She took my photo with a Polaroid camera. She seemed more intrigued by the idea that the repair had been delayed than that the chief of mission had disappeared.

"When will they fix it?"

"I have no idea."

"Why did it take them so long?"

"They've been scouring the bottom of the sea."

"How long have you known Conway?"

She pronounced his name in three quick syllables.

"Only a couple of months."

"But you come from the same place?"

"Not exactly."

"What does that mean?"

I shrugged.

"Did you have disagreements with him?"

I laughed. She didn't. She asked me again. I pondered telling her that he had, at one point, changed his name. It set off a series of triggers in my mind. Doubt and deceit slouched alongside one another. Perhaps he had used his original name to get past the airport manifests?

The fan stopped whirling.

"Do you have any idea where he may be?" I asked.

She jiggled the wire until the blades spun again.

"The ocean currents are strong here," she said.

"Meaning?"

"I'm sure he will turn up soon enough."

I tried the airport a second time. A small bribe got me access. I was sure the manifests would reveal something. But there was nothing under either name. The heat bore down. If only I could escape from it. I went out and walked along the beach again. It was strewn with rubbish. The detritus of the sea. I went south, all the way to the landing station. The building was set on its own, just behind the dunes. A bungalow. Surrounded by a barbed wire fence. A generator hummed to the side. All the traffic of the world could slip out of the sea, and into that small building, then out again, in a fraction of a fraction of a second. All the switches. All the routers. All the wires. All the ones and zeros. Ordered and reordered. In one place. Anonymous. Squat. Gray. There were no windows. No chance to look inside. A couple of cars were parked outside. I tried the intercom. No answer. I called to a short-haired young man in a crisp white shirt as he left the station. He shook his head at me and hurried to his car. Two boys remained, kicking the ball against the fence.

I looked out to the Georges. There she floated, a few hundred meters from shore. Samkelo was in charge now, with Abdul. I would not be allowed back on board. Once I had made the decision to leave, it was out of their control. I didn't relish the idea of getting back on board anyway. When I left, I had used the rope ladder down and tumbled pathetically the last three rungs into the coast guard dinghy. I'd smashed my camera in the process. All of us in the gutter. I had left most of my clothes in my cabin. But I still had my computer. And I had taken my letter to Joli.

I waited for the foghorn to go off, but the Georges just floated. I thought of Petrus down in the engine room, working hard to keep the boat in place. He would return someday soon to his motherless country.

At the hotel bar I noticed the young detective sitting, watching me in the mirror. I went across and sat beside her. I had nothing to hide. She introduced herself as Akosua. I ordered a soda water. A gin and tonic for her. Akosua had nothing new to tell me. No new developments. In fact, she had forgotten that this was even my hotel. It was a pure coincidence that she had sat down. She preferred hotel bars, she said. No local men to prey on her. She wore an engagement ring. If the world does anything, it confuses.

"I talked with the wife," she said.

"Partner."

"Same thing."

"And?"

"She's in London."

"And?"

"They've had some problems apparently. They were taking some time apart."

"I knew that."

"You didn't tell me."

"I wasn't really sure. At first."

She swirled the straw in her drink, then pointed it at me. A drop of gin fell and hit the table.

"She's quite famous, it seems."

"She's getting that way."

"A million followers, more," she said.

"I don't really know all that much about it. Technology doesn't really do it for me."

"And you're writing about fiber optics?"

"More the human element."

"Good luck with that."

She let the red straw hover just above the table.

"He probably swam somewhere," she said. "That's what I figure now. Or he hired a boat to get out of here."

The idea hadn't even crossed my mind, for some reason. A boat out of the port. It made perfect sense. If anything made sense.

"Either that or he's fallen off the face of the earth," she said. "If it has a face."

Upstairs, I wanted to email my editor, but realized that the internet was still down. The ceiling fan spun. I watched a caterpillar crawl up the wall and crawl back down again. My head pounded. I was in a small room. What was it Pascal had written? All of our problems stem from our inability to sit quietly in a room alone.

In the morning I went along the beach to the landing station once more. Men slept sprawled under the palm trees. The boys passed a football along the hard shore, away from the fence. The heat seemed to rise from underneath the sand.

I returned later. A scrum of cars and TV vans had gathered outside the landing station. Police vehicles with their lights spinning. A black Mercedes. The boys pressed themselves up against the fence, staring through the gray diamonds, their fingers clenched high on the wire. It was hard to tell if they were on the outside looking in, or the other way around. I walked around to the front of the station. A press reception, it seemed. Politicians and businessmen. Akosua stood beyond the row of microphones. She wore a man's gray suit and a gun holster. She was there to guard the politicians. I was stopped by a security guard, his hand hard on my chest, but Akosua waved me through. Not a single person from the Georges was there. The press conference was finishing. The internet was returning. Things were now repaired. That was the message. As if it had all happened magically. Nobody mentioned Conway. Akosua took me aside and said that it had been classified as a *domestic misunderstanding* and that he had obviously gone home. Curious word, home. Wherever that was for him. He floated between places. Like data. Amid the flickering lights.

So much for the speed, the connectedness, the dawn of progress. I think I might have preferred to find myself sleeping under a nearby tree, my legs stretched out, a hat down over my eyes.

We were led through the landing station. A photo opportunity. The station was about the size of Conway's bungalow in Cape Town, not much more. A maze of blue and yellow and red wires. High metal shelves. Neon tape on the floor. Arrows. Warning signs. Long rows of fluorescent lights. Air-conditioning ducts. Flashing lights in a mesmerizing row. I scribbled my notes. *Human bypass. On the outside, looking in. The face of the earth. If it has a face.*

———

It was only when the Georges left Accra that I realized the flag she flew was from Mauritius. It was a four-banded flag: red blue yellow green. I wondered what that tiny piece of cloth in the Indian Ocean meant apart from a gesture of convenience, or a way to hide. It was a long way from Brussels, Cape Town, London, or, indeed, Dublin. Everything, a misdirect. The flag hardly flapped in the breeze as the Georges pulled away from port.

She disappeared out over the horizon, a low gray thing. To the untutored eye—which I suppose mine still was—the Georges could have been any sort of vessel at all, squat and gray and meaningless.

3

I spent the next three weeks trying to figure out how to shape the article. I had no desire to return to Ireland. I rented a seaside condo on the outskirts of Accra. Near a fishing village further south of the landing station. A wide, unimpeded view to the Ghanaian coast, where the Atlantic threw itself down. The complex was walled and gated. Two discs of gray lawn flanked a flagstone path. An ancient yardman came and tended to it in the early morning. He used a watering can as he shuffled around. A watchman, Paul, patrolled the periphery. He wore green woolen slacks and circled endlessly, stopping only to dump the sand from his shoes. The condos around me were empty except for a heavyset politician who came and went at all hours of the night. His red Mercedes crunched down the driveway.

The condo was large. Everything echoed within it, not least my doubt. White walls and floor-to-ceiling glass. The furniture was cheap and the sofa stained. Ants made faithful lines around the edge of the kitchen counters. But there was air-conditioning and a dehumidifier. I set up a desk looking out to the water and cracked open the sliding glass doors in the morning. The sea air jagged me awake. The waves combed the days. I sat for hours on end, listening to their rise and fall, watching the seabirds plunge and rise.

The first part of the process was simply taking notes. I put them down in a file marked Madame Georges. There were blackout times on the electricity. I tried to make sure my computer battery was fully charged.

The early choices in any story present vectors that can spray in dozens of different directions, a rorschach of possibility. My mandate was to talk about the wires, and how they got broken, and the boats that went out to repair them at sea. On one hand, it seemed quite simple. I would open with a teasing narrative of the boat in Cape Town, quiet and unassuming under the gaze of Table Mountain. I would switch to the massive underwater mudslide thousands of kilometers to the north in the Congo channel. The story would return to the boat out at sea. There was the history of cables to flesh out, the first transatlantic ventures, and the role of fiber optics in breaking down time, distance, and, indeed, money. I had lined up phone interviews with cable experts, hydrologists, a young American professor who specialized in technology and the new colonialism. I was still very much convinced that my story would be a portrayal of the heroics of our unsung rescuers. I settled early on a headline: *No Rest for the Wired.* I played around with it for a while, changed the font size, boxed it off, deleted it, wrote it out again.

The story would follow the descent of the grapnel and explain the repair. Fair enough. As a writer, you find a box and then you try to place the story within it. The great hope is that it doesn't begin to leak from the edges. You prefer a glass box, you settle for a dented metal one, though most of them are just made of paper, easily mildewed and ripped apart. I envisioned a long piece. I had been commissioned to write eight thousand words, though Sachini had told me that if I wanted to stretch it to ten thousand, I could. If anything, there was so much more that I wanted to excavate, especially the new cables that were planned around Africa at the cost of billions of dollars. The same corporations who controlled the cables controlled the information too. It was a well-dressed shell game. All the myopia. All the greed. A new cable would make billions of dollars for its owners. It was also quite possible that the information within was owned or tapped, or both. The old colonialism was dressed up in a tube. It snaked the floors of our unsilent seas.

All I had to do was one single thing: get the fucker written. Put the words down. It was as simple as that. Of course, nothing is simple. I recalled once being at the dentist for a root canal, and while he silenced me with a drill in my jaw, he floated the idea that he would have loved to be a writer but for the fact that he just didn't have the time. I pondered telling him afterward that I had contemplated a career in elite brain surgery but just didn't have the time. The moment passed and I had to pay his outrageous bill anyway.

I wrote the lines, chopped them, razored them, turned them inside out. *The cloud lives under the sea. The light bouncing through the wire—billions of pulses per second—has met a sudden and sharp darkness. Everything, in this exponential age, depends on speed.* The idea was to get the boat out of the port and then turn to the wider world of the fiber optics. I got a couple of phone interviews under my belt, and it felt to me as if the piece had enough muscle and sinew to start putting it together. It wasn't too much of a stretch to remember that in *Frankenstein* Mary Shelley wrote that the fallen angel becomes the malignant devil.

My problem was obvious: I had no idea what to do with Conway. He—or rather, his work—was at the heart of the story. I wanted the reader to have a protagonist to hang on to, especially given how complex the whole technological world happened to be. My guide to the underworld. But Conway had skipped out on his own story. I had promised him that I would not get into anything personal, and that it was only his working life that I was interested in, but that had become tangled now. I spent a good deal of time trying to figure out how I might weave Conway into the story without bringing attention to his problems at home, his disappearance, or, worse still, his possible demise. *Tell me about a complicated man, how he wandered and was lost.* The story would drift away from repair, which was the theme I had thought I wanted. My own odyssey was caught up in itself. If Conway was dead—officially dead, his bones washed up on the shores of Accra—I would, in fact, be able to incorporate him, and perhaps even Zanele, in the narrative flow, but anything else would just draw attention to itself and become a rogue wave. I toyed with the idea of following Petrus as a central character instead, the quiet hero in the engine room, with a dash of tragedy thrown in, or even Samkelo, the right-hand man, but in truth I hadn't made all that much of a link with either of them while out on the boat, and I didn't think they would suffice for what I wanted to say. Still, I had to admit that what I wanted to say was now in its own turbulent flux. I avoided responding in any decent detail to Sachini and told her instead that I was in the heart of a *creative contrition.* She answered with a couple of smiling emojis—in other words, she didn't really give a toss. But I liked the idea of having my back up against the wall, and I felt certain that I could eventually crack the code.

Early on, I had focused on the idea of firefighters at sea. The emergency run. The chief and the loyal men who followed him. The dousing of the underwater flames. The joinery. The known repaired by the unknown. It was a direction Sachini had liked, and I wanted to figure out how I could ease the image into the story. *A five-alarm fire. The camaraderie of singular men. The clarion call of the broken.* My mind kept drifting backward to 9/11, to the firefighters and what they did on that day and in the months afterward. I began to land, in my memory, on a photo I had seen of a falling man, not a fireman at all, but a waiter or a cook captured in midflight from the towers, departing the earth not so much as a stone but as an arrow. He was photographed almost casual in his plunge, a white tunic, black pants, his arms at his side, his left leg bent, at the edge of the buildings. There was something angelic about him, as if that flight might never end. It had made the front page of a newspaper I worked for in Dublin. I had brought the paper home and placed it on my desk, but the newspaper itself was upside down amid the pencils and the books and the tea-stained cups, and it had stayed that way for weeks. I was unable to move the paper from where it lay, or unfold it, or turn it to its obvious conclusion. Back then, I saw the falling man every morning as I wrote, and in his position, it looked strangely like he was ascending, a reverse gymnast, scaling the towers. I learned later that the photo was banned from being republished in most newspapers for fear that the man's family might see it, and there grew a resistance to the image, as if to say that we don't fall, we can't fall, we never fall. All of us, of course, are capable of the most extraordinary self-deceit. Over the years the photo trawled the dregs of the internet, the shock sites where the image was repeated alongside the sonic booms of falling bodies, and the crash and recrash of the towers, the glaucoma storm of debris, the pornography of death, the trucks rattling off to the dumpsites, full of ash and bone, and it dawned on me that the falling man could well have been one of the images being hauled through the wire at that very moment, outside, in the waters in Accra, into the anonymous landing station and beyond. The image had become, literally, the stuff of light. It carried the code of the falling. I recalled, too, that the newspaper disappeared from my desk at the end of the month when the part-time housekeeper simply whisked it away, and it was gone, but not gone, remembered and not remembered, down there among the wires, exactly like Conway, who had been turned completely upside down in my mind.

I expected a knock on my door at any moment, a forlorn Akosua, saying that the currents had finally delivered Conway, bloated and lifeless. But the watchman circled the condo, and the yardman watered the grass, and the waves rolled to shore, and the nights darkened, and the sun rose on the inevitable, and on all its echoes too.

I watched the clock circle. I conducted my phone interviews. I rearranged my notes. My one solitary triumph was not drinking. I took a daily walk, around by the nearby fishing village, where I bypassed the local liquor store. I could still hear the siren song, soggy as it was, but I had continued to lose weight and for the first time in many years was able to do a series of pull-ups on one of the ceiling beams.

My only visitor was the watchman's sister, Veliane, who cooked for me in the afternoons. She called me Professor and took great care with the meals, which were small and healthy and precise. She was in her late thirties, and she had, it turned out, studied mathematics at university but had been unable to find any work after graduating. She had written her thesis about Batchelor's law and fluid dynamics, and when I said to her that a friend of mine had mentioned that turbulence was more difficult to understand than relativity, she dismissed it, with a wave of her spatula, as utter hogwash. There was a law for everything, she said. It simply had to be found. She was sharp-faced and wore a tiny tattoo of a coffee cup on her shoulder, which I found incredibly endearing. She said she was constantly trying to figure out what the cup contained. I thought about inviting her to dinner some evening, but I was fearful that it might take away from the magic of her daily arrival and the routine it had established.

I woke early in the morning and wrote, or tried to write, until noon or so, when she cooked lunch. She lingered afterward and we drank tea. At first she would not sit down at the table with me. She thought it impolite and remained standing at the kitchen counter. I implored her to join me. Shyly, by and by, she did. She insisted on clearing the table first but then she sat down with me. She was even shyer about receiving money for her work. I had to pay it through her brother, Paul, the watchman, who I was sure took a steep cut. Still, I have to admit that I ached a little every day when she left.

I could find little of anything new on the internet relating to either Conway or Zanele. She had, it seemed, suspended her private accounts, though she was still acting and had been offered several significant roles. Conway had had no social media presence at all. I sent emails to an agency address where I thought they would get to Zanele, and left several phone messages, beseeching her, or her representatives, to contact me. *Rouse your soul to frenzy.* I sent long emails to Samkelo and Abdul too. They didn't respond. I was able, however, to track the journey of the Georges online, which felt curiously intimate. My old suitcase. My clothes. They existed, now, as flashing cursors, inside my computer. It felt that I had lived, over the past two months, another life altogether, a vortex existence. It would soon spin me out once more. One of the few people who contacted me was Elisabeth, the publicist in Brussels, who was insistent that I show her any drafts of my story prior to publication. I surprised myself by being relatively polite. There's an odd grace in not just settling for the simple *Fuck off.* I told her that I would, of course, send her a draft at some point but would not entertain any editorial changes, to which she replied: *Please send now.*

And then, out of the blue—creating the upside down in me— Zanele called.

It was late afternoon. I was at my desk, putting a polish on a somewhat tedious paragraph. Veliane was in the kitchen, preparing a stir-fry. Out the window, a lone dog was prowling the beach. The number came up as *Unknown.* I answered it and put it on speaker in case I had to write notes. She gave her full name, Zanele Ombassa, and I was immediately transported back to the Cape Town kitchen when her voice had struck me as pure windfall.

I stammered ridiculously. She responded that she had gotten my emails, then allowed a silence as if to say that the responsibility to talk was now mine, not hers.

"I'm so sorry about Conway."

"Thank you."

"Have you heard from him?"

"I believe you were with him when he left the Georges," she said.

"Not with him, as such. I mean, we were on the boat together, yes. But he left that night. The coast guard searched for a week or more." I was hesitant and I stumbled. "They sent out divers. I asked around at the airport. There've been no reports. I'm sure you're . . . Have you heard anything from him?"

"I decided to stay here, London," she said. "With our kids."

"I was under the impression—"

"Conway asked me," she said, and her voice rose an octave. My immediate thought was one of pure amazement, that she had actually talked to him, and that he was alive, and possibly he was with her, and all the elaborate worry could immediately be put aside.

"He said that you weren't going to write about him," she said.

"Not directly, no. But how do you mean? How did he ask?"

"He doesn't want any reports."

"I understand, but when did he ask you? . . . Is he there with you? Can I speak with him?"

"Conway's not here," she said.

Veliane had come out from behind the kitchen island, where she was chopping vegetables. She wore an apron over her long kente skirt. She stood gazing out through the huge plate glass window toward the beach. The dog had crested the ridge of the dunes and was making its way through the long grass. I had left the gate open earlier in the morning after my walk along the beachfront.

"Can I ask you, Zee, how did you talk to him?"

"Sorry. What did you call me?"

"I don't mean to be . . . familiar. But I'm just wondering. I was scared that he had drowned, nobody heard from him . . ."

"He doesn't want to be heard from."

"I understand that."

"I need your assurance," she said, "that you're not going to make a fuss about all this. We've gone through a lot."

I thought for a moment about taking Zanele off speaker, but Veliane didn't seem in the least bit concerned, or even listening. Instead, she had taken off her apron. Her dress was orange with sewn-in waist beads. She made her way toward the sliding glass doors as the dog came up along the flagstones. It was lean and brown and scruffy, with a severe limp that made it appear it had been in a recent fight. Veliane had taken a couple of scraps of gristly meat from yesterday's leftovers. She slid open the glass door with one hand and stepped out onto the veranda. The dog looked at her warily. She crouched down to meet it at eye level. Her colorful skirt spread. Beyond her, the sea slid along in its relentless blue and gray.

"Can you tell me where he is?"

"Even if I knew, I couldn't tell you, Mister Fennell."

"Anthony."

"Conway and I have both been through a good deal."

Veliane was on one knee in front of the dog. She put a scrappy piece on the ground. The dog came forward, step by careful step, the forelegs moving like slow pistons. I was sure Veliane was going to drop the other small pieces of meat on the ground and retreat, but she remained in place, her hand outstretched. The dog snapped forward and struck at her hand. She tumbled backward but rose quickly and brushed the dirt away. The dog turned and sprinted toward the dunes.

"I'm glad to hear that he's okay."

Zanele didn't respond.

"Is he still in Africa?"

"Really, that's Conway's business," she said. "But if you hear from him, I'd be grateful if you'd let me know."

Veliane came back through the sliding door. She was clutching her hand, near her wrist. The dog had clawed her and there was a small patch of blood on her forearm. I caught her attention. She shook her head to say she didn't need help.

I leaned closer to the phone on the table in front of me. "Do you think he's gone back to Ireland?"

"No," Zanele said. "I really must go."

"Can I ask you about his other name? Banks?"

"I have no clue what you're talking about."

"I don't have your number."

"You can send me an email. Like before."

"I'm sorry."

"There's no need to be sorry," she said, and the line snapped quickly dead.

Veliane took a hand towel and wrapped it around the heel of her bloodied palm and her wrist. I put the phone down and scribbled some notes in shorthand. Out the window, along the dunes, the dog was loping away. Veliane went outside a moment and called her brother, Paul. She gestured calmly to the fence and he nodded. She came back inside, the hand towel stained slightly red.

I sat a moment. Conway was alive, but Zanele wasn't willing to tell me where he was, or else she just didn't know.

When I turned again toward the kitchen counter, Veliane was plating the food.

"Are you not going to join me?"

"Not today, Professor."

"How's your hand?"

"It's just a tiny nick," she said.

"You should get that looked at. I'd be happy to pay for any shots you might need. You never know."

"It's really nothing for you to worry about."

"It's a wild dog."

She washed her hands in the sink. "I'll bring the towel back tomorrow."

She made her way toward the door and then turned. She lingered a moment. Her eyes were deep and brown.

"Your lady friend?"

"She's an acquaintance."

"She's from South Africa?"

"Yes."

"I don't like her," she said. "She sounds slick. Polished."

She deftly closed the door behind her.

It was true. Zanele did sound slick and polished, but there was no reason for me, or Veliane, or anyone else, to have anything against that. There was nobody Zanele could trust, least of all me. She had moved away from her home. She had been attacked. She was under scrutiny. Her relationship had fallen apart.

I watched Veliane walk away through the condo gates. She had put on a bright headscarf. She was all color as she moved through the heat. It was a one-kilometer walk to the fishing village and I thought about getting in my rental car and driving her home, but the moment had gone, and an early dark felt like it was settling in, and the evening was a blanket that tamped everything down save the low murmur of the sea.

———

The phone call had answered little for me. He was alive, but she did not seem to know where he was, or at least Zanele was not willing to tell me. She didn't seem to know about his other name. Nor was she able to tell me definitively why he had disappeared. Still, the idea that he had found himself a refuge somewhere was a sort of balm to me. Conway had survived. Maybe that was enough. I was pretty sure that I would be able to finish my article now. I could fold him in. The narrative was straightforward. He was the chief. He marshaled his team. At the end of his stint, he had guided the Georges into port to initiate the final repair. He had to leave the ship for personal reasons. There would be no mention of Zanele in the article. No abandonment of ship. No domestic misunderstanding.

This was the truth, or as close to the truth as I wanted to get. No need to talk about anything else. I could cleave to my principles. I could keep my idea of Conway entirely intact. He served my article. And I could remain true to my word.

I worked through the night and was surprised that Veliane didn't show up the next day. I found her brother in the toolshed, getting ready to mow the lawn. He had, it seemed, taken over the duties of the yardman too. Things were shifting now. There was little order. I was frazzled. I wanted some continuity.

"Is she okay? Your sister?"

"She had a dog bite."

"I know, but did she get it seen to?"

"She will be back in a couple of days."

He pushed the lawn mower out of the shed, cranked the engine, raised the dirt on the small patch of gray lawn.

I sent her notes and left messages. I didn't hear from her. I'm not sure what I had expected anyway. It was companionship, nothing more. This time around I wasn't fooling myself. But there was a substance to her that I missed, a kinship between us. Those afternoons when Veliane sat with me were among the sweetest and least complicated that I had known for quite a while.

I saw the dog on the beach a couple of times, and once, when it approached the gate, her brother lashed it with a stick until it ran off howling.

I zeroed in on finishing the story. I had blocked out most of the rest of the world. The condo had grown messy. I filled my fridge with leftovers. The dehumidifier spilled over. I didn't care. A writer's craft is one that operates in fits and starts. Time swells outward. You catch a voice and you run with it. The rags of language begin to fall into place. The frayed ends start to come together. A line that was tossed away suddenly fits in a new paragraph. A contrapuntal rhythm takes hold. The facts and the figures begin to make sense, or at least they come close enough. The here and there of choice. *Satellites are puny and expensive compared to cables. It's so much more than a simple repair. The new geography is placed upon the old.* I knew it was working well because I wanted to return to it again and again. I rose late at night to record an idea. I opened my laptop while still in bed in the morning.

I finished a first draft late one morning, close to noon. I had no idea even what day it was. I read it aloud a number of times, as I always did with my work, trying to catch the hiccups. I attached it to an email and sent it off to Sachini. I felt a pulse of satisfaction move through me. An electric salve. I had finished, or at least I had taken a good step toward finishing. There would be the usual give-and-take, the sharpening of the language, the fact-checking, the copyedit, the little curlicues to put on the text. Small worries. I was comfortable with the role that I had given Conway in the story. Things hadn't fallen apart.

There was a measure of sadness in having finished the story, and a tiredness too, but it would open up again once it hit the web, and then it would zip around in the world in the very tubes it portrayed.

———

The smoke drifted. It became the smell of Accra to me. A blend of woodsmoke from the cooking fires and the acrid taunt of tires burning. I sat outside on my uncomfortable metal lawn chair. The smells wafted along the coast. It wasn't a lazy smoke, more an underlayer, but I could feel it coat the back of my throat and wend its way into my lungs.

I had a few days left. I had to admit to myself, on rereading, that the article was a tad anodyne, but it was just about done and dusted. Sachini had suggested a few more edits, but mostly they were pedestrian, a nip here and a tuck there. She wasn't convinced anymore by the fireman analogy, but she still felt it would resonate with readers, and she was prepared to let it slide. She had a team of designers working up a short interpretive slideshow to go alongside the text, and the whole thing would be out on the web in a couple of months. Odd to think how slow the process was. Another boat heading out to a break.

The challenge was to avoid a celebratory drink. I had booked my flight in advance. Accra to Paris to Dublin. I thought of continuing the letter to Joli, but Accra, or at least the waterfront condo, didn't seem like the correct place in which to write to him. I left messages with Veliane to see if she could come out to cook, or even just visit, but she didn't reply. Her brother said that she had found a new job but he didn't know where. How was her health? She was just fine. No complications from the dog bite? Oh, no, none at all. Was it an office job? No idea, sir. Could he give me her email? Of course he would. Later, he said. I nodded and thanked him.

One thing I had learned about West Africa is that *later* seldom comes. The hour arrives, but the promise lags behind.

I had food delivered. The curtains stayed closed. The world tightened. So be it. I left my rental car idle. Nor did I want to take long walks on the beach. There was something increasingly sinister about it, the gray sand, the pileup of rubbish, the palm fronds whipping along in the wind. I had begun to realize that the dog was not just a single dog but a series of them, wild and skinny and unleashed. There were times, too, I would see groups of men near the compound wire. Barefoot and bare-chested. Lingering at first, then moving along the water's edge. I disliked my own distrust. Voices seemed to flow away and then return. It was an echo, partly. But inside the echo there was a voice not quite my own. I knew I didn't belong there. I felt so very pasty sitting in my chair. Cowardly too. There I was, the great truth teller stuck in his seaside condo. Hardly the Hemingway I wanted to be. One thing would cure that, of course. Still, getting off the booze was one of the few fights I had won for myself in the past few years. I had gone out on a boat, and had kicked the habit. Even if the article wasn't all that I had imagined, the triumph was that I had repaired myself, or at least healed a part of the wound, and I could get back to writing novels or plays. But a drink. A drink. Another drink, maestro, please. Put your lips to the shotgun. Behan had once said that one was too many and a thousand not enough. The old beloved triangle. The geometry of booze.

It was time for me to batten down the hatches. Maybe I wouldn't go into town at all. I would just curtail myself and eke out the last couple of days in the condo, keep the doors locked, scan the beach with binoculars.

I had written an article about the great expansiveness of global information, the world unfurling through a wire, the acute sense of time meeting time, and here I was, in a sort of advance lockdown. The intrepid writer heats his leftovers. Drags his metal chair out onto the lawn. Watches the watchman. Pines for the companionship of his young cook. Turns to the cool side of the pillow. Other voices wake us.

———

I drove to the liquor store in the fishing village. A shady little place near the docks. A yellow inflatable waving man whipped in the breeze, advertising a Mexican beer. The path was littered with cigarette butts. The fishermen sat outside, passing a bottle of rum. They nodded as I went past in my cargo shorts and sandals. Hardly the Papa I wanted to be. A bell on the door rang out. The smell of boric acid hit me. The owner looked startled. The white man cometh. Like the hours. He greeted me loudly. Too loudly. Too cheery. He had a gaunt face and sad eyes. I wanted to put him at ease, quickly deepening my accent, eager not to be just another blow-in. No, not Irish whiskey, thank you. Not beer either. A case of wine please, sir. French. No, not white. If not a Bordeaux, at least a deep Burgundy. He only had Australian plonk, which I enthusiastically pretended I did not hate. It was astoundingly expensive and I tentatively asked for a discount on the case. He looked at me as if to say that, yes, he would give me the discount, but later, sir. It was all so very efficient. I had cash. He didn't count it out. Later indeed.

There was a growing crowd outside the store. The inflatable man whipped in the wind. I had a feeling they had been placing bets on what sort of liquor I might buy. The wine would have come low on the list. I wasn't sure what to do, but a part of me wanted to acknowledge my own miserable failure of succumbing to the booze, so I carried the box back inside and bought two oversize bottles of white rum. The owner counted the cash this time. I asked him to give the bottles to the men. Surely there was a hierarchy out there that I would not understand. He nodded and said he would help me with the case. We emerged and I popped the boot on my car. He put the case in the back and glanced at the rum in my hands. "Do it yourself," he told me. His smile was expansive and wicked. He had pinned me down. I scanned the faces of the men. I picked out the oldest. That, I thought, was the wisest way to go. He struggled to get up from his broken-down chair and he thanked me excessively, even bowed, which embarrassed me further, and I played on the whole genial expansive Irishman thing once more by holding my fist to my heart, saying *Sláinte* over and over again, until they repeated it, mangling it, and we all laughed, as if we had known each other forever, and the old man bowed once more, then spat on the ground. I turned and beeped the car door open with my key chain, and I sat there, so very incomplete.

These things happen. They cannot be explained. Veliane trudged past. There is no other word for it: she *trudged*. I wish I could say that she floated or glided, or I found her on a park bench reading a book of poetry, or she emerged from the dunes after an afternoon swim, her shoulders glistening, but, no, here she was, and she was laden down with two shopping bags, which gave her a lopsided effect. She wore a blue dress with beads again sewn into the waist, but she did not seem like the woman who had come to my house to prepare days and days of healthy meals, nor the young mathematician who had brightened my afternoons by remaining for a cup of tea, nor the kind soul who had gone outside to feed a ravaged dog.

We caught each other's eye and her face flushed. There was something unsaid that had gone between us on the day that Zanele had telephoned, when she had found her slick and polished.

"Paul tells me you got a new job."

I was aware of the fishermen behind me, carefully watching the encounter, already passing the rum among themselves.

"It didn't quite work out," she said.

"Would you like a lift?"

"Where?"

"Wherever you're going. Those bags look heavy."

"Oh, I'm just fine, I'm going home. But thank you."

She put the shopping bags on the ground. She glanced at the liquor store. The penny slowly dropped. I had told her many times of how I had triumphantly battled the booze. She looked at me again and seemed to soften a little bit, to ease back into herself, or at least the self I had once experienced.

"It's good to see you again, Professor," she said, but I had a fair idea she didn't really mean it. She leaned down to pick up her bags and made her way up the street. I got in my car and put my head against the steering wheel. The radio was on. Some inane pop tune. The same tune that was inevitably being listened to just about everywhere, at the exact same time.

Veliane disappeared around the end of the block, toward the edge of the village.

I popped the boot one more time, stepped out of the car, took the case of wine, handed it to the astounded old man and his friends. They were already a good way through the rum, and I suppose that, for them at least, the day had truly opened with promise.

———

I found her on the very edge of the village. At the head of a dirt road that led past the local dump. I parked the car. The smoke was thick in the air. Little columns of darkness rose up from the hills beyond the dunes. A slag heap.

She didn't seem at all surprised that I had caught up with her.

"You live around here?"

"Professor," she said as she flicked her eyes inland. "I don't think it's such a good idea. My family is quite conservative. I'd rather not be seen walking ..."

She had no need to finish her sentence.

"I just wanted to say that I was sorry about the dog and what happened."

"It wasn't your dog."

"You didn't come back," I said.

"You were busy."

It was true. I had been busy. I had been on the phone. I hadn't bothered to drive her home with her bandaged hand. I had let the moment slip. I had ignored her.

I had the urge to ask her why she still lived here, in this small African village by a slag heap, and what was it that rooted her here, when she had gone to university and studied the idea of fluidity, and if there wasn't another life somewhere else, her, with her shoulder tattoo, and the whirl within, and her gift for taste, and her stern kindness, and everything about her that was increasingly difficult to pin down.

"I'll just walk with you a little way?"

She shook her head no, and took a half dozen steps away from me. The light was hard and true. She moved on with the bags, but then—sharply—turned from the dirt road in the direction of the hill.

"Follow me."

She stepped toward where the smoke rose. I hurried to catch up. I reached for one of her bags. The hill was sandy. The grass was long and tough. The one bag weighed me down. I peeped inside. Nothing extraordinary. Some vegetables, glass bottles of spices, two tins of tomatoes, a box of tea bags.

We crested the hill. The smoke was thick in my throat. My eyes stung. Beneath us, then, in a field about the same size as the Georges Lecointe, was a garden of ash. Behind it, the village dump. Huge mounds of bags. Two dump trucks. Some rusted shipping containers. A row of burned-out cars. The earth was scorched in patches. Black cinders rose on the wind and sailed elaborately on the air.

At the far end of the dump, a group of men and women were gathered around barrels.

"Careful where you step," she said. "The ground's hot."

Little stalks of burned grass crunched beneath my feet. The remnants of broken concrete blocks. A few pieces of plastic pipe lay shattered and forlorn. A crushed shopping trolley without its wheels. A gutted mattress, the springs sprung. A scattering of paint cans and cracked flowerpots.

"Watch for broken glass."

I walked in her exact shadow. The beads moved at her waist. She stopped as if to catch her breath.

"All the minerals," she said.

I wasn't quite sure what she was referring to. She combed her hand on the hip of her dress and gestured somewhere out beyond the smoke.

"You know where they come from, Professor?"

"Of course."

"And you know where they go?"

"Well, the obvious places, right? They don't end up here, that's for sure."

"Wrong," she said.

It wasn't a lecture, but she was sharp and clear and the words pierced me. The greed, the mining, the plunder. All the roads gouged into the forests all over Africa. All the stories that we had ignored down through the years. Gold. Bauxite. Aluminum. Cobalt and copper. Vermiculite. Diamonds. Uranium from the Congo. I was reminded of Zanele and her four billion tons of industrial waste. Maybe it was only women who stayed focused on these things. The true stories of our times. The way the land gets taken. The stripping down. The leaving. The poisoning.

We stepped closer to the men and women perched over the barrels. Nearby there were two little children, young girls, in identical pink dresses smeared with dark streaks.

A whoop of joy came from the dump, and I noticed a group of boys, like small birds, combing through the refuse.

The ribbons of smoke rose. The cinders caught in Veliane's hair. She didn't seem to notice. At the far end of the row, two men were burning tires. They were filthy and smoke-blackened, reaching into the barrel with long metal tongs.

A little stir went among the men and women, but Veliane waved at them and in that wave there was some sort of communication that I knew I would never understand.

Over the first barrel, set slightly aside, and cooking on woodsmoke, was a strange shape, turning on a spit.

"What is that?"

"A goat."

"They're cooking a goat out here?"

"Why not."

"Your lunches were slightly more hygenic."

I was immediately aware of my flippancy, but she gave me a forgiving smile, and I liked her all the more for that.

She turned and pointed down along the row of barrels. For a split second it confused me. Things should have fallen into place earlier, but I had missed it.

Two very young men in soccer shirts were hunched over a folding table next to the barrel. They were slicing something with razor blades between their fingers. As if they were opening a thin snake. It took a moment to realize exactly what it was. A little larger than a garden hose.

They were meticulously separating the strands, pulling the wire apart. At the second barrel another group of men worked the gutted portion and held it over the fire. The liquid was dropping down into a small coffee container. At a third barrel, right next to it, two other men, bare-chested and precise, were carefully shaking a sieve.

"How did they get it?"

"Your friends left it behind."

"In the sea?"

"Your broken cable, Professor."

"They salvaged it?"

"If you want to call it that."

"They're separating the strands?"

"And they smelt them down again."

"Good God."

"Then they sell it. The outer rubber is good," she said. "And the Kevlar. They can get a few pennies for that. There's some copper too. A thin sleeve of it. It's not as good as the old wires. The old wires had more copper. There was worth in them."

"Your minerals."

"Yes."

"And the glass?"

"The glass is useless. Melts to nothing."

I had the brief thought that everything the glass had once held was nothing too: all the algorithms of the void.

"How much do they get for the smelt?"

"Maybe a week's worth of food."

"A week?"

"If they're lucky."

"How do you know all this?"

"I saw them bring it out from the sea."

"When?"

"After your ship left."

"The discarded wire? They left it on the seafloor?"

"Yes, you did."

She had told me once that there was a law for everything and that it simply had to be found, but there didn't seem to be any law for this. *Yes, you did.* The Place of No Return. It confused me a moment. The smoke shrouded us. The boys continued slicing the wire.

And then I knew. A few birds darted out against the sky. I was reminded of the birds in the colonial hotel.

"When was he here?"

"He slept on the beach," she said.

"When?"

"For a couple of days."

"He dove?"

"Yes. He brought it up in sections for the boys."

"Is he still here?"

"No."

"Did you talk to him?"

"Nobody did. Except the boys."

"Where is he now?"

"He's gone."

"I wish you had told me."

"I didn't think it was anyone's business but his."

"When did he do it?"

"Three mornings in a row. The boys brought him out in a rowboat. He was quiet, they said. Hardly uttered a word."

"How did he do it?"

"They had a hacksaw. And he used a rope. Tied it around the cable. He brought it up in sections. Sometimes he was down there a very long time."

"Are you sure he's gone?"

"Yes."

"How did he leave?"

"He took a boat. North. Along the coast. He told the boys that it was time to leave. He said he was sorry that he had so little to give them."

"Did they say anything else?"

"He told them not to cut the new cable."

"Why?"

"Because if they didn't do it correctly, they might get electrocuted."

"Is that all?"

"Yes."

"Can I talk to the boys?"

"You can, but . . ."

She turned then, away from me, and shrugged.

On one side, the dump. On the other side, the sea. It didn't look quite so vast to me anymore. I heard the heave of surf landing on the shore. One of the cinders from the barrel caught on the wind and flew into the side of my face. I felt a tiny burn as Veliane brushed it away.

"Go home, Professor," she said to me.

———

All of us live in at least two worlds. I now know exactly what it was like for Sheen when he caught sight of himself in that mirror. The sweat poured down his face, his chest, his balls. He drew his fist back. His mind processed the gulf between himself and his reflection. His body calculated the distance. His fist whipped through the air and his mind was precisely aware of when the body should stop, but nothing stopped, neither mind nor body, and he drove his fist through his reflection.

It was a standing mirror, a vanity, and it rocked a little, as if surprised. It wasn't just a touch against the glass. It was a punch that wanted to go beyond itself, into those places where it had come from, the boy the man the actor, those places he had been, those places he hated, the person he once was, the memories he now despised.

I could see the night sea out the window and my own reflection, and I wanted nothing other than to shatter that too. When I hit the glass, it vibrated as if a little amused. I hit it again. It wobbled. The

177

frame of the window let out a low moan. The glass settled. The reflection shimmered. The yearning distance remained. I waited for the blood from my knuckles, but it did not come.

I leaned against the mocking glass, face-to-face, the green eyes, the gray eyes, and the seascape quivered out there beyond us, reliably distant, the splash of waves, the piss of light from the moon, the drift of smoke from the hill.

I turned around and went back to my table, but I could still see the seam of the dunes, the torn fence, the grass bent by dogs, the veranda, the metal chair forlorn on the lawn, the plate glass window, the leak of light across the floor from my computer, which I absolutely wanted to smash, but knew I wouldn't.

PART THREE

1

I said at the outset that if I take liberties, and leave gaps, then so be it. There is so much that we cannot know. The mind begs for logic but gets the actual world. We fall back on invention. The days come and go. They bird themselves against the window and end up at our feet, stunned.

Conway's disappearance came in the spring of 2019. The virus came along less than a year later. A nasty little shit of a thing, it crushed time, obliterated chronology. If a small, round camera eye were to open and shut in my memory, it would capture so many disparate scenes and freeze them in terrific clarity—I remember the photographs of men and women in hazmat suits outside the seafood market in Wuhan, and I remember the video of the man who sang to his wife from across a balcony in Mantua, and I remember the deserted streets of Dublin in the slant gray rain—but the exact chronology is almost impossible to recall.

The clocks fell in upon themselves. Everything went fast and everything went slow at the same time. Months leapfrogged one another. Even whole years seemed to disappear. Time stepped up behind us and delivered a blow to the back of our heads. Logic was mangled. The times were concussed. Even now I find it difficult to tell how far away, or close, those Covid days happen to be, but I have tried, in whatever way I can, to reconstruct the last year of Conway's life.

It is generally presumed that what happened to Conway was a descent into pure madness, and what he did was the act of a man who had lost the proper run of himself. But all living things contain a measure of madness. Without it the world couldn't function. It's the only answer we have for reality. There is not a single one of us who has not danced in front of that mirror or caught our reflection in the plate glass window. The stray wrinkle. The too-full shirtfront. The wild eye. The detail that sends us toward the edge. Others have tried to fill in Conway's movements and his whereabouts, and they may be correct—he was said to have spent a few weeks in a cottage in the Shetland Islands, and there are photographs of someone who might well be him in the docklands of Marseille, and he most certainly spent some time in New York—but the facts, or the lack of them, also speak to the notion that he knew exactly what he was doing, and that what he was repairing was destroying him, and us, too.

———

Mostly, I reconstruct it from his final days. I can't explain why he chose Egypt as the place he wanted to sabotage the cable except that it was the nexus point for so much of the world's traffic. There were two landing stations not far from one another. Several cables came together near Alexandria and they branched to Europe, Asia, Africa.

He was just one man. That was his genius. If he had tried to operate in a group, or with any other people, then he would most certainly have failed.

His disguise was simple. There appeared to be nothing clandestine about it. Almost everything he did, he did out in the open. He rented himself a tiny apartment on the western outskirts of Alexandria. One room in a small white towerblock not far from the marina. He posed as a local fisherman. He could get away with being Egyptian. His skin was dark and windburned. He appeared to be deaf, but he understood Arabic and the language unfolding around him. He was lean. His hair was slivered through with little runs of gray. His shirt was torn. He did not wear the knit hat anymore. Rather, he chose a ragged baseball cap. His linen pants were cheap and dark and baggy, but they were carefully selected to be quick-drying. His sunglasses were knockoffs. A gold coin with the Eye of Horus hung around his neck. He wore a simple blue Covid mask.

The virus had brought a quietness to the streets, but the worst of the lockdown had already passed. It was a good time for loners. The virus gave him a helpful distance. The land had a poisoned aspect: it held our illness. But the sea was deemed free from it, and the small boats were allowed out into the harbor and beyond.

He had studied the manners of the local men. On land they walked coiled and half-bent and aloof from themselves. But at sea, he noticed, the men moved fluidly as if an ease filtered up from the waves underneath. Their faces appeared different out on water: open, untethered.

His skiff was patched together, wooden, painted a greenish blue. The outboard engine was old, but he replaced the gas lines, the filters, the lubricants, the spark plugs, the gaskets. The secondhand gas tanks were faded pink with age. He rowed the boat out of the harbor, then coughed the engine to life further along the shore. A thin trail of smoke drifted behind him. He felt his body unloosening as he went along the coast. The boat had been named in the past, by some other owner, but the lettering on the hull had faded. He had wrapped cloth bracelets around the tiller. He had aged the bracelets, treading them underfoot, so they appeared tattered. He kept a radio in the well of the boat—it was one of the few things that attracted attention, but he had signaled that the deaf can feel vibrations through wooden boards. The locals thought of him as a man who must have experienced some vast grief.

The Mediterranean was clear and blue. Close to shore, it shone. He immediately knew the language of the currents. He gauged the depths at a glance. The shallows and the drifts and the reefs. The surges between sandbanks. Bars, troughs, faces, berms. The oscillating waves. The art of the undertow. The sudden shelf where the catch would be enough for the day. He used a sandbag anchor attached with a nylon line. He appeared languid, trailing his hand in the water, but he was reading every movement. He approached the shore near the landing stations but stayed away, in the beginning, from the area of the cable. One landing station was west of the city. The other was far to the east. To get from one to the other involved a loop far out into choppy waters. He spent most of his time in the western water, where it was quieter and shallower. He used a wooden pole with a sharp double blade fixed to its end. The pole suited his purpose of hiding in plain sight. Many of the locals still fished that way. He leveraged the pole to get in and out of the boat. He carried his catch in a red cooler to the market, where he exchanged it for whatever small and simple things he might need: oranges, toothpaste, a razor blade.

When he guided the skiff back to harbor, he pushed his sunglasses to the brim of his hat, stopped, and rolled himself a cigarette. He had begun to smoke in public, though he was worried about how it might intrude on his capacity to dive. Everyone in the harbor smoked. It authenticated him. He nodded at them as he left the marina. He nurtured a slight limp as if there had been a childhood polio. In the streets he slowly shuffled along, carrying the cooler. Small ovals of sweat gathered under his armpits. He passed the mosque. He had the air of the ascetic. He kept a cross in his pocket in case he was challenged. He did not need the complication of pretending to be Muslim. Still, he bowed his head until he had gone beyond the shadow of the minaret. His apartment block was near the roundabout at the edge of El Alamein. He limped along the broken pavement, up the crumbling staircase. One room. On the top floor. With a single mattress and a plastic bedside table. He never slept any more than four hours. Nobody ever visited his apartment, but he was careful to choreograph it to look staid just in case there was a raid, or if curious children broke in.

Everything about him suggested the ordinary. He had no phone, no computer. He had become bare. He had thought through every apparent misdirect he might need. The torn shoes. The worn socks. His fingernails that were kept raggedly short.

His strategy to hide in plain sight was, of course, open to disaster. A comment in English might turn his head. He might react too suspiciously to a knock on the door. A voice in a stairwell might cause him to start.

He kept the explosive flares hidden, but not too hidden. They were simple auto flares. They could be bought anywhere. It would not be unusual for a fisherman, even a poor one, to have several. He had waterproofed them himself. There were marine flares available also, but they were propulsive and would not suit his purpose. He thought he might have to improvise a sparking fuse, but all that would take was a little ingenuity. The rest of his material he created in the open. He knew full well that if someone sought to raid his home, the materials would be found.

I imagine he was not sure what he would do if he was caught: he had lost so much already. But suicide was not in Conway's vocabulary. Nor arson. Nor prison.

He had a single picture of Zanele on the bedside table. He was, I am sure, worried that it could get her in trouble with the authorities if he was ever caught, but she was beyond famous by then, and there might have been many men who would keep a picture of her close by. It was the same photo that I had seen when she left for the airport in Cape Town, her hair cropped close to her scalp.

The look that had become her staple. *Unreachable by Machine.* The irony would, most likely, have torqued him. The photo was, by then, over two years old. At night he might have turned it away so that she gazed in another direction. The only other photo that he had in his apartment was of Thami and Imka. It was the only thing kept in his tattered wallet, which was later found on the bedside table.

———

Others had attempted to sever cables in the years prior. Vietnam. Norway. Serbia. The most notorious case of them all was that of a group of Egyptian men in 2013. They were arrested at sea, not far from Alexandria. They had dived from a motorboat. Using scuba gear. Hydraulic cutting saws. They were apprehended offshore and their photos published by the Egyptian military. Within days their story was on websites all over the world. Three men, their hands zip-tied, looking forlornly into the camera. It was suggested by some that they were stealing copper. Others said that they were trying to disrupt communications, or that they were ISIS, or Muslim Brotherhood, or government saboteurs there to silence political dissent. When they were arrested, they were wearing plain clothes: T-shirts and sneakers and jeans. Hardly militant or even maritime fare. They did not seem organized. Their look into the camera was one of bewilderment, as if they had been duped. The news of the arrest faded alarmingly quickly. The story, like the cable, was suddenly half-buried. The men were wiped from the system. No public trial. No record of their names. No follow-up from any of the international newspapers.

Conway would have known all this. The group's subterfuge had worked against them. Their mistake was to use scuba gear and to work at night. The gear was cumbersome. To dive with a tank was nowhere near as efficient as a freedive. It was slow and open to failure. Their cutting equipment needed power, and power drew attention to itself out on the water: the lights, the noise, the fluorescence, the churn.

It was possible that after the men were arrested, they were quietly executed. Hooded and gallows-marched and hanged. Conway would not have been beyond thinking that the same fate might wait for him.

He knew that to do the job properly, one had to live in a dual reality. To be seen and unseen at the exact same time.

———

I can imagine him, in the apartment, turning to the wall. A lizard scampering by his head. He reaches out to grab it, but it scuttles away. His body is still out of rhythm. If he is going to destroy the cable, and get away with it, his whole being has to be perfectly in tune.

There is still work to do. A grace to achieve. The whole of him has to fall into place. There is a need for balance. He does his sit-ups, his push-ups, his pull-ups. He works with two bags of sand wrapped in burlap and duct tape. He goes through a series of repetitions. Morning and night. Even in the heat. He must be careful that his body is not too defined, but he has to develop the stamina too.

Most of all, the breathing. He does his exercises in and out of the water.

He switches off. Calms his mind. Fills his lungs. Inhales long and slow. Thinks of nothing but the fill-up. In his mind he sees a gauge. A fuel tank filling. He uses every ounce of oxygen. It rises from his toes, descends from his shoulders, slides from his spine, gathers in the tank. His rib cage expands. The wall of his stomach grows thin until it almost disappears. He takes the last amount of oxygen in audible gulps, his tongue clicking against the roof of his mouth. The tank full. Beyond full. Close to overflow. He closes off his throat.

He has a watch, but he doesn't use it. He counts it by his pulse.

A moving calculation. The longer his breath is held, the slower the beat of the heart. He inhabits the inner space. A lullaby cadence. Everything leaves him until only a small corner of his mind remains. The imagined gauge lowers slowly. Half empty, three-quarters empty, seven-eighths empty, fifteen-sixteenths. The only thing he knows is the release. It's a gateway in his head. It will open. He does it slowly, calmly. The body pulsing. The mind awake. The brainspeak returning. The perception reawakened. He is up to eight minutes. He wants to make it to eight and a half. With the exertion of the dive, that will still mean only a short time at the cable. Four and a half minutes, maximum five. The brain will desire, the body will follow. Even walking home from the harbor, he holds his breath and counts it out with paces. Everything else disappears. A walking man, not breathing.

On the boat, too, he does the exercises. He rows out into the quiet bays he has found near the western landing station. Where there are no strong currents. He drops the sandbag anchor to the seafloor. With his wooden pole. Long, bladed, sharp. Cored and reinforced with a thin sliver of steel. He wears goggles and nose clips, but no fins, no weights. He presses his tongue to the roof of his mouth. With careful control. Forcing air to flow to the middle ear. Equalizing. He dives to the depths and sits on the sandy floor, clears his mind of everything except the knowledge that he must rise at the right time. Ten meters. Twenty-five. Forty. The ocean pulses around him. All specimen of fish and flora. The maze of bubbles. A surging shoal. Jellyfish. A long weed exploring the back of his neck. He lets his mind empty of all but the gauge. This is key. To teach the body to relax. To be entirely calm. To get close to nothing. In the blue light that he thinks of as jazz.

———

He prepares the materials late at night: iron oxide and aluminum powder. Together they will create thermite.

He uses rusted iron, gathered from the marina. Nails that he has soaked in jars of salt water. Bits of old anchor. Iron parts taken from smashed boats, the rust scraped off and chopped up finely with razor blades. At his kitchen table. In the light of an old lamp. His eyeglasses perched at the edge of his nose. The red shavings of iron oxide fall in a small pile. He sweeps the piles carefully into paprika jars kept on the shelf above the sink.

He wears his Covid mask to avoid inhaling any stray specks. The times are speaking to him.

For the aluminum powder he has bought rolls of silver foil from the nearby supermarket. He smooths the sheets out and feeds the foil through an old wooden-handled coffee grinder. A pyramid of silver shavings. He adjusts the grinder and passes them through again until they are as fine as sand. He chops them once more into powder. Almost dust. The pile shimmers on his kitchen table. He does not mix the powders yet, but together they will flare at a couple of thousand degrees. The job is to get it into the water, to ensure that the mixture is dry before he ignites it. He pores over several problems in his mind. How to carry the bag underwater. How to keep the bag from being bulky. How to keep the device in place. How to make a practice run. When to do the mixing. How to create a neck weight, a fitted collar, to help speed his descent. For this, he decides on a bicycle tube filled with small steel balls. He wonders if he might have to develop a chemical pencil to delay ignition and buy time to swim away from the burning. Perhaps the flare will give him enough time to ignite the elements. Rust and metal and fire. The natural world, too, speaks.

———

No sea charts or cable maps. He doesn't need them anymore. He has figured out exactly where the cables join one another and how far out from shore, a single ridge of rock that the cable must navigate. At this point the cable is thicker than most others under the sea. Gathering four in one. A mother cable. A gateway for data. So many wires coming together in one place.

It is always a surprise to him that the stations are only lightly patrolled. Yet he has seen this in many places. All around the world, they are left unguarded. Even here, where there have been attacks before. He has noticed that the coast guard will send a boat into the bay on occasion, and sometimes there are soldiers squatting on their haunches on the coastline. But there are whole chunks of the day when there is no surveillance at all. He has seen kayakers and canoeists near the landing station, even sunbathers on the beach, the cable silent beneath them.

In the beginning he keeps his skiff far away from the landing stations. Two hundred meters out from shore. One hundred and fifty meters east. Then he begins to edge closer, narrowing the triangle each day. Figuring out the currents. The depth he will need to achieve. Getting closer each time.

His simple wooden boat. His primitive methods. A flash of fish on the end of his spear. He creates no room for suspicion. Anyone watching him would think he was no more or less skilled than any of the other locals who fish the same way.

Days pass into days. It is a drifting game. He builds his routine. Out from the harbor, there are many other fishermen going at the same time. They nod to each other in the gathering light. They, too, are hard, taciturn men. They go in pairs or triples. If they find it curious that Conway goes alone, they say nothing about it to him. He is, after all, deaf. Or so he has led them to believe. He moves away from the shipping channels. He is aware that his radio is the one thing that could be challenged, and he plays local music on it, the lyres, the lutes, the cymbals, which he pretends to absorb as reverberations through his body. In truth, it is a radio capable of tuning in to all the marine chatter along the coast, and he clicks it on whenever he is alone. He wants to monitor how they talk about him. Mostly he is ignored. This is, of course, exactly what he wants.

The more habitual he is, the better. Nearly always he takes the same route from the harbor, south past the towers, beyond the beaches, past the little slice of wetland where the white egrets soar, a few hundred meters from shore. The landing station is recognizable by four things: a high fence, a generator, no windows, and a couple of manhole covers within the perimeter. An architecture repeated all over the world. A casino of sorts. All the information humming away inside, the constant rolling dice of the binary.

Only twice has he been ushered away by the coast guard. The suspicion has worked in his favor, given him a chance to reinforce his deafness. He has ignored all the sounds they make, the horns, the shouts, the warning signals, but when they come in sight, and grab his attention, he becomes quickly deferential. He clasps his hands in apology. He makes the sign of *Hear no evil.* They nudge right up against his wooden boat. Warn him away. He makes words badly, haltingly, masking his Arabic, blaming his deafness for the mangling. What comes out is incomprehensible to the guards. But he has the right sounds, the proper timbre. Perhaps they think of him as a simpleton. This, of course, is his great success. To be nothing in their eyes. Day after day. The guards letting their guard down. Allowing his presence. The harmless one. Pathetic even. A deaf man diving for his sustenance.

He drops the sandbag to anchor. Packs his lungs. Down he goes. Pushing himself to the depths. Forty, fifty, sixty meters. The height of a twenty-story building. The deeper dives are easier for him. After ten meters he reaches neutral buoyancy, the point when the sea accepts him and begins to drag him down. He has one goal. To hit the ocean floor. He has not yet touched the cable, but he knows that it emerges from the ground at a rocky ledge only two hundred meters from shore. He familiarizes himself with the landscape: the sand depth, the plants, the texture of rock. He rises from the ocean floor and pops up out of the water, using the nylon line for guidance. There is difficulty in getting back in the boat on his own. But he has prepped his body. The bow is where the skiff is most buoyant. He rises from the water, places the spear across two iron pegs that he has drilled into the wood. He lowers himself again in the water, puts his foot in a loop of rope that he has hung off the side, then explodes upward, using the reinforced spear for leverage, like a thin pull-up bar. He drags his chest, his stomach, over the bow, keeping himself low all the time. He takes his place on the bench, careful not to look around too furtively, especially if there is someone on the beach, or a fisherman in a nearby boat. The boat moves slowly. Stops again. Down he goes once more. His agility serves him well. The work of repetition.

2

It occurs to me now that I am not sure what words to use anymore. *The bombings. The burning. The explosion. The chemical cutting.* When all was said and done, it was puzzling to me that nobody had ever really thought of his exact methods before. There were comparisons, of course, to Ted Kaczynski and even to the 9/11 bombers, and there were online gatherings where every theory under the sun was drawn out, and his every action dissected, with analysis of closed-circuit cameras, sifting of bank accounts, shipping logs, hacked emails, maps of the harbor, charts of the water depth, aerial shots of the landing stations.

My own article, *No Rest for the Wired,* buried deep on the internet as it was—forgotten and largely unread—was suddenly discovered and rehashed. My portrayal of Conway as a fire marshal of the sea was easily ridiculed since he became, instead, the prime arsonist. I was invited onto TV shows and podcasts, but a lethargy of nostalgia held me back. I wanted to think of the other Conway, back on the ship, committed to repair. I had the easy excuse of Covid. It was yet another thing breaking us down.

Even in my retreat, Conway's story surrounded me. His link with Zanele put her under another microscope, but at that stage she had a publicity team behind her and, if anything, they were the firefighters putting out the flames. *No comment. No comment. No com-*

ment. She had moved into a different sphere. I could see her face on the magazine stands. She had developed a line of skin care products, an aloe that she used after the acid attack. The origin of the salve stretched back to her youth, when she had spent time in the aloe fields near her township. I walked past the newsagents in Dublin and saw her face staring out at me. I recalled talking with her in her kitchen. *We can hardly congratulate ourselves for the mess we've left them, can we?*

Conway didn't belong to any political group, and he didn't leave any manifesto behind either. Nobody really knew, not the police, not the psychologists, not Zanele, certainly not me. The lack of obvious motive reinforced the notion that he had gone mad or that he suffered from some acute form of schizophrenia, a hollow man, headpiece filled with straw. I talked afterward with doctors, and an array of theories abounded: that something physical in his brain could have snapped, a disruption of the communication between the neurons, a spike of chemicals in the amygdala, an arterial blockage that had perhaps been caused by his years of diving. There was my own theory of the broken heart, the *tako tsubo,* which had surfaced in my mind on the very first day I met him. There was the heroic element of it too, as if he was some sort of Hayduke incarnation, or a Letzte, a millennial portrait, a new mythological figure to hang on to, the destruction as an artful creation.

The thing that I tried to cling to was that Conway didn't want to hurt anyone. That was not his intention. There were no dead bodies. Nobody got caught with any flying shrapnel. He didn't attempt to take out the landing stations themselves, or the people who worked there, or those who worked the ships, or even those who called the shots from Brussels. He didn't go for the full deep-sea disruption with a grapnel, which surely must have crossed his mind.

If he had cut a strategic underwater cable at a greater depth, it could have taken months to fix. That sort of sabotage was within the realm of the possible for him. He could have hired a boat and gone out into the middle of the ocean with a cutting grapnel, low-ered it, disrupted the absolute depths. He had that knowledge and ability, but he didn't do it. Instead, he cut the cables close to land. At a reasonable depth for repair. And he did so without machinery. No wires. All of it, especially himself, stripped down to the core.

Conway had become the loner, the idler on the edge, and the only insight I have into his thinking is the one into my own, this imaginative leap that takes me further downward.

3

He wakes in the early hours. He is already dressed. Shirt, trousers, socks. He pulls back the sheet and steps into his boots. He walks out onto the balcony in the dark. A sharp morning. Four o'clock stars to the east. A waning moon falling to the west. Not a sound around except that of the unseen sea. Its metronomic rise and fall. He steps back inside. Sits at the table. Reaches for a bowl of fruit. Dates, figs, a pomegranate. He forgoes his morning coffee. He must keep the heart rate low today. Avoid dehydration. The diver's promise to the dive itself: *We descend together.*

He has already filled the red plastic tanks with petrol. Dropped off the two neck collars. The cooler too. With the radio. Late last night. When nobody was around. It was a gamble to leave them overnight in the boat. Still. It had to be. He tarped them and put a few stray rocks on top. He pulled himself into the chill and walked home. Sat at the table. Wearing his Covid mask. Made the final adjustments to the waterproof backpacks and the flares. Something comically primitive about them. Floppy waterproof bags. An inch of flare sticking out the side of each. Rubber sealant around the holes. The thermite already inside. In plastic milk containers. One kilogram in each. The rest of the flare in the heart of the thermite. A final check: compass, headlamp, nose clips, goggles.

Now the morning cold stuns his cheeks. He folds his jacket collar down around his neck. Lifts the brim of his baseball cap. Better not to look furtive. He has figured out a system of carry. It all goes inside a burlap sack. Slung over his shoulder. He must be careful not to snap the protruding flares. Everything else has been practiced, just not the carry of the flares. One wrong bump. One fall. Some random Covid check.

Along the crumbling balcony. Through the shattered glass. Around the piss-stained corner. The rubbish. Graffiti tags tugging him downward on the stairs. Orange juice bottles. Discarded posters. Flyers for the Brotherhood. He is careful not to step on any of the faces. Even with nobody around. No desire for insult.

Down by the roundabout, he hears the muezzin's call. He has grown used to it, the low-pitched timbre, its waking notes, its haunting praise. Almost as if it is a trigger for the light. Soon the heat of the day will begin to gather. He walks along the broken pavement toward the fishing end of the marina. At the east end, the larger boats, the cruise ships, the military boats, the twinkling lights. At the west, the smaller boats bob in the dark.

A smell of tidewater. Gasoline. Rusted chain.

He is startled a moment by a figure stepping toward him. As if rising up out of the sea. The man asks for a cigarette. Tight hat. Thin body. Almost himself. Or what he used to be. He realizes that he has left his tobacco behind. Not a good sign. To have forgotten something, especially a ritual thing, a marker, a part of the disguise. He pats his empty pockets and the man turns away sharply, but not without glancing at the burlap sack.

Down to the boat. The tarp still in place. The stones holding it down. Carefully, he lays the burlap sack on the slip. He removes the tarp, makes room in the boat, places the sack gently on the boat's bench. He removes his jacket, slings it in the well of the boat, pauses to gauge the position of the moon. Still forty minutes until sunrise. He drags the boat down the slip. Low tide. The water laps quietly. He is ahead of his normal schedule. The other fishermen are only now filtering down toward this broken end of the marina. It will give him time to get out on the water.

He pushes out from the slip and rows the first section, following the moon's glimmerline from the east. Out from the harbor, he coughs the outboard alive. A burn in his eyes from the smoke. Along the coastline, in the dark. Precise now. Concentrated. Parallel to the shore.

He aligns the boat in the direction of the landing station. A twelve-minute trip from the marina. The light begins to lift itself up around him. Low tide. Gentle waves. A shallow undertow. Perfect conditions. He knows the exact location of the manhole covers, right in front of the building. Directly out from them, the cable will flow. He has calculated it all carefully. He turns the boat out from shore, consults his compass. Precision. Calm.

He cuts the engine, drops the sandbag anchor.

It hits at forty-seven meters.

How quickly the light arrives, how sharp.

Conway strips off his shirt. Pulls the waterproof backpack tight across his chest. He cannot dive straight into the water. He adjusts his goggles, nose clips, and headlamp. Tightens the collar weight around his neck. Eases himself off the side of the boat, careful not to dislodge the flare. The backpack is heavy across his stomach. He must hold on to the side of the boat in order not to be pulled too quickly down. He waits for his body to adjust. Inhales long. Exhales slowly. The water laps around him. He takes a huge breath. Lets it expand. Begins to pack the air. Sip after sip. In his lungs, of course, but in his toes his feet his calves his thighs his balls his gut his spine his shoulders his throat his mouth his eyebrows his brain even the tip ends of his hair. Every small capillary filling. One final sip of air. Eyes closed, he lets go of the boat, turns in the water, kicks down into the blue. Headfirst. The backpack against his stomach. He pushes into the breaststroke. The arms wide, the feet in rhythm. The collar pressing against his neck. The weight of

it. Pulling him down quicker than he thought. The first squeeze
of the deep on his body. The push through the heavy water. Another wide stroke. Another. This is the hardest part of the descent. A
half atmosphere down. The backpack shifts to accept the challenge.
Pushes against his chest. The collar on his neck. The deeper he goes,
alongside the nylon rope, the fiercer the pressure. Into the crush
of the sea. His lungs contracting. Pushing through and down. The
tightening of the diaphragm. Ten meters. A safe spot. An equilibrium. He reaches free fall. Another wide stroke. He is ancient
now, he is whale, he is dolphin, fifteen meters, twenty, no thought,
twenty-five. The place where the sea accepts him. The applause of
gravity. Moving fast in the pulldown. His blood shifts. The whole
of him contracts toward an inner core. He arrows deeper. His lungs
small. His throat cut off. Sinus, air, depth. So much space pressing
against his skin. An ease to the descent. Seal. Minnow. Lumines-
cence. Beam. Dust. Flake. Light. Sounds carried from so far away.
Another wide stroke. Churn. Thirty meters, thirty-five, forty. Past
the blue light. A darkness gathering. To do only one thing. To reach
the shelf of rock where the cable is exposed. All intuition. The spray
of light from his headlamp. Close. He hits rock sudden and hard.
His hands roll. Abrupt. No gloves. A miscalculation. Disoriented.
A bloom of silt in the air. A flash of eel. A scrape on his knee. A distant sound. He can't tell what. A ticking. A bareness down here. No
canyons, no holes, no underwater trees. Just the ridge of rock. His
hands running along the edge of it. Stay calm. His mind moves the
oxygen through his body. To the heart. To the mind. Stay calm. The
fuel gauge ticks down slowly. Calm. He has given himself a minute
thirty to find the cable. Kicking along the ridge. A foot above it.
Fingers along the rock folds. It takes no more than twenty-five
seconds. He has calculated perfectly. Here. The shock of touch. The
hard casing. Rubbery. Cold. Reinforced so close to shore. A thicker
cable than out at sea. Cables within cables. A thin covering of sand.
Slick underneath. Faster faster faster. What hath God wrought.

He floats above the cable. In the vast pressure. Removes his neck collar. Drops it on the rock next to the cable. A small thump. A roll. He reaches to unstrap the bag. Fumbling. He's ahead of time, yes. He places the bag above the wire. There she be, yes. Impossible to lift the cable, but perhaps he can slide the strap underneath. The bag in danger of drifting. He must weigh it down, yes. Reaching for the neck collar. Chest thumping now. Too much thinking. The burn of oxygen. Don't think. He places the collar on the backpack, yes. The flare still intact. Once the thermite ignites, it will burn quickly. Clean through the cable. Two thousand degrees. He pauses. Knee against the rock. Looks back along the cable. The ocean and the ocean and the ocean. Hand against the flare. The ring key. The improvised chain. He turns sideways. Finger in the ring pull. It has come to this. He angles his head away. The pull is solid. Nothing at first. No sound. No light. The underwater pressure will help ignite it fast. His chest constricting now. The hammer hold of his pulse. Using too much of the tank. Then, suddenly, a spark. A drill line of them. A spray of light. A sizzleshot. It has caught. He is far too close. He turns his head. The bag flares. An array of sparks rises upward. A spatter of molten iron. Two three four feet. Soaring up. Need the anchor line. Where is it? Don't panic. A hot burn at the back of his calf. A tap of fire at the back of his head. Wide stroke. Looking for the rope. Stay calm. Another sweep. His arm touches. Here. Nylon, yes. He pulls. A half glance below. All is lit below. A cone of uplight. A terrible beauty. Fire. Spark. Particle spin. White light in the blue. Turn again. Upward, go go go, yes. Tongue mouth brain. Fuel gauge just over half. Need more. The danger now. The ascent. Against the pressure. So much air. Push. Wide. Stroke. Push. Wide. Stroke. Gauge. Pumping through the sinuses. The fire below will last forty seconds or more. The rope guides him. Calm now rise. Calm now rise. Calm now rise. Calm now risc. Fill every capillary. Up from the blue. Light. Shoal. Particle spin. Surface. Flood of sky. Arc of cloud. Spray. Release of breath. No blood. Off with nose clips. Goggles, headlamp too. No throat squeeze, no sinus eruption. Here I am, yes. Brain cells filling. Replenish. Re-create. Fingers and thumb. He turns in the water. Boat drifting. Not too far. A perfect anchor drop. Not a stir on the ocean. Gray expanse. No glow from below. No other boats. Nothing. Pivoting slowly. Land. Sky. Stunted trees. The landing station on the shore. Same as it ever was. Old song. And you may ask yourself was I right was I wrong. The breath even now. Blue boat in gray water. Nose clips in his hand, goggles around his wrist, he takes slow, sure strokes over toward the small wooden boat. Calm now. So much light. He makes the okay sign to nobody but himself.

4

All conjecture, of course, the dive down, the dive up. But what we do know is that Conway blew the first cable at 8:23 A.M. on September 18, 2021. It was severed through using a thermite mixture. I have talked with divers who were skeptical that Conway didn't have an accomplice of any sort, given the extreme danger of the dive, but all the indications are that Conway worked on his own, solitary and purposeful. At the depth he was working, and with the exertion that he undertook getting the thermite in place, he must have sapped his reserves in extraordinary ways. On the ascent, it wasn't the bends that Conway would have been subject to—I soon learned that nitrogen narcosis is rare among freedivers—but rather a possible blackout, his lungs squeezing, or his trachea tearing.

Still, I tend to think that he rose from the first dive perfectly intact, maybe even surprised at its ease, coming out in a shower of droplets into the wide roof of Egyptian blue.

What is certain is that, after blowing the first cable, he is able to get back into his boat. Emerging from the water, he is no larger or more visible than a seal. He reaches in for his fishing spear. He uses it to help leverage himself up. He makes his way into the well of the boat and lies there a moment, soaking wet, eyes closed. The radio is tuned in to local marine and police chatter. He knows that it will be a few hours before the crew in the landing station can pinpoint exactly what has gone on and where the break has occurred. The most obvious guess will be an anchor rip or a tangled net from a large craft. This is what the coast guard will be looking for. He, on the other hand, is still considered an ordinary fisherman. In an ordinary boat. On an ordinary day in September. Perhaps there are a few bubbles of air, or some specks of molten dust still rising from below, but there is no other surface evidence of what he has done, and very few people around to see him anyway.

Just forty-seven meters beneath, the thermite has expired and the cable is cut. The waterproof backpack has been burned, along with the neck collar that held the bag in place, and the steel balls that he used as weights have been scattered after the bicycle tube burned. There are no remnants of the flare. No fingerprints. The thermite is, in many ways, the perfect underwater crime. It leaves only little metal fragments on the ocean floor, around the rock ridge, and a black scorch mark on the rock.

The oxygen moves through him. His diaphragm begins to accept his breath. He lies back in the boat and takes stock of what remains. The other backpack, the extra neck collar, the goggles, the nose clips, the compass, the sandbag, the radio. After a while he rises from the well of the boat. He pulls on his shirt, his baseball hat, his sunglasses, makes himself into a fisherman again. He pulls the improvised anchor in and moves directly north from the landing station into open water. It is his intention to also blow the cable, or multiple cables, leading to the second landing station on the far eastern side of the city.

It is, in his small boat, a three or four-hour journey that will force him to loop out and around the harbor of Alexandria, first north, and then east, navigating the shipping channels and the outer waters. The early chop is easy. The boat slices it smoothly. Further out, the water roughens, and he begins to muscle the engine along, straining through the loudening chop. He is worried that the effort draws too much attention to himself, but there are several other small vessels out beyond the harbor, a sort of chaos that helps him hide. Much of the chatter he hears on the radio is in English, but what I like to think is that he doesn't listen for any news at all, at least for a couple of hours. Instead, he allows himself to move through the silence, away from the shore, the landing station growing smaller in the distance, the waves rising as he goes further out, the lurch and the swirl of the Mediterranean, the city of Alexandria becoming a distant thing as his boat hits the waves, a one-foot swell, a two-foot swell, and he is soon soaked beyond the skin, his left hand on the tiller, his right hand on the gunwale, straining to push the boat through. He knows that this next dive will be deeper. It is possible that he might black out and never be able to come to the surface. Or rise to the surface spraying blood from his nose and throat, even his eyes.

He has calculated the distances. He will have to dive further out from shore. To a depth of over sixty meters. With a tiring body. And a tiring mind. The water will be choppier. Colder too. And darker. On the eastern side, the cables are toward the busier end of the harbor. That, he knows, means more boats. The possibility of a patrol. Especially now that the first cable is down.

His is a small boat rising and falling in a wide gray sea. It takes all his strength just to keep the craft in place. He keeps himself low and centered. The waves smash the hull. One after the other. They send the bow high in the air. The thrash of each one moves through the tiller, up his forearm, upward through his jaw, into his eye sockets. He angles the boat into the waves. The inevitable next. And the next. And the next. The water slams his face, creeps in behind his sunglasses, drips relentlessly down his cheeks. The salt accumulates around his eyes. The sting of it. The taste in his mouth. The clog in his nose. The noise of the boat, the screech, the drum, the whistle. The cracking, the slapping, the creaking. As if at any moment it might break apart. The sloshing of oily water at his feet. He glances down at the waterproof bag. Still intact. His mind roams through the coordinates. He must get near the landing station. Align with the other manhole covers. Calculate the distance from shore. Pinpoint it. Scan the horizon for any coast guard activity. He clicks on the radio again. There is some chatter in Arabic. News of the cable break is out on the airwaves. He must be careful now. He knows there will be frantic phone calls. A scramble for answers. A search for a fix. They will be checking the equipment. Looking for an elemental error. A power failure. A local malfunction. They will call all the landing stations on the far end of the cables. Shoot the light down the wire. Ping it. They will get closer and closer. Testing and retesting. Surprised by its proximity. The technicians will step out of the windowless landing station to look at the sea. To search for the offender. Nothing out there. Some distant tankers. A large cruise ship. Little specks of fishing boats. No obvious culprit. The day as bright as any other. The heat gathering. The strange mystery of it all. What, then, is that tiny skiff but a speck of nothing? And, beyond that, nothing else, nothing.

We know for certain that Conway was warned off by a coast guard boat when he began the southward swing of his loop, nearing the waters around Abu Qir. The boat approached at twenty meters, its presence alone issuing a perfunctory warning. It quickly turned away from him, but his photograph was taken and later circulated online. In it he looks tiny and ragged. The black cap, the sunglasses, the open shirt, the thin rack of chest bones. Nothing in his boat suggests the need for alarm: a burlap sack, a fishing spear, a red cooler, two discolored petrol tanks, some odds and ends. He is dismissed. Their concern is with trawlers or any craft that might drop a large anchor. He goes further south. His loop avoids the harbor, though he can see the container ships, the tugboats, the working craft, all plying their trade in the harbor. His old world drifting in the distance. The noise diminishes as he angles again and goes further east, up the coast. He pilots the boat three hundred meters from the beachhead. He slows, waits a moment, exhausted.

Here, the egrets soar. Couples walk the beach hand in hand. The boys fly plastic kites above the tamarisk trees. The girls in headscarves hug their knees. A soldier with binoculars stands on the roof of the landing station, and another patrols the shore, zigging, zagging, along the water's edge, up to the tree line, down along the beach once more. Perhaps they recognize the boat, perhaps they don't. He has spent a good deal of time in the area. Besides, there are other craft in the water: kayaks, catamarans, canoes, even jet skis. What can one deaf fisherman do? He has marked out the area of the manhole covers in his memory. He knows exactly where they lie, on the eastern side of the landing station, and so he guides the wooden boat further into the bay. The cable is buried directly beneath him. He has calculated the distance at which it emerges from the seabed. A sort of buoy system in his mind. He is wary of any mistake. He surely has only a few dives in him. He drops anchor. Fifty-eight meters. It holds for a second, then descends again. Sixty-two, sixty-three, sixty-five, sixty-seven meters. His exact calculation.

His first dive fails. He reaches the ocean floor easily, begins scouring parallel to the shore. The darkness gets him. He cannot find the cable. Just rock and sand. He comes up gasping for air. Take your time. Recover. Breathe. He checks the backpack. Still watertight. No activity on the shore. He climbs in the boat, adjusts the positioning. Further out, a deeper dive this time. The second, too, fails. He falls, exhausted, into the well. The blueness above. The light weakening.

He sees, then, the coast guard boat returning his way. Sleek and gray. The small turn of its satellite antennas.

A blast of its horn.

An officer on deck.

Churning through the water.

Two officers on deck.

A perfect vee in its speeding wake.

Three officers now.
A seagull above.
Strange beauties.

———

I have no idea why he makes the decision to continue—maybe the madness, the schizophrenia that so many people attributed to him, but I can't access that no matter how hard I try. It pierces me, yet it doesn't hold. I don't think Conway was insane at all. He continues, I suppose, because there is something there that he believes, or something that he can't believe, or perhaps these two are the same thing to him.

He prepares the backpack across his chest one more time. Glances up. Puts on the neck collar. The headlamp. Secures the nose clips in place. Glances again. Pulls down the goggles. Goes to the far side of the skiff. Away from the coast guard. Holds on to the gunwale. Lowers himself down. Another blast of horn from the boat. There is hardly enough time to pack his breath. He descends. The colors fall off one by one. The reds at seven meters. The yellows after twenty. The greens after thirty. But the blue remains with him. Down and down. A single color for him to inhabit, until that, too, begins to fade away, the absence a presence, and he hits the dark.

Conway had told me—back in South Africa—that he was free of everything when he dove. That to him it was like floating in space. It was not an outer space, but an inner space. A liberation from himself. He was free in the mind and the body. Something happened to him when he was at depth. Down there, with even the blue gone, it was difficult to think anymore. The heart rate could be reduced to something close to that of a coma, ten beats a minute or even less. He said that there were times that he had to remind himself to come up. He approached a meditative bliss. I didn't quite believe him then, and I certainly didn't understand it, but I have pondered it since, and a part of me wonders if that is what happened to him. The concentration that was required would no doubt have taken a chunk out of any reserves that he might have had. His heart rate—higher in that moment with the approach of the coast guard—would have sapped a great deal of his energy. Just the sheer weight of the task was enough to put a stress on every part of his body. A fourth major dive within hours. This one at a depth of sixty-seven meters, almost half again more than the first dive.

He blew the second cable successfully, and all that was discovered afterward was the floating boat, the goggles, and the shattered headlamp. There was no body found, and that, of course, just added to the myth. The currents in the channel outside the landing station were severe, and it was possible that the body was carried out to sea. But there were several other scenarios. The coast guard dove after him almost immediately. They found no sign of him. Later came the scuba experts. Slow and careful and forensic. His headlamp was discovered on the ocean floor. The glass in the lamp was shattered. That in itself was a clue. And one side of the goggles was scorched. Which suggested that Conway had lingered too long and too close when he ignited the second bag of thermite. He might have been in the process of turning his face away from the lit flare. The second bag was under even more pressure than the first. You squeeze something down, your heart, your mind, your thermite, it will want to explode outward. The tiny makes the epic. It is quite possible that the thermite combusted with a force that surprised even Conway. He might have been blown sideways by the ignition, or caught by the quick upshoot of flames, which would, no doubt, have disoriented him and severely depleted his supply of oxygen. Perhaps the blast caused him to gasp or gulp, and his control abandoned him, and his breath might have galloped, that wild horse, in the light of the underground burning. In the surrounding darkness—since at that depth, and that time of day, heading toward the late afternoon, the light had almost completely left him—he might have been disoriented. He could have begun swimming laterally, or discovered himself, in midrise, doubting his actual direction. Or he might have descended rather than going upward, a reverse Icarus, no sun but the dark, another myth burning in the wrong direction. But it is also possible that he knew what awaited him above and that he found a peace with the moment and that he was taken with the sight of it all, and he paused above the burning, or surrendered himself to it, oddly beautiful, even in the smash-up, in the face of the dark, the white sparks rising up from the bottom of the ocean, the shards of light reaching up, the destruction of the cable underneath, the sudden disappearance of all the noise of the world, the rest is silence, a sort of clarity coming to him, a sense of relief even amid all the clamor, and he might have known from the fuel gauge in his mind that he just didn't have enough to get him to the surface, or he might just have told himself that it was not time to rise anymore, all had been done, all had been seen, and he didn't want captivity, and he didn't want fame, and he could see no further way with love or hope or time, and so he remained, near the bottom of the ocean, where he had already told me, in the course of the repair, that things in the underneath betray all other categories.

EPILOGUE

I have always had an odd relationship with London. I had gone there as a young man to be away from the squinting windows. I had lived a rather raucous life on the edges of Brixton, and it had all eventually descended into cocaine and empty bookshops. Later I began to like the veneer of politeness that the city suggested, the little scarf of fog that hung around the Thames. I enjoyed walking her quieter streets, around Kensington and Chelsea, especially late at night, when the curtains were drawn and a little light leaked out from the windows. I tried to imagine the dramas unfolding in the terraced houses that had become among the most fashionable addresses in the city. I knew the area quite well and indulged my fantasies for a short while when I had an affair with a poet who lived in a high-windowed flat on Ovington Street.

This time around, fifty-one years old, the city appeared to me in a heap of broken images. My nerves sizzled. The heat crawled behind me up the stairs to the apartment I had rented in Pimlico. Dropped its weight down on my shoulders. Crawled across my scalp and slunk into my cranium. There was no air-conditioning. I filled the bath with cool water. When I looked outside to John Islip Street, the birds looked motionless. Even the shadows seemed combustible.

Night was only a slight relief. The morning crept up on me, a slow drumming between my ears.

I had, I thought, arranged a meeting with Zanele in London, but her handlers had begun to freeze me out. They gave no reason. I had been at pains to say that the pretext for the meeting was personal and that I didn't have any intentions to visit as a journalist. I had taken all my Covid tests, I said. I offered to sign an NDA. I wanted to adopt a position that wasn't even vaguely threatening. I mentioned Imka and Thami in a casual, offhand way. The assistants remained aloof, on the surface of things.

I still had that nagging sense of guilt for having denied my son while I had been in Zanele's kitchen years before. But that person seemed entirely different: he, or more accurately, I, was out there somewhere, still watching the gray waves roll by. Time and Covid had put a new foundation beneath me. I had sent my letter to Joli. He hadn't responded at length, just a quick acknowledgment, but I felt sure that the words had landed. I had continued to temper my drinking. Kept my weight down. Put manners on my hair, clipped it close to the temples. I had developed a pandemic interest in choreography, perhaps as an outreach to Joli's mother and our past. Freelancing for an online news journal kept me above the waterline. I had even begun to write about dance. Most everything was quietly unrequited—the middle-aged desire to choreograph, to be a proper father, to experience love—but I had, at least, tried. I felt the balance and unbalance of the perpetually falling man.

Conway's story still reached in beyond my rib cage and turned my heart a notch backward. Each time I thought of him, there was a squeeze of the arteries.

It was almost a year since the bombing in Egypt, and he had entered into folklore. I had come to London, I suppose, to put it all to rest. But Zanele, or rather her people, were not returning my calls anymore. I had begun to realize that nothing, once begun, ever properly finishes.

———

The news of the *bombing*—and that is the word that most of the world heard—had shot through the media within a couple of days. It hit all the major websites, amid the stories of the pandemic and the hurricanes and the evacuations and the drowning of refugees and the other sundry horrors that the world delivered. *Major Mediterranean Cables Bombed. Attack Disrupts Global Networks. Undersea Cables Sabotaged in Egypt.* It was attributed, of course, to terrorism. The bombers were clothed in the inevitable language of kaffiyehs. It was some rogue Islamic group that wanted to take the system down. An offshoot of ISIS. The Brotherhood itself. There were a few others who saw it more globally. It might have been a Russian ploy, or it could have been a Chinese hack, or even an American operation, since the bombing had disrupted the cables that went all the way to Afghanistan.

In the early days Conway was not identified as a subject. None of the news of the mechanics of the attack had been revealed. Nobody could really conceive of it being a simple one-man job. His body had not surfaced, but his boat had been found floating, and the divers went to the scene of the underwater crime. They would piece it together slowly, as would observers on the internet who took it on as a global crime.

But the real penetrative shock came when it was revealed, just two days after the attack, that a similar device had been found in Cornwall, England, strapped to an underwater cable, at almost the exact same distance from shore as the one in Alexandria. The likelihood was that it had been planted by the same group. It was discovered first by three scuba divers who had heard about the destruction and had gone, for curiosity's sake, to see how easy it might be to dive down to inspect their own local cable.

There is a video that was posted by a young Englishwoman who looks petite alongside two tall, burly men. They film themselves at the beach, laughing and joking as they struggle into their neoprene wetsuits. At one stage the woman turns to the camera and says that she is about to explore the murky underdepths, which rang a distant echo in my head. The filming stops, the video is cut, and they are suddenly on a small motorboat going out from the shore. The footage, obviously from a camera strapped to the woman's head, is amateur and jarring. Their voices compete with the rush of speed and wind until they are far out in the water. They guide the camera in the direction of the landing station at Porthcurno, but in the light fog there is little to be seen. Besides, the lens has a severe lack of depth, which somehow makes it feel entirely honest, as if unfolding in the eternal now. In the footage, they make several attempts at diving for the cable. The extraordinary thing—and this observation is made several times by the young woman quivering in the cold—is that there is no security in and around the landing station. No boats out on the water. No patrols.

They continue their dives without luck until one of their last forays, later in the day, with the gloaming approaching. The two divers, the woman and the taller of the two men, move into the blackness with the tanks on their backs. They finally stumble upon a reinforced portion of the cable, thick and dark in the shimmer from the flashlight. They follow the length of the cable. There is no sound, but a sign language goes between them: hand signals, thumbs up, thumbs down, index fingers sliding along their palms. *Descend. How much air do you have? Follow me. Stop.* And then—quite suddenly—there is a halting of the bodies. A flurry of bubbles. A turn sideways of the camera. Panic. A hand sweeping in front of the lens. A movement back and forth. A jarring shock. The camera switches again in the direction of the cable and—almost impossible to discern in the underwater fuzz—there is a black backpack suspended just below the cable. At first it appears, in the cone of flashlight, like some form of rectangular fish hovering, but if the footage is paused and examined carefully, one can see that the backpack is attached by a series of large plastic zip ties. Everything else is difficult to make out. The divers dart upward until they realize that they may be ascending too quickly, and they have to hover above the bomb, or at least what they think is a bomb. There is no underwater sound, but the alarm on the man's face is palpable. The woman directs her companion sideways, away from the cable. Her movement is nimble. When she turns again, her co-diver lumbers behind her.

The camera stops—or at least the footage is edited in this manner—and the next thing we see is that they are back on land, in a small car, driving very fast, looking for a place with proper cellphone coverage in order to call what they refer to as the bomb disposal unit. Later that night there is static footage of them interviewing each other in what looks like a seaside bungalow, at a long table with plastic chairs and a row of beer bottles. The taller diver now oozes a haughty confidence. He goes into elaborate detail about his dive, and how he discovered the bomb. He reports that the device has been defused, and acts as if he himself had been the sapper, working away meticulously at the wires. The young woman visibly rolls her eyes.

It was, in fact, experts from the Royal Navy who defused the bomb the following day, although, as it turned out, there was nothing to actually defuse. The bag was filled with sand. A copycat device. There was no way to know if it was the same brand of backpack that had been used in Egypt, since the Egyptian ones had been burned to nothing. But it was logical to assume that the same perpetrator, or perpetrators, had been involved. It suggested to some that the Islamic group had penetrated the local area. It didn't matter that there was no actual bomb. It was a clear indicator that the saboteur had, at the very least, contemplated blowing the cable. The shock, of course, triggered a series of investigations near all the landing stations around the world. Ten other bags were found, two in Florida, two in Long Island, two in New Jersey, two in Marseille, one off Norway, one in the Black Sea, all of them made from the exact same material, zip-tied to the cables.

I was convinced that one would eventually be found in South Africa, and another off the north coast of Ireland, or somewhere else that mattered to Conway. They never were. There is no logic. The world is messy. The answers lie in the beyond.

The speculation was that the bombers—they were still plural at the time—had been trying to take down the internet all around the world in one simultaneous act. But there were no timers in the bags, no black matches, no batteries, and most tellingly, no flares. In each case, the backpacks were filled with sand. The authorities hid that simple fact from the general public, insisting instead that the threat had been neutralized, only finally admitting that they had, in fact, been dummy bombs. Nobody could quite understand why the plot would be so intricately counterfeit, and why someone would go to the great difficulty of diving all that way just to hide something that was likely never to be seen. It triggered speculation across the internet: everyone with an opinion, of course, the obscene certainty of our days.

When it emerged, weeks later, that it was Conway who had ignited the Egyptian device, there was a splutter of confusion. The evidence against him was overwhelming. The Egyptian coast guard had discovered the floating boat, the goggles, the radio that was left in the cooler. They traced the boat back to the harbor. From there they were able to reverse engineer Conway's path from his apartment to the harbor using closed-circuit camera footage. He disappeared at times, but then returned when the camera angles caught him, often out of focus, with his burlap bag over his shoulder, and his baseball hat low on his brow. The apartment was full of clues—which convinces me that Conway planned to return, even if he did decide, in his last moments, to contemplate the fire, or assess the beauty, or the violence, of it all. I presume Interpol was involved in this, along with other agencies, the alphabet soup of who we have become. FBI, GIS, MI5, BNI, SSA, DSGE. There was no passport left in the apartment, or identification of any sort, but in the end it must have been easy enough for them to piece together the various clues to arrive back to a chief of mission on the Georges Lecointe, a man who had gone missing in Ghana.

The search for Conway was extensive. Helicopters. Divers. Nautical experts who knew the currents. His missing body fueled reams of speculation, of course. A whole host of theories sprang up around him.

It was news for quite a while, especially in Ireland. The newspapers excavated what they could. He was indeed from Rathlin Island. His family, the Bankses, had lived there for generations. A Protestant line originally, but they had married with the McPhails, the McGowans, the Walkers, the Kellys. His father was an underwater welder who worked in the oil fields of the North Sea, and his mother was a sound engineer from Norway: she had been engaged in whale research. He had no brothers or sisters. His was a quiet boyhood by all accounts. A wanderer and a swimmer and a diver. But his mother had died in a boating accident when he was just twelve years old, and his father disappeared, never to be heard from again, two years later. Alistair Banks himself left Ireland when he was seventeen, first for the North Sea and then, a short time later, for southern Louisiana, where he became John A. Conway by deed poll and signed up for the U.S. Navy. Nothing was known of what he did there. He was described by the papers as a chameleon, a charlatan, a con man.

When Zanele was finally hauled into the frame, the journalists reasserted the notion of the consummate con man, mostly for themselves: the story sold well. He had conned a famous actress, faked his name, his background, his status. She didn't give any interviews about it, just made a statement that indeed they had been friends and had known each other over the years, and she was mourning his loss, and had nothing else to say, please leave her and her family in peace. But even she must have known that there was never going to be a time when she would be entirely left alone. She had performed plays by Ntozake Shange, August Wilson, and Suzan-Lori Parks, and a Pinter series that had won her several awards. She had made two feature films. She had also written a series of essays, mostly about the climate and different forms of change, including one about her township, *Where We Come From,* and one about freediving, *Where We Came From,* a powerful exploration of how the body undergoes a mammalian response when underwater, a master switch in the human body where it devolves back to earlier aquatic states. It did not mention Conway, but I could feel him diving alongside her, an evolutionary descent toward a quieter place. *This is the world as it is. Impossible. And fucking beautiful.* Another essay detailed how she had grown up not ten kilometers from the sea, but she had never visited it until the age of fourteen. The collection came in for considerable attention, especially among young readers who saw her as a grounding voice in a brutally confused time.

These were the fragments. The shrapnel pieces. They arrived from all directions. When they were put together, they made a mosaic, and after a while, I began to see the outline, or at least a large part of it.

It didn't come like a burning bush or a pillar of light, but Conway had stepped into that hotel in Cape Town, years before, and he stood on the shore of his loneliness, and he had said that he liked things that worked, and what he had hidden was that nothing was working, and it was all falling apart at his fingertips. He forged on because he believed that perhaps something would change. But time took hold of him and turned him inside out. Things began to slip further and further. His brain quaked. It must have been an interior landslide. He lost equilibrium. He was unable to tell up from down. He tried to hold on. He was profoundly principled and yet at the same time altogether unreliable. He had a magnetic effect. I recalled how much the women seemed to hover in his orbit: the waitress in the hotel, Petra, the scientist who had riffed on turbulence. Perhaps Zanele had been unable to deal with his rootlessness. Maybe he was simply unknowable. In the end she had left him and she had found refuge with Mmodi. Time wasn't able to keep up with the truth. But neither was repair. That might have been Conway's undersong. I still don't know exactly what he was searching for—it wasn't redemption and it wasn't revenge, but he had made a career in repair, most likely because he was aware from the very beginning of what was happening to us all and he wanted to warn us.

There were numerous supposed sightings of him in various parts of the world, in San Francisco, in Buenos Aires, in Berlin, and he attained a notoriety that took over parts of the internet, mostly in those dark and hidden areas, until his skeleton—along with the Eye of Horus necklace—washed up in a bay in northern Libya five months later, most of him still left at sea.

He was found, finally, by children.

———

I had sent the initial email to Zanele in order to arrange a visit. She had replied that she would be glad to see me some day in London. It may have been one of those offhand emails that one later learns to regret—*it went to spam, the deposit is on its way, I'll do it next year*—but I had taken her message entirely to heart. I had been surprised to hear from her directly, and perhaps it fueled my fascination, but it seemed earnest, and I felt quite keenly that it was important to see her, not for any grand public profile or exposé, but for the simple human instinct to resolve it all.

Time, as I have said, was contorted. We were all standing six feet apart. We were meaningful and meaningless at the exact same time. Every interaction mattered. And yet nothing mattered at all. Our certainty and our doubt. I let the months slide. I sent her an occasional email—it wasn't beyond me that it bounced along on the seabed—but I didn't hear back. It was early in the summer of 2022 when I finally felt that it would be a good idea to take a trip to London.

I had been writing a piece about Alonzo King Lines Ballet—they had cooperated on a piece with an Irish writer I vaguely knew, and they were due to perform it at the Barbican Centre. I hoped to find something in flight. I felt it would be a perfect time to fling the metaphorical stone at all things that fly. I wrote again to Zanele but the personal replies had stopped, and I entered the complicated back-and-forth with her assistants. Then the silence. The term, I suppose, was *ghosted*. I was disappointed, but I was fully prepared to understand her and accept it. If Zanele did not want to see me, it was disappointing, but I could move on and leave well enough alone.

I arranged an interview with the Irish writer. Truth is, we were of the same generation but didn't much like each other. Envy is a dark ink. He was a middle-class Dubliner who had written a free-verse poem on spiritual themes and what he called the divergence between what people see and hear. A dandy, he wore a thin purple scarf even in the heat. I attended the rehearsal in the morning, then got myself dressed for the opening performance. I took the Circle Line and emerged at the Barbican in another wave of swelter. The pandemic had waned significantly, but the audience was still required to wear masks.

It was all rather disturbingly triumphant—the performance was sinuous, and the dancers eddied onstage. It finished with a standing ovation. I found it hard to disguise my discontent. My writer acquaintance was the sort who had never really met anyone he liked better than himself. He had promised me that I would be welcome at the after-party. I searched him out in the lobby, but because of Covid regulations, the location of the party was being kept secret. Preposterously, most people had already taken their masks off. They were shaking hands and leaning close to one another. I walked through the crowd, looking for the scarf more than the man, and brushed against Aubrey Mmodi, who, even with a mask on, was instantly recognizable, his hair slightly graying, his body agile underneath his black silk shirt. I wheeled around to look for Zanele. All of us moving in an underwater shoal. The maskless and the masked. Shoulder against shoulder. The disconnected dance. Trays, waiters, laughter. After a moment I spotted her. She was in the corner talking with the Irish writer, who had somehow found himself a kufi to wear. He had been to a tanning salon. He appeared orange. I sidled up and caught his attention over the shoulder of Zanele. He made a tiny but elaborate gesture to shoo me away, a half-polite *Fuck off,* but I stepped forward anyway and hovered behind them, close but not too close. The writer shot another piercing look at me. Zanele must have sensed someone, because she turned ever so slightly, and I lightly touched her elbow and told her my name. "I just wanted to say hello again." She bent forward and asked me to repeat my name. A brief wash of confusion went across her eyes, but then she reached for my forearm and said, "But of course." I instantly looked for the spot on her neck where the acid had been thrown. It was a small discoloration, shaped like a descending bird. "I fear I owe you an email," she said.

She turned her back to the writer. He immediately paled. I said something along the lines that I was very sorry for her loss and hoped that she was finding solace in her work. All quite banal. She responded with no great emotion. I said that I had enjoyed her collection of essays, especially the freediving one, which reminded me of Conway. A sudden gravity came over her and she said, "Oh," and it was plain to me that his name had touched a chord. She lowered her mask, asked for a pen, fumbled in her handbag for a piece of paper, then leaned toward me and said: "You'll come visit me tomorrow?"

I watched as she crossed the lobby toward Aubrey Mmodi. He put his arm casually around her waist and guided her toward the door.

I had no idea whether it had been pure politeness on her part, or if she existed apart from her handlers, or whether it was a matter of surprise to see a face that connected her back to her past, but she had given me her address and a proposed time in the early afternoon, and I had every intention of going.

"What the fuck was that about?" the writer said to me as Zanele walked out the door, but I handed him my glass and moved on, out of that current.

I wandered back to Pimlico in a daze. Not even the heat bothered me. I pulled my bed to the open window, where a slight breeze kept me company.

———

The cast iron and granite of Battersea Bridge cantilevered over the water. Behind that stood the bascules of Tower Bridge. A small flock of terns skittered out over the Thames and made parabolas on the air. The water ran beneath the bridges, brooding and tidal.

I made my way down Cheyne Walk. I was already cursing my choice of shirt, a light blue linen. I could feel the ovals spreading at my underarms. The flags along the light poles did not flutter in the heat.

Zanele Ombassa was living on a houseboat on the edge of the river. A sign at the yacht club entrance warned that the area was private, but there were no security guards, no fences, no locks. Twenty or more boats were lined along the waterfront.

There was something exclusive and yet also unassuming about it, a house that rose and fell on the tides. The walkway was carefully kept. The other boats were brightly painted, their open decks scattered with chairs and potted plants. I counted out the numbers.

Hers was near the end, a pilot boat with a red wheelhouse neatly trimmed with white. It lay low and long, as if it might have to sneak out into the river and escape at any time.

Even here the security was minimal. Just an intercom system and one small gate. It was a man's voice that answered, and he repeated my name as if surprised to have a visitor at all. He took a few moments to buzz me in.

The door opened. The brightness made it so that I could not recognize who stood in the shadows.

"You're very welcome," Zanele said after I negotiated the short gangplank. She wore no mask and she gestured to me that I could take mine off too. "I hope you don't get seasick."

I suddenly recalled the two afternoons cramped in the shower stall of the Georges Lecointe.

"Kidding," she said. "But fair warning, the boat does get a little creaky at flood tide."

"Excuse me?"

"The river's on the rise for the next few hours. You hardly feel a thing. But it's when we ebb that it all feels entirely strange." She took my elbow and guided me into the boat.

"How long have you lived here?"

"It's temporary," she said. "We're renovating another place."

Kensington, I thought, or somewhere nearby in Chelsea: the black ironwork gates, the whitewashed façades, the high windows.

"We have a new house in Gqeberha," she said, and her tongue clicked. She saw my confusion and added: "It's the proper name for Port Elizabeth." And then: "Follow me."

All along the walls of the corridor were children's drawings, framed. One of them, I noticed, was of a tiny ship out at sea, a thin line drawn to the bottom of the page. It stalled me a moment, and I thought about taking a photo, but Zanele had already disappeared, and I hurried to catch up.

"You're moving back to South Africa?"

"Kind of," she said. "We've another place out by Cornwall. Where the kids can run wild. They like it there too."

"Just to clarify," I said, "I'm not here to write an article."

"Oh, I don't really care, Anthony," she said, and her voice was suddenly sorrowful.

She guided me into the small inner kitchen. It was dark and neat and somewhat cramped, with a high porthole window. I studied her in the weak light. Her grace. Her ease. Her head was still perfectly shaved, and she wore two small silver earrings.

"You can write what you want," she said. "I'm beyond that. It doesn't bother me what they say anymore."

Perhaps it was what I should have expected: it wasn't the first time she had thrown me off balance, but quite plainly I had misread her. I had expected a large glassy boat. With mahogany cabinets. Silver capstans. Glinting lines of light. But here it was, a simple place, elegant and understated.

"Come meet Aubrey," she said, balancing a jug of water with glasses.

Mmodi was sitting on the deck at the stern, by a fan that sprayed droplets of cooling water. He appeared moody, but he stood to shake hands. The two children, Thami and Imka, were at a folding table, playing dominoes. They were just home from summer camp. They turned and waved at me. It all seemed so very ordinary. No maids, no security cameras.

I stood for a moment in the cool of the spray and I made small talk. Mmodi was terse and uninterested. He seemed glad when Zanele returned, carrying a plate of sliced lemons.

We went to the front of the boat, where another small table was set up under a wide red umbrella, out of earshot of her family.

"Excuse my fingers," she said, and she dropped a slice of lemon in my glass, handed it to me. "Well, then . . . ?"

The simplest way forward was to compliment her work, but she had mostly brushed that off the day before, and it seemed an early cul-de-sac. Still, I admired her directness.

"You're quite brave," I said. "Living out in the open like this. I thought you'd be surrounded by handlers."

"Oh, them," she said. "They're just doing their jobs. Nothing brave about it. All that"—she waved one arm in the air as if she might collect the word there—"hullabaloo."

"Was he ever caught?"

"Who?" she said. "Oh, him, yes. He was just a kid. He was sick. He got charged but went to some mental facility. It wasn't any grand plot. He's out now somewhere. It doesn't worry me."

"I was on the Georges when it happened."

"Of course."

"We were all very concerned."

"I don't really talk about it all that much. There was a lot going on at the time."

She watched a passing boat as it made its way toward Battersea Bridge. A pulse of wave went underneath us. She seemed just as capable as me of sitting in silence.

Eventually I said: "I'm sorry about what happened."

"There's no need for you to be sorry. Conway and I just couldn't quite figure it out. For a long time I didn't want to think about any of it. I suppose we end up surviving by our ability to forget."

"Is that what you've done?"

"Quite plainly, no," she said, and she swept out her arm, encompassing the boat, the rising river, and, with a flick of the wrist, my presence. "All this time, I haven't met any other people who were on the boat with him."

"You didn't hear from anyone? Brussels? Nobody?"

"I got a postcard from someone named Petrus, I think."

"The engine man. What did he say?"

"Something about his mother. I can't quite recall. Isn't that terrible? These things, they fade away."

"And what about Conway's possessions? Did you get them?"

"I didn't ask for them."

"I used to see him writing in notebooks."

I had often had the thought of his notebooks surfacing. I would be able to comb through them and make sense of it all, the gaps, the cracks, the hanging edges.

"They're probably gone now."

"I think he was pining for something," I said. "I saw him one morning standing out on the deck. He was just staring east. It still haunts me."

"When?"

"I don't know. A few days into our journey."

"Along the coast? Mid-Angola?"

"Yeah, more or less, I suppose."

She shivered a moment and ran her hands along her forearms.

"How was he, those last days on the ship?"

"He surprised us all when he disappeared."

"Conway was well versed in the art of disappearance."

"What do you mean?"

She closed her eyes and there was a pressing silence. Another small wake from a passing boat trembled underneath us.

"Can you tell me what happened?"

"No," she said.

"But you knew he was alive. That time when you called. You said he asked not to be written about. You said he didn't want to be heard from."

She held the rim of the water glass against her lower lip.

"What other disappearances were there?"

"Conway was an actor," she said. "Probably a better actor than I could ever be. He could fit himself into just about any situation that came his way. Except he was never quite fully there. Always hovering outside himself, if you know what I mean. He never lied to me. There was always a truth there. Even just a hint."

She didn't elaborate. I waited, but she said nothing more.

"I wanted to tell you something. From that day. In Cape Town. You asked me if I had children. I didn't exactly tell the truth."

"Oh, that's okay," she said.

"I have a son. In Chile."

"That's nice," she said, and it angered me how easily she was able to slough it off. She looked along the length of the river. "I mean, London is sometimes so beautiful that it is difficult to remember that it is built on a whole empire of lies."

I wanted somehow to pierce her in the same manner that she was capable of piercing me. I floundered around, and I stuttered, asked her about the early years.

"It's a long story, but nothing washes away your childhood. I was an only child. I had no father to speak of. I'm sure you've read about the townships."

I had: the shanty houses, the dirt roads, the coal fires, the garbage bags scuttering in the sky.

"I was sixteen when I left. They gave me a scholarship to a high school in Jacksonville. I stayed with a professor who was an Elizabeth Bishop scholar. I went on to college in Key West, where I studied theater. I met Conway in Key West when I was just nineteen. First time I saw him was next to the boardwalk. A beautiful woman had dropped a wedding ring off the dock. She was incredibly distraught. And nobody could find it. He came along and just climbed in the water. He was under way too long. I was part of the crowd that had gathered. Someone had already called for an ambulance when he rose with the ring. Everyone applauded. I could tell he didn't like the applause. The woman tried to give him money, but he didn't want it. He glanced at me, walked away, looked over his shoulder again. There are times you just know. The next morning I saw him again. He was going diving with friends. He wore a plain white shirt. I will never forget that. He was shorter than me, but he never cared about that sort of thing. He wasn't of this world. He wanted the elsewhere. He taught me how to dive. I had never been in the actual ocean, even though I grew up ten kilometers from it. But here it was, another ocean. And here I was. I had never met anyone like him before. We went out on the water every day. You know, there's a samba moment just before you lose consciousness. It's a term in diving. Samba. You lose control of your body. In shallow water mostly, or when you resurface. You can't keep your eyes open. And then someone blows air into your eyes to waken you. I can still feel that. He would waken me in the morning. Just a gentle breath into the eyes. He was working in the oil fields at that time. You wouldn't know it, but he had a lot of money. He gave it away. But he gave all sorts of things away. He couldn't hold on to anything. Not me, not anything. He went back to Louisiana. We wrote to each other. He went missing. And then he appeared again. Months at a time. And then he was off somewhere else."

"So it's true? The oil fields and everything?"

"Of course."

"He was in the Middle East? After 9/11?"

"That was much later. I think he went there in 2004, maybe later."

"Why?"

"I don't know. Maybe because of me."

She said it plainly, without drama or sorrow, but it rang authentic and it echoed a moment, and I liked her again. "I really shouldn't talk about it when the kids are here. They're going soon. Aubrey's taking them to the park."

There was a squeal of delight from the front of the boat. Mmodi was spraying the children with water from the hose.

"See?" said Zanele, as if it explained everything.

She rose and walked up to where they were gathered. I saw her kneel in front of Imka and adjust her dress. The kids each draped their arms over her shoulders. She stood and nodded at Mmodi—no kiss—and then she escorted them down the gangplank toward the pier. It was almost as if I was the one who lived on the house-boat and was watching her go.

She returned with another jug of water, fresh lemons, limes.

"Angola," she said immediately, settling into her chair. "There's an island there. It used to be Portuguese. It's deserted now. Ilha dos Tigres. It became a ghost town after it was cut off from the mainland in a storm. Destroyed. No fresh water. All the people left. We went there together one winter a few years ago. We loaded up an old tug and dropped anchor. We stayed three weeks. There was nothing like it. Sand blowing down the street. The churches under two feet of it. Still the paintings on the walls of the churches. The wind coming through the keyholes. Not a person around. We survived on tinned food, condensed milk. We slept in a church. We hung a mosquito screen from an upper balcony. That was the best time we ever had. We were still quite young."

"When was this?"

"We even thought about abandoning the tug."

"I guess I just don't understand the chronology."

"This is long before the kids . . ." She trailed off. "We kept splitting up. And he would leave again. Over the years. And I would ask him back again. We wanted to give it another try. But we both knew. By the time I got to Brighton. Before then even. He knew. Aubrey knew too."

"And on that deck he was looking out at Angola?"

"I have no clue, Mister Fennell. You were the one who saw him."

It was difficult to forget the sight of Conway standing there, some sort of green light out there for him. The ocean and the ocean and the ocean.

"And Ireland? He was from Rathlin Island?"

"I never went there with him. There was a part of him that he wanted to protect. He didn't talk about it."

"But it's true that he grew up there?"

"Why wouldn't it be?"

"His mother was killed when he was a child?"

"Yes, but I wouldn't retreat to the couch for that one. It wasn't something he ever mentioned. It didn't define him."

"But how did it happen?"

"All I know is that the boat overturned on her. She was a sound engineer. She was recording at depths."

"Was he with her?"

"I told you, Anthony, he never told me all that much more about it."

I was flattered, of course, by the reversion to my first name and the ragged edges of the new pieces of information that she was giving me. She had invited me in. And yet there was so much more that I still couldn't fathom. I glanced at the seawall.

"The flood tide lasts six hours," she said. "The ebb, six and a half."

I wondered if later the low tide might reveal something more, a hidden pattern down in the dark mud of the Thames.

"All that travel of his, during the pandemic. He seemed to go from place to place. But there's no footage of him in Marseille. Or Cornwall. Or other places."

"People ghost around," she said. "He was trying to make a point. He wanted connection, just not the way he was getting it."

"And you say he wasn't in touch with you?"

"I didn't say that."

"You said he was an actor."

"He was."

"He must have traveled a lot. In order to put all those dummy bags in place."

"Like a dress rehearsal," she said.

There are moments when the truth seems to come tumbling down even before it is said. Zanele liked grand themes. A vague terror seized me: Could it be feasible that it was all part of her ongoing theater? Perhaps she had worked in tandem with him. Maybe it was all just one vast art scheme that she had orchestrated herself, a comment on who we were, our breakdown, our dissolution, our severance from ourselves. She had mentioned a house in Cornwall after all. And she too was a diver. It wasn't beyond the realm of the possible that she had planted at least some of the other devices, maybe even alongside him.

"Why did he choose the places for the dummy bombs?"

"I don't know. But most of them were nexus points. Where a lot of cables came together."

"Why didn't he just continue doing it?"

She shook her head.

"Any idea why he decided on Egypt?"

"Maybe he got tired. Maybe it was enough. Maybe something in him snapped. I don't think I'll ever know."

"Were you involved?"

She just smiled.

"Conway was deep in his own mind," she said. "He had his own theories. That's where he was diving."

"But you weren't involved in any way?"

"Mister Fennell," she said. "I talked with him at times when he was traveling. He was drinking a lot. He was hiding out in places. I think his compass had long since disappeared. Literally."

"Did you know what it was that he was doing?"

"I had no clue."

"You said you had a house in Cornwall?"

"He stayed there for a while. But I wasn't there with him. He was welcome to stay. Aubrey knew he was there. The kids too. None of us saw him, but we all knew he was there."

"But—"

"Don't make the world narrower than it already is."

"Of course, but what I'm asking is . . ."

A rill of impatience trembled in her. "I didn't aid him in any way, if that's what you're asking. I didn't orchestrate anything. He did what he did on his own. I have no doubt about that."

Just then there was the blare of a ship horn from far down the Thames, and it hung in the air.

"But what was the point if it was all going to be repaired?"

"Maybe that was exactly his point."

"How so?"

"Sometimes I wonder if there are still some dummy bags out there."

The thought stalled me: if anybody knew, she knew.

"Are there?"

"How would I know?" she said. "In the end I think he was just trying to find a way to get by. He was quite simple. In the best sense, I mean. He liked the world. He just couldn't hold on. It was all so stupid, the world, but it mattered too. Still does."

I was surprised to see how much the boat had risen in the time we'd been talking. By the markings on the wall, it had climbed almost two feet. A part of me might have preferred to seep slowly down into the mud. But Zanele had landed on a notion that I thought I might be able to carry with me: the wonder of things is that they were ever created in the first place. Maybe that was the simplicity we needed. Everything is made to be disassembled. Not all of it can be repaired. All there is is the trying.

It was still bright when we heard young voices filtering along the slipway. Three silhouettes appeared on the gangway.

"I'll be right there," called Zanele.

I wanted to startle her with some last-line wisdom, but none came. She lifted her water glass and drained it. I thanked her for having spent the time with me, and then she took out her phone. I was sure she was just checking her messages, but then she said, "Do you want a selfie?"

I presume that I must have visibly bristled, because she appeared slightly startled and her body turned defensively away. She was no doubt used to people taking selfies with her, and it was no more than an automatic response.

"I was just thinking you could send it to your son," she said.

I knew it the moment she said it. Mine has been a lifetime of dropped connections.

You can ache for years and not even know that you've been aching. The ache has gone so deep that it seems to come from another life, one not even remembered anymore. Then, when it spins back up in your mind, you can choose to shove it back down into the territory of a deeper ache, or you can try to coax it into some sort of meaning.

I crossed toward her and she half embraced me. She held the camera out and clicked the button.

"I'll send it to you immediately," she said.

Take a hair from your head. Better still, an eyelash. Study it. That is the width of the glass tube that carried the photo that Zanele took, the same one I sent later that evening to my son to tell him that I was on my way to Santiago.

The tubes are tiny. They are hollow. They weigh nothing. All they carry is light. I can't presume to explain this.

It is one of the things that still continues to fill me with wonder.

ACKNOWLEDGMENTS

It struck me, as I finished this novel, that this was a chance for me to directly thank you, my readers. The distance between us is only a story. And a novel is never complete without each of us bridging that distance. The Peruvian writer César Vallejo says that mystery joins things together. So I am deeply grateful. Thank you, dear reader, for completing this story.

My agent, Sarah Chalfant, kept this book afloat. She was tireless and inspirational. She and everyone at the Wylie Agency deserve my deepest thanks. There's a barstool at the Modern where we will continue to gather.

My thanks to my editor, Jennifer Hershey, for her guidance and patience, to Wendy Wong, to Andy Ward, to Alison Rich, to Windy Dorresteyn, to Lucas Heinrich and to the whole wonderful crew at Random House. And to Nigel Newton, Allegra Le Fanu, Alexis Kirschbaum, and the wonderful team at Bloomsbury in London. Also Caroline Ast, Diane du Périer, and every single person at Belfond who makes France a second home. And Thomas Uberhoff and the crew at Rowohlt, who have supported me down through the years. And of course the wonderful Jaco Groot in Amsterdam, along with all his team. To the folks at Feltrinelli: *grazie mille* for finally making it happen in Italy. And all the other publishers who have helped pull my literary world together.

On the houseboat and beyond, thank you Alexandra Pringle and Rick Stroud. For the Milford digs, Josh Sapan and Anne Foley. For the tower, Susie Lopez and Caoimhghín O'Fraithile. For the cottage, J. J. Abrams and Katie McGrath. And thanks to Sally, Roger, and RoseMarie for the safe havens. Sean and Freda too. Family, all.

On the cable boat, and underwater, there are many whom I would like to thank. First and most important, Didier Mainguy and the crew of the Léon Thévenin: you are not in this novel, but it would have been impossible without you. Thank you Benedicte Bigot, Michel Sénéchal, Serge Vales, Samkelo Ndongeni, and all the good folks at Orange Marine. Tim Stronge at TeleGeography was a fantastic resource for all things cable-related. As were Nicole Starosielski and Patrick O'Rourke.

Thank you to Jonathan Ledgard, who helped me truly submerge. I was inspired by Craig Sinclair, Marie-Anne Cambon, Jennifer Morgan, Ibrahim Hani, and Sam Robinson. I read so many great books on diving and cable technology that it would take a long time to enumerate them, but a special mention to James Nestor, Adam Skolnick, and Andrew Blum. A nod, of course, to Joseph Conrad and T. S. Eliot.

There were so many who shaped the manuscript as it tacked along. Of course, thanks to Dan Barry, always the sage counsel and friend. Also Max Krupnick, my assistant, who did so much of the deckwork. Chris Booth was so generous with his editing and vision: a lifetime of connections, indeed. Terry Cooper, for the wise words. John Ismay for his expert advice. Thank you, Bob Mooney— you're a gentleman and a scholar. Phil Brady. Amanda Rabadeux. Ronan McCann. Evan Camfield and Amy Schroeder for the eagle eyes. And Diane Foley, thank you for allowing me another story that helped prop up this one. Loretta Brennan Glucksman, for being there. Tim Martin at *Alexander* magazine, gratitude for your vision. Thami Ndimande in Soweto. Zukiswa Allah, Babalwa Tetyana, Yamkela Vayo, and all in Gqeberha and Joe Slovo.

Colm Mac Con Iomaire and Sting and Gregory Alan Isakov: you continue to enter the words. Gabriel Byrne, Meredith Fages,

Michael Proskin, Jim Marion, Lisa Reynolds, John Quinn with your late night talks. And always Danny McDonald and the crew at the best bar(s) in New York.

Liz Brack and Rob Kovell, you stepped along the gangplank. Thank you Gideon Stein, generous as always. And Greg Khalil too. Jennifer Murphy, you gracefully held it all steady. Lila Azam Zanganeh. Cormac Kinsella. Louise Dobbin. Siobhan Dalton, gratitude for the sailing lesson. And Victor Fruhinsholz too. I fear that I have forgotten some. Still, I am grateful to all.

Lisa Consiglio, always the visionary. And all the crew at Narrative 4: every book is your book.

There are times we all become the sons of our sons—JohnMichael, this really would not have been possible without you. And crucially, as always, deepest thanks also to Allison and Isabella. And of course Christian, to whom this novel is dedicated.

ABOUT THE AUTHOR

—

COLUM McCANN is the internationally bestselling author of the novels *Apeirogon, TransAtlantic, Let the Great World Spin, Zoli, Dancer, This Side of Brightness,* and *Songdogs,* as well as three critically acclaimed story collections and two nonfiction books, *Letters to a Young Writer* and *American Mother.* His fiction has been published in more than forty languages. He has received many honors, including the National Book Award, the International Dublin Literary Award, a Guggenheim fellowship, and an Oscar nomination for the short film "Everything in This Country Must." He is a member of the American Academy of Arts and Letters, as well as the Irish association of artists Aosdána, and has been named a Chevalier des Arts et des Lettres by the French government. In addition, he has won awards in Italy, Germany, and China. A contributor to *The New Yorker, The New York Times, The Atlantic,* and *The Paris Review,* he is the co-founder of the global nonprofit story-exchange organization Narrative 4. He lives with his family in New York.

columccann.com
Facebook.com/columccannauthor

ABOUT THE TYPE

———

This book was set in Caslon, a typeface first designed in 1722 by William Caslon (1692–1766). Its widespread use by most English printers in the early eighteenth century soon supplanted the Dutch typefaces that had formerly prevailed. The roman is considered a "workhorse" typeface due to its pleasant, open appearance, while the italic is exceedingly decorative.